Only Jody Knows

Only Jody Knows

CRAIG B. EWALD

Library of Congress Control Number: 2021911768

HARDBACK: 978-1-955347-97-6
PAPERBACK: 978-1-955347-96-9
EBOOK: 978-1-955347-98-3

Ordering Information:

For orders and inquiries, please contact:
1-888-404-1388
www.goldtouchpress.com
book.orders@goldtouchpress.com

Printed in the United States of America

Chapter

1

I could hear excited shouts from the grandstand, sounds of people watching the rodeo as the afternoon sun cut through the mountains onto the brightly colored tents of the fair. We had been here since early morning, and now I was tired and thinking of my comfortable slippers inside my back door at home. I had been showing some of my cattle and was pleased that I had won a few ribbons. But now, my good clothes were beginning to irritate me, and I wanted out of them. Everyone dressed up in their Sunday best for the Wyoming State Fair.

I waited for my wife, Martha, to finish discussing the cooking awards with several ladies she had met, prowling around only a few feet away to let her know that I was ready to go. I waved to a couple of friends I knew over by the beer stand. One was Dr. Robert Heidbreder, a dentist; the other was Caleb McMillan, an auctioneer. Both were from Sheridan. They acknowledged my wave but did not approach me. The last thing I wanted to do right now was strike up a conversation. As Martha would say, I was "in one of my moods," tossing my thoughts around as I waited. In the distance, the Bighorn Mountains stood in shadow, blue-black against the reddening sky. As I looked beyond the tents and awnings to the far-reaching expanse of the yellowing Wyoming countryside, a barker from a nearby sideshow was shouting to a small group of interested people. Eventually his words filtered into my thoughts.

"He predicted President Roosevelt's victory for a second term," he was calling out. "And he predicts that he will go on to win an unprecedented third term three years from now. With his amazing powers he can see into the future and explore the mysteries of the past. Come in and challenge the spectacular Martin Darden with your questions. Ask him about your future, or question him about the past. His answers will amaze and astonish you. If you think this is a hoax, he will return your money. So let the amazing Mr. Darden answer your questions. Hurry, hurry, hurry; the show begins in a few minutes."

Tired as I was, I listened. Somehow, with the words, the smoke from the carnival torches, the bright colors of the tents, and my mood, I was taken back to another September day, another place—a memory forgotten many years past. I looked into the distance and saw not the rolling Wyoming countryside but the South Dakota plains of my childhood: golden fields of corn and wheat, cattle grazing for miles under the warm September sun, and trees beginning to show the colors of the coming of fall.

And I remembered a question about the past.

Martha came up beside me. "Ready to leave, dear?"

"Let's go in and see this fellow Darden," I said, straight out.

"But, Ralph, you don't believe in such things. And I don't want any of our friends to think that we believe in this nonsense."

I grabbed Martha's arm and headed for the tent as if I hadn't heard a word she had spoken.

I bought two tickets, and we went in. It was a small tent, with uneven rows of chairs facing a raised platform. There were about twenty people sitting there, waiting. Waiting for what, I wasn't sure. We found two chairs near the front, joining the others in the warm interior. My hands were sweating, and I felt quite nervous, even a little excited. Soon the barker came out; he was Darden's assistant, and he handed us small envelopes and cards to write our questions on.

"What are you doing?' Martha asked an amazed look on her face.

"Sh!" I hushed her and wrote my question. The barker took the envelopes, checking each one to see if it was sealed, and put them in a black hat that he placed on the table. The barker then announced Darden, who immediately came out.

I was disappointed by his appearance. He was under medium height, dumpy, and his clothes seemed too big for him. He was bald, and what little hair he had was brown. A big cigar protruded from the right corner of his mouth. In his right hand, he carried a red handkerchief to wipe the gathering perspiration from his forehead. This guy didn't look as if he could predict yesterday's weather.

The crowd politely applauded his entrance and waited; the air was electric. Darden began by telling what prophecies he had made that had come true, and he mentioned some predictions for the future. He stated that some fellow in Germany named Hitler would be making trouble for all of us. It was plain foolishness. I was sure I had wasted my money.

Taking the top hat, Darden picked out one envelope. He opened it and read the question. It wasn't mine. Somebody wanted to know about a brother overseas. Darden closed his eyes and in a low voice answered the question. I paid little attention to the response. I could only think of my own question, wondering if he would pull it—and, more importantly, if he could answer it.

He worked his way through the envelopes, opening some, holding others to his perspiring forehead. People were murmuring; some nodded their heads in approval.

A lady behind me said, "That's wonderful, but how could he know that? Only I knew that."

I waited, hoping each envelope would be mine. Had the envelope gotten stuck in the lining of the hat where it would not be felt by his searching fingers?

Darden held yet another envelope to his forehead and closed his eyes.

"This question is about a young woman. It asks if I believe her to be alive, and if so, where is she now? If she is dead, how and when did she die? Her initials are S. W."

I was amazed. That was my question, and he knew my question without unsealing the envelope. He opened his eyes and stood motionless for a moment. He said nothing. I had known he couldn't do it.

"Before I proceed to answer this question, I must have the correct initials of the woman. The initials given to me are not correct. Will the person who wrote this question please give me the correct initials?"

I was astonished! How could he know? I hesitated; I didn't want to make an ass of myself, yet the desire to know was killing me.

"J. B.," I blurted out, not caring what the others thought.

Darden looked straight at me, a strange look on his face.

"This is a very interesting question," he said, closing his eyes and tipping his head back. He winced and made several strange faces and weird noises in this position. Pausing for a long moment, he began speaking as if to himself.

"I see a dark night. There are six burning torches spread far across the rolling countryside. I see something tied to a piece of barbed wire. There is something in it, but I can't make out what it is. Things are not clear, and I am having difficulty making it all out. I see a boy standing on a bluff overlooking …"

Chapter

2

"**C**ome on, Ralphie. Why are you always the last one ready whenever we're going someplace?"

I hated to go to dances anyway. Since I was the youngest in the family, Mom and Dad wouldn't let me stay at home all by myself, even though I was eleven years old.

"I'm coming," I yelled from the upstairs window. I went back to the mirror and finished combing my hair. I grabbed the sweater I had received last Christmas from my sisters. It would probably be quite cool on our trip home, even though it was the middle of September and the days had been warm.

I went down the narrow stairway in three big bounds and proceeded through the sitting room to the kitchen and the back door. I grabbed an apple from the bowl on the huge kitchen table Father had made last summer.

"Come on, Ralphie," yelled my oldest sister Elsie, a look of impatience on her face. "Let's get going. I don't want us to be the last ones there."

I shoved the back door open so hard that it made the door bang into the wall of the house. I ran across the porch and jumped to the ground and ran over to the wagon.

"You slam that door one more time like that, Ralphie, and you will get a switching you won't soon forget."

"Gee whiz, Ma. You wanted me to hurry too, didn't ya?"

My older brothers Eddie and Art grabbed me by the arms and hauled me up over the side into the wagon.

"Okay, Bob. Let's get going," called my father to the people in the other wagon.

We were headed down to the Smith ranch. The Bucklin family had arrived a few minutes earlier. We were all going down there together. The Bucklin's had the ranch to the east of us, and they had stopped to join up with us.

"Father, can I ride with Jamie?"

"No, you can't, boy. You stay right where you are. I'm not going to have you boys roughhousing in the wagon and getting dirty before we even get there."

I knew better than to argue. Father's word was law as far as we children were concerned. But I did want to play with Jamie, who was my best friend. He was a year younger than I was, and he had red hair and freckles. He was always getting teased about those freckles. He was a thin boy, and I beat him almost every time we wrestled, which was often.

I wanted to ride with Jamie because I knew that we would have to go to bed about an hour or so after we arrived. That's the way it always was at the dances. The younger kids were put to bed in the house so that the older kids and the adults could attend the dance. Jamie and I couldn't even sleep in the same room because we would never get to sleep. We would wrestle or have pillow fights with the other children our age. I knew we would be arriving between eight and eight thirty, which would mean that Jamie and I would only have about one hour to mess around.

It would take us an hour or so to get to the Smith ranch. It wasn't that far, but the last two miles or so were hilly, and the horses went slower. My parents talked about who was expected to attend. My older sisters Elsie and Lydia were wondering what boys would be there to dance with. Eddie and Artie were hoping it would still be light so that they could play some ball before the dance started. They were old enough that they did not have to go to bed and could dance if they wanted to. My two younger sisters Minnie and Lottie were hoping that there would be time to play a game of "pump, pump, pull-away." It was a game that all of the younger children liked to play—especially us boys, because we could run faster than the girls and would usually win.

We were approaching the last big hill before we got to the Smith ranch. I always got a little excited, because from the top I could see the Missouri River and the trees that lined it, which were nearly three miles away. From that hill on, there were rolling hills and valleys all the way to the river. I had only been to the river on two occasions, and both times it was to get trees from which we would build barns and sheds. I always felt a strange excitement when I saw the big river. There were rattlesnakes there too.

From the top of the hill we could also see the Smith ranch. It sat in the first distant valley to the right of the road. You could look down on the house, the barns, and the sheds. There were lots of trees surrounding the house. A row of Russian olive bushes lined each side of the barnyard for forty yards. It was only a mile or so more until we were there.

As it turned out, we had left a little late, and as we headed down the hill we could barely make out the river in the distance as we were looking into the evening sun. The fluffy clouds that had been white twenty minutes earlier were now bright reddish-orange. I could see the lights of the Smith house peering at us out of the dark valley like holes in a pumpkin face. A broad beam of light spilled out of the twin barn doors sixty yards behind the house. That was where the dance would be held.

As we moved down the lane toward the barn, I heard Mother and Father recognizing the wagons and horses already there. We pulled off the lane between the house and the barn, and Father tied the team up to one of the trees. We children all piled out of the wagon and ran to the barn to see who else was there.

"Come on Jamie, I'll race you to the barn."

"Now you stay in bed, Ralph. I don't want you and Jamie playing around. It is going to be late when we get home tonight, and I don't want you causing a fuss."

"Aw, Mom, can't we stay up a little longer tonight? We always gotta go to bed early. Why can't we play some more?"

"It is almost ten o'clock, and that is past your bedtime. I don't want to hear any more of it."

With that, Mother closed the door to the sitting room. There I was with five other boys, all of them younger than I was. My mom figured I was old enough to watch after them but not old enough to stay up later. Jamie was in the bedroom across the hall from me. He was with three younger boys and two older girls about thirteen or fourteen. The girls were to watch after Jamie, me, and the others.

7

Mother had ruined all of our fun when she separated me and Jamie. There was nothing else to do but turn down the kerosene lamp and go to sleep. I took off my sweater and rolled it into a ball for a pillow. I pulled the suspenders from my shoulders and let them fall to my side. I took the quilt Mother had brought for me and spread it out on the floor. Placing the sweater at one end, I laid down on the blanket not too far from the door. I pulled half the blanket over me and reached over my head to put out the kerosene lamp sitting on the chair. The room was now pitch dark. I closed my eyes and settled back. I could hear the fiddle music coming through the window from the barn not very far away.

"Ralphie, wake up. Come on, Ralphie! Wake up." I felt a jab in the middle of my back. I rolled over, and there was Jamie on all fours, hovering over me.

"Come on, Ralphie, but be quiet."

"What's the matter?" I questioned.

"Let's sneak out to the barn and see what's happening. Tonight there is supposed to be a special occasion from what my dad said the other day. I want to see what it is."

"Don't you have any ideas? I don't want to get caught. We would get switched for sure."

"No, but I want to find out what it is. Are you coming or not?"

"Okay."

I sat up and pulled my suspenders up over my shoulders. I pulled on my shoes and laced them quickly, one ending up in a knot. I grabbed my sweater and put it on. Following Jamie, I got on my hands and knees and crawled the few feet to the door and into the hall.

Jamie turned and shut the door as soon as I passed through. We both stood up. The hallway was dark except for the light that was coming from the kitchen. We moved slowly and quietly down the hall to the kitchen. Several boards squeaked and groaned beneath our feet as they reluctantly accepted our weight upon them.

When we got to the kitchen door, Jamie peeked in. It was empty. A single kerosene lamp sat on the table in the middle of the kitchen. We quickly proceeded across the room to the back door. Jamie peeked through the doorway to see if anyone was on the back porch.

Sixty yards beyond the porch was the barn. A beam of light pierced the darkness from one of the big doors that had been left ajar. We could hear the fiddles and clapping quite clearly now.

"Come on, Ralphie; I can't see anyone."

We opened the screen door and slipped through.

"Let's sneak around to the side so we won't be seen. We can use the wagons and trees as cover."

"Okay, Jamie."

We jumped off the porch and ran to our left to a big cottonwood tree that sat thirty feet from the back porch. The tree hid Jamie and me easily it was so big. From there, we moved farther to our left toward another tree that had a team of horses tied up to it. It was easy to hide behind the wagons; no one had seen us yet.

It was nearly a straight line ahead to the west side of the barn. There were several trees with wagon teams hitched to them that we were able to use for cover as we proceeded to the barn. It was quite dark, and the moon had not risen yet. This aided us in our journey. As we approached the last wagon, a door on the west side of the barn swung open. We dived under the wagon.

Two people stepped out into the darkness. It was hard to see who it was in the dark, but we could tell that one was a man and the other a woman. We could not make out their faces since the light had not fallen on them. They talked in hushed voices. We could not make out what they were saying. They stood there for several moments facing each other. They finally stopped talking. The man moved quickly to the woman and placed his arms around her. In the darkness we could see two figures blend into one they kissed. It lasted only a few moments. They separated very quickly and opened the door. The light filled the doorway exposing the two people about to reenter the barn.

It was Jamie's sister, Jody! The man I had seen before on several occasions. He had passed by our house and had gone to the Bucklin's house. I had seen him at the Bucklin's when I had gone up to their house to play with Jamie.

"Did you see that?" I exclaimed.

"I sure did. Boy, if she knew I had seen her kissing, she would tan my hide. I sure got something on her now. I wonder what Dad would think if he knew that?

I wondered what I would do if I saw any of my sisters or brothers kissing someone. I suppose I would not say anything to my brothers because they would probably beat up on me. At the same time, I thought my brothers would side with me in teasing my sisters if I told them I had seen them kissing a man. I just did not begin to understand this fuss about kissing.

"Who was that with her?" I questioned Jamie.

"John Northfield. You have seen him before. He's been spending quite a lot of time at our place lately. My ma says he's sweet on Jody. He's got a big ranch west of the Missouri about seventy miles from here. Sometimes, his friend Chris Jennings comes with him. I really like Mr. Jennings because he plays ball with me. Mr. Northfield never wants to play ball; he only wants to be with my sister. Mom always says I am not to bother them."

"Don't you like him?"

"Aw, he's okay, I guess; but he doesn't pay much attention to me. Come on. Let's see what's going on."

We crawled out from under the wagon, brushed the dust off of ourselves, and then ran the remaining distance to the barn.

"Do you want to go in this door?" I asked. Jamie's sister had.

"I don't know. Let's open the door just enough to see if we should go in here." We would have a good vantage point from the west door to see the entire inside of the barn. Jamie reached up and grabbed the latch. With a low grunt he tugged on the door. It was stuck. He tugged again, and again. Apparently, the door had been slammed hard enough that it was jammed too tight for him to open.

"Let's go on around the back. I don't want to get caught trying to open the door," I said grabbing his arm.

"Okay."

When we got to the northwest corner of the barn we encountered a wooden fence that extended north into the darkness. It was a livestock pen. Right where the fence joined the barn there was another door. It was bigger than the first door, and instead of swinging open on hinges, it rolled on tracks paralleling the side of the barn.

"Let's try this door," I whispered in a low voice.

"Okay, Ralphie."

I grabbed the handle, head-high to me, and pulled. Slowly and quietly, the door rolled back on the tracks. When it was open enough for us to get inside, I let go. We peeked through the door and saw no one. What we saw was a large penning area. It was a shelter room for the cattle. There were several troughs to our left that held grain and hay for the livestock. The pen was partitioned off from the rest of the barn by a wooden wall about eight feet high. From the top of the wall to the ceiling above there was nothing. The glow from the dance lit up the ceiling above us. Occasionally, strange shadows would flash there when someone passed in front of the light.

"There's a ladder leading up to the hay loft. Let's hurry up there so we can see what is going on; no one will know we're there."

"I'll follow you, but for Pete's sake be quiet, and don't let anyone see you," I said softly.

Off we went, clinging close to the door and wall of the barn. Jamie led the way. We reached the ladder with no trouble. We were right next to the wall separating us from the dance. We could plainly hear voices on the other side of the wall, conversations of people no more than four or five feet from us.

"You are up first, Jamie, and when you get to the top of the wall, look around a bit to make sure it's safe before going up the rest of the way. After you get into the loft, I'll follow."

Jamie started up. The rungs of the ladder were quite far apart. For us, they made climbing the ladder difficult. Slowly, Jamie proceeded, trying to be sure to not slip off or miss a rung. He finally was high enough to look over the wall. His red hair flamed brightly as the light struck the top of his head when he appeared above the wall. You could see every freckle as plain as day on his face. He looked down at me and signaled that he was going up. He grabbed the next rung over his head and lifted his right leg upward to the next rung. Pulling himself up, the upper part of his body was fully exposed in the light. He grabbed the next rung and the next—one more and into the loft. He made it; no one had seen him.

Now it was my turn. I raised my leg to the first rung, and up I went. When I reached the top of the wall, I peeked over. There were people directly below me on the other side of the wall, as I had expected from the voices we had heard. There were people clapping their hands and stomping their feet. Five men were on a small platform, forty feet from us, playing fiddles, banjos, and a harmonica. "Chicken" Charlie Zimmerman stood in front of them calling out instructions to the people dancing. I had heard him do that before at other dances. Old "Chicken" was really good and very funny. He would stomp his feet and strut like a chicken. Everybody loved him.

I suddenly remembered that I shouldn't be gawking. I waited until everyone seemed to be looking the other way. When that moment came, I grabbed the next rung and started up. I was sure I would be spotted, but, unbelievably to me, I wasn't. My heart was pounding, and my hands were wet, but there I sat, next to Jamie in the loft.

"Whew. I never thought I'd make it without getting caught," I said to Jamie.

"Come on, Ralphie. Let's go to the edge of the loft where we can see everything."

We got up and climbed over the bales of hay to the edge of the loft. From here we could see the entire dance area. The other side of the barn was identical to the side we were on. The only way we could see the people standing beneath us would be by looking through the cracks in the loft floor.

Looking over the edge, I could see my brothers, Artie and Frank, dancing, as well as Elsie and Lydia. Mom and Dad were in the corner opposite us, not too far from the fiddlers. They were talking to Jamie's mom and dad. Not too far from them, a big table had been set up. It was covered with pies, cakes, chicken, and homemade bread. There always was plenty of good food at the dances. Pots of hot coffee sat at one end. Scattered around the barn floor were bales of straw. Some of them were covered with the brightly colored quilts and blankets. These served as seats.

We peered down, watching the dance in progress. Round and round the couples went, dipping, leaning, swirling, and whirling. The music went faster and became louder as the dance drew to its climatic end. When the last note was struck, the twenty dancers and the onlookers broke into clapping and laughter. Most of the dancers exclaimed how out of breath they were. The music subsided as quickly as it had begun. Jamie and I made sure we made no motion that would betray our presence.

"If I could have your attention for a moment, I would like to make an announcement."

It was Jamie's father speaking. He was walking over toward the small platform as he spoke.

"I believe that most of you are aware of what I am about to say. I am not a man of many words, as you know, so I will make it short. All of you know the members of my family: my wife Amy, my daughter Jody, and my son Jamie. We are a close family, but, as it happens in life, families separate as its members get older. This is what my announcement is about."

There was a low murmur among the people gathered. I noticed that some heads turned toward Jody, standing off to the side. She was standing with the man we saw her with outside—John Northfield.

"I would like to invite you to our daughter Jody's wedding to John Northfield, two weeks from this Sunday. Some of you have seen him around, I'm sure, but John has a ranch about one hundred miles west of the river, not too far from the town of Red Elm. They will be getting married about eleven in the morning, so you are all invited. We'll have food and maybe some beer for the men."

At the conclusion of the announcement, there was mild applause. Elsie and Lydia rushed over to Jody and hugged her. They seemed very happy, and everyone was smiling and laughing as they stood around her. Even from where we were, we could see that she was embarrassed.

Several of the men had John Northfield pinned against the wall. They were shaking his hand and slapping him on the back. Everyone seemed quite happy about the announcement.

Chicken Charlie had returned to the little platform and announced that there would be one more dance and then everyone would eat. The dance would soon be over. Hearing that, I poked Jamie in the ribs.

"Come on, Jamie. We better get back to the house. You heard what you wanted to, didn't you?"

"Yeah," he returned, rather disappointed.

"What's the matter?"

"Oh, I just don't like him too much, that's all. I wish she was marrying Mr. Jennings instead."

"Oh, there isn't any point in getting upset about it. After they're married you will hardly see either one of them. And when you do, he'll probably be a lot nicer to you anyway."

"Maybe you're right; I don't know."

With that remark, he picked up a small bunch of hay and disgustedly threw it down. Forgetting himself for a moment, he threw it right over the edge of the hayloft, down onto the dance floor.

"Jamie, what are you doing?"

I nearly tore his sleeve off trying to get him back to his senses.

"What?" he said, not realizing what he had done.

"You just threw hay out of the loft, stupid."

"Boys, you get down here right now!"

It was Jamie's father. He had spotted the hay and then us. We were in trouble.

When we climbed down the ladder, our fathers were waiting for us. Dad grabbed me by the collar and led me back to the dance floor. We were followed by Jamie and his father, who had a hold of Jamie's left ear.

"What are you boys doing up and out here?" We were questioned by Mr. Bucklin.

"We just wanted to see what was going to happen," Jamie answered. "After all, I heard you and Mom say something real important was going to happen tonight, and we wanted to see what it was."

As Jamie spoke, I looked around. Everyone was watching us. Some people had their hands over their mouths as if they were trying to hide something. I looked at Jamie, and he was rubbing his hands and swaying back and forth a little. He was nervous, just like I was. We were afraid of being switched.

Jody appeared, just as her little brother finished talking.

"Father, don't be too hard on him. After all, a boy's curiosity is not to be contained," she said, pleading for our innocence.

He thought for a moment and then replied, "You boys go over to the table and get a piece of apple pie and a glass of milk. Then go sit down out of the way of everybody. I don't want people falling over you. There ain't no point in going to bed now, is there?"

Jamie and I looked at each other. We were grinning from ear to ear. We wouldn't be getting a switching. Instead we'd be getting a piece of pie and a glass of milk as a reward for our endeavor.

It was the best piece of apple pie I'd ever had.

Chapter

3

We got up earlier on the morning of Jody's wedding. Chores had to be done so we could get ready and be there by ten forty-five in the morning. Needless to say, it was pitch dark. I fumbled in the darkness for the clothes I had left at the foot of my bed the night before. Across the room, I could still hear Artie snoring, even though I could not see him.

I located my clothes and set them down beside me. Just as I pulled my undershirt on, Mother called from downstairs for all of us to get up. My sisters were already up, helping Mother in the kitchen.

"Come on, Art, Eddie. Mom wants us up. Let's go," I said, real loud.

"Shut up, Ralphie," returned Eddie in the darkness.

With that, I proceeded to dress. Unfortunately, I could not locate one sock. I stuck my head over the end of my bed, and, with both hands, I searched the floor for my elusive sock. I could not find it.

"Come on, Eddie. Light the lamp. I can't find my other sock," I said, very annoyed.

In the darkness, I could hear Eddie fumbling with a box of wooden matches. Several times he struck the match against the box until a sudden spark followed by a flash of light shot across the room. Eddie was sitting up in bed. He leaned over and lifted the chimney of the lamp on the chair beside him. The flame jumped from the match to the wick when he drew the match close. Eddie put the match out with one hand and raised the wick with the other while leaning on his left elbow. As the wick grew out of the lamp, the flame and light increased.

I searched the floor again, this time with my eyes. I quickly spotted the sock under Frankie's bed. How did it get there, I wondered? I retrieved the sock, finished dressing, and headed for the door. When I opened the door, the smell of freshly baked bread filled my nose. It made my mouth water. I turned around and made an announcement to my half-awake brothers.

"I am going to feed your breakfasts to the dogs, you lazy buzzards."

I jumped through the doorway, narrowly escaping a pillow that Eddie flung at me. I bounded down the stairs to the kitchen, laughing louder than usual.

"What are you laughing at, Ralphie?" my mother inquired when I reached the kitchen.

"Oh nothing," I replied, not bothering to reveal my own little joke.

"Well, go wash up then and don't dawdle around."

I proceeded to the stove, where a kettle of hot water was sitting. I grabbed a hot pad from a nail on the wall beside the stove. Very carefully, I wrapped the pad around the handle and gently lifted the kettle from the stove. It was fairly heavy and quite full. I turned and walked slowly to the back door a few feet away. I was careful not to shake or tip the kettle. There was no way that I wanted to be scalded by hot, boiling water.

I pushed the screen door open with my rear and proceeded to a small table that sat on the back porch against the wall. Over it hung a large wash basin. When the basin was removed from the nail, it revealed a small mirror, which Artie and Dad used for shaving. I set the kettle on the floor by the table and grabbed the basin. After placing it on the table, I lifted the kettle and poured in some steaming hot water. I set the kettle down and turned, looking out into the darkness as I waited for the water to cool a bit.

The sky was very overcast. Nowhere could I find a star. Off in the distant north, I saw a large bolt of lightning flash across the sky. In a few moments, I could hear the low rumble of thunder pass overhead. I remembered my mother telling me that thunder was nothing more than potatoes rolling across the sky. I thought of that and was not frightened. There was a little breeze, and the clouds, which were black and puffy, bubbled and churned over each other like the boiling water I had just poured. There was no rain.

I turned back to the basin. A light steam continued to rise from the surface. Carefully and slowly, I put my first finger into the water. It was hot but not hot enough to prevent my other fingers from joining the first. Soon I was splashing water all about. I had it in my hair and eyes as I cupped the water in my hands and threw it onto my face. Water ran down my hands and arms to my elbows, getting my shirt sleeves wet. I always hated to get my shirt sleeves wet. Even when I rolled them up, they would come undone and fall back down over my arms. It was an uncomfortable feeling to have wet shirt sleeves.

With my eyes shut, I searched the wall with my fingers for the soft touch of the old towel that hung on the peg beside the mirror. I kicked the kettle while doing so, and—wouldn't you know—water popped out of the spout onto my pants leg and into my shoe. Wet sleeves and now a wet shoe; what more could there be? Finding the towel, I quickly brought it to my face to wipe the water out of my eyes and hair. At least I could now see what I was doing. I dried off, and just as I was about to hang the towel up, the back door opened.

"Ralphie, I don't see the soap on the table. Did you forget to use it? Mother says to be sure to wash with soap and behind your ears. And how did you get so wet?"

It was my sister Elsie. I gave her a hateful look and a threatening gesture with my fist. Quickly, I pulled the bar of soap from the washstand drawer. I tiptoed over to the window on the other side of the washstand and peeked in. Mother and all of my sisters were busy. I returned to the stand and tossed the soap into the basin, causing water to fly all about. I lathered up the soap and stirred the water until it was a milky white color. Upon completing this, I proudly surveyed my work, deciding it would fool everyone into thinking I had washed with soap. I dried my hands off once again and hung the towel on the peg. Just as I finished, Eddie and Artie came through the door onto the porch. Ed walked over and picked up the basin with both hands. He moved a few feet across the porch and dumped the water out of the basin onto the ground. He put the basin back on the table and picked up the kettle. He poured some more water into the basin and handed me the kettle.

"Take this back in the house, Ralphie, and put it on the stove. How did you get so wet, anyway?"

I rolled my eyes in disgust and grabbed the kettle from his hands, not bothering to answer.

After breakfast, we all went about the business of doing our chores. Eddie and I were given a special assignment of catching three chickens and getting them cleaned and dressed for frying. We decided that we would be sporting about it and would catch three chickens that were running loose about the farm yard. It would be too easy to catch them if they were already in the coop.

We carefully surveyed each bird. We wanted one that appeared to be fat and that had a nice full coat of feathers. I always thought the chickens were sickly when they were molting their feathers with the changing seasons.

We selected our first chicken. It was a big hen that was scratching the ground in front of our largest barn. We decided we would chase her inside where we could catch her easier. We checked the barn to see if any doors or windows were open. Everything was closed except for the big double doors the chicken was standing in front of. We circled around to get in front of her; slowly we approached her from the front, trying to force her to retreat straight back through the double doors.

As we got closer, the hen suddenly became aware of our approach. She cocked her head to one side and studied us for a moment. Then she turned to our left and started to slowly strut parallel to the barn doors. Quickly, I moved to my left to cut her off. It worked. With a flutter of wings and wild cackling, into the barn she retreated. We followed quickly so we could close the doors to prevent her escape.

Once inside, Eddie and I had little trouble catching her. It was a matter of forcing her into a corner and grabbing her. We had little difficulty in doing so, but we would display the scratches we received from her as medals of bravery for being the conqueror.

We bound the chicken's legs with a piece of string so she couldn't run and tied the string to a support in the barn. We only needed two more. Without a doubt, our system had worked, so we decided to employ the same tactic again. We opened the doors wide, went outside, and started looking for another plump chicken. We spotted our quarry near a tree not too far away and forced her toward the barn. We worked her between the doors easier than the first. Within a few moments, we had our second chicken.

We congratulated each other on our success and went about our business of finding the third chicken. By this time, we were practically old hands at chicken catching. In no time at all, we had herded another chicken into the barn. We closed the doors and worked her into a corner. In short order, the chicken was tied like the previous two.

"Come on, Ralphie. Let's take them over to Mom."

"Is she gonna chop their heads off?" I inquired.

"You know doggone good and well she is, Ralphie. You have seen her do it lots of times."

"Yeah, think maybe this time she'll let me do it?"

"Ralphie, how many times have you had the chance to do it? You chicken—ha, ha—out every time you get the hatchet in your hands."

"I bet I do it this time, Eddie. You wait and see."

"Okay, I'll bet you a licorice stick on it."

We picked up the chickens and headed back to the house. We had a chopping block a few yards from the back porch that was used specifically for situations like this. We set the chickens down and called to mother in the house. I felt a touch of sorrow as I looked down on the would-be victims.

Shortly, Mother came out. She carried a large pan and a long thin knife with her. She ordered Eddie get the hatchet that was over by the wood pile. I was instructed to go to a shed and get a box or a burlap sack to put the feathers in. Eddie and I both returned about the same time. He handed Mother the hatchet.

"Pick up a chicken, Eddie, and put his head on the block," Mother requested.

Eddie picked up the biggest chicken, grabbing hold by its feet that were still tied together. He pointed it head downward until its head and neck rested on the chopping block. As Mother raised the ax, I turned my head slightly to the side, wanting and not wanting to look at the same time.

"Wait a minute, Mother," said Eddie, pulling the chicken off the block. "Ralphie said he could take care of this today, didn't you, Ralphie?"

I pursed my lips and gave Eddie an ungrateful look.

"Sh ... sure, Ma," I retorted, hoping some moisture would return to my dry mouth. "I'll do it if you really want me to. If you're too busy in the kitchen, I will."

"I know you would," she said, patting me on the head, "but I don't want you to get blood all over you. It is getting late, so why don't you go in and change your clothes for the wedding?"

"Well, if you think you can handle it, I'll do as you say, Mom."

Eddie licked his lips and patted his stomach, an indication to me that he thought he had won a licorice stick. I ignored his gesture and continued talking.

"Why don't you go get dressed, Eddie? I'll hold the chicken," I said, feeling suddenly brave.

"No, you go on in, Ralphie," Mother replied. "Eddie and I can handle it for now."

I put down the bag I was holding and headed for the kitchen door. I pulled the door open and stepped inside. I turned and looked back at them; Eddie was already holding one chicken minus its head. It was flapping its wings wildly. Somehow, that didn't bother me so much. I always seemed to marvel at the actions that a chicken went through after its head was gone. I even was amused when they were let loose to flutter and run wild immediately after the execution. I turned and went to my room.

After dressing, I came downstairs and went to the parlor. Lottie and Lydia were looking at an old family photo album. I went over and picked up a Sears Roebuck catalog off of the table in front of our large picture window. All of us took great pleasure in leafing through the catalog. We thought it was great fun to see all of the different things that were available to buy. All of us had our favorite sections in the book. My sisters and Mother looked at the dresses, shoes, and cookware in just about that order. Dad and my brothers looked at the guns, traps, and many tools that were offered. My favorite section was the toys. Every time I went through the toy pages, it seemed as though I picked out a favorite different from the one the time before. I was interested in the guns also. I wanted one very badly, but Father said I would have to wait until I was twelve to have one like my brothers did.

I wanted a shotgun, a 12-gauge. Although I didn't have one, I had shot one last winter. It was my father's old single-shot 12-gauge. He told me to put the butt of the gun up tight against my shoulder when I got ready to shoot. That gun sent me flying when I pulled the trigger. I was positive I had broken my shoulder from the kick. My brothers just about died laughing at me lying flat on my back on the ground. Even Dad thought it was funny, and he told me I'd have to wait till I was older and bigger to have my very own.

Even though I couldn't have a gun, Dad let Eddie and me join Artie and him when they went hunting. We had lots of pheasants and rabbits around. There were lots of deer too, especially down by the river. It wasn't uncommon at all to see them early in the morning or late in the evening in the fields. Dad and Artie went deer hunting over to the river last winter and stayed overnight. They would hunt the deer with Winchester rifles, and they got one last year.

In the fall, we would have ducks and geese down along the river. They would land in the water and stay for a while on their way south. So we had plenty of game in the area; we all looked forward to the winter months when work slowed down and there was time for hunting.

"Come on, children, it's time to get going," Mother announced as she entered the parlor.

We all stopped what we were doing and headed for the back door. The wagon was waiting for us. Sometimes we would have walked over to the Bucklins on a nice day, but since it was a mile or so away and it was still overcast and looked like rain, Dad had decided to take the wagon. We had rain slickers and blankets in case it did rain.

Mom, Dad, and Artie rode in the front. The rest of us sat around in a semicircle, our backs leaning against the sides and back of the wagon. I could smell the wonderful odor of the chicken Mother had cooked coming from the large basket sitting under the wagon seat. I was hungry for some of it already.

I squirmed around in my place, trying to forget I was hungry. Besides that, my neck hurt from the stiff, starched collar of my shirt. I always felt cooped up in a good shirt; I hated to dress up.

When we arrived, I saw several wagon teams tied up to the corral to the right of the house. In front of the house was a hitching post with six horses tied to it. There was a small group of people standing on the front porch. Off to one side there were several boys playing catch. One of them I made out to be Jamie, so before the wagon even stopped, I climbed over the side and jumped to the ground, ending up on my hands and knees. I got up quickly and brushed my pants off, hoping

Mother hadn't noticed. I headed off to my friend on a run. I could hear Mother yelling at me to not get dirty.

I greeted the boys with a cheery "Hi" and asked the one with the ball to throw it to me. He let the ball fly in my direction, only to have it go over my head. No sooner had I retrieved the ball when we were called to the house by Jamie's mother.

When we entered the parlor, we heard a discussion going on between Jamie's mother and father. The other people were gathered around listening.

"I don't care what you or she thinks, it is absolutely ridiculous for us to all go out there when it can possibly rain," exclaimed Mr. Bucklin.

"But that is what Jody wants, dear," Mrs. Bucklin returned. "After all, it is her wedding day. You wouldn't want to spoil it for her, would you?"

"Amy, let's be reasonable. We have a big house, there is plenty of room, and we will not get wet; why can't she be married in here?"

"You know how she feels; she has always thought of and loved that big old tree by the old well. You put a swing up there for her; she played there when she was little, and she has fond memories and feelings for that old tree. After all, it is starting to turn color, and you yourself always remarked how beautiful that tree is in the fall color.

"I know, I know, Amy, but it is going to rain. Do you want everyone to get wet? They didn't come over here to get wet, you know.

As they spoke, I watched them, along with everyone else. Mr. Bucklin was a big man, much taller and broader than my father. He had a full head of brown hair, with heavy side burns. His eyes were dark brown and deeply set in his face. He spoke with a stern expression that made his eyes appear more menacing than they really were. He had bushy brown eyebrows and a thick red-brown mustache. He always appeared to have a dark tan, even in the winter time.

By contrast, Mrs. Bucklin was small and frail. She had deep brown hair. It was always neatly fixed into a ball on the top of her head. She had blue eyes and was very light skinned, even pale I thought. She came from England, and I loved to hear her talk since she spoke with an accent. She was very quiet as a rule, and I couldn't recall her ever raising her voice in anger at Jamie and me. I believed her to be a strong woman even though she did not look it.

About this time a third person entered the conversation. It was John Northfield, the man Jody was to marry.

"Mr. Bucklin, your daughter and I are to be married today. I am sure you approve of this marriage from the friendship that we have shown each other. Most people today just run away and get married. Your daughter loves you and does not want to hurt you. Otherwise, we would have run away. She will be leaving this place she knows as her home. She has only seen a picture of her new home. She has pleasant memories here, and they will become fonder after she leaves. Let her be married as she likes—out by the tree by the old well. I want her to be happy, and this will make her happy."

Mr. Bucklin looked at Mr. Northfield as he spoke. He appeared to be annoyed at what his future son-in-law was saying, but he listened carefully. When Mr. Northfield finished speaking, Mr. Bucklin put his right hand to his chin, lowered his head slightly, and remained silent for a moment, deep in thought.

"Okay, John, I suppose it will make her happy. But for heaven's sakes, let's all get out there right away so that we can have the ceremony before it starts to rain," he announced to the entire room. "I will bring Jody along in a few minutes."

Mrs. Bucklin and Mr. Northfield smiled at each other, displaying satisfaction in the victory they had won in having the wedding outside. Everyone started to move out onto the front porch. Jamie and I stayed together as we left the parlor with the other people.

Once outside, Jamie announced a challenge to me to race him to the well. He seemed quite happy, I thought. I guess he didn't realize that his only sister would be leaving him today. It seemed strange since Jamie was not fond of his future brother-in-law. I agreed to the race, so we decided to start from the hitching post in front of the porch. We both agreed that we would place a hand on the rail and start on the count of three. My sister Lottie agreed to be the official starter.

"Okay, are you ready, Jamie?" she asked.

Jamie nodded.

"Are you ready, Ralphie?"

I nodded that I was.

"One ... two ... *three!*"

Off we went, headed for the left side of the house. Our destination was the old well, which sat about one-third of a mile or so behind the Bucklins' biggest barn. We rounded the corner and ran straight back through the farm yard. Off to our left from the back of the house was a chicken coop. To our right were the barn and the corral that our wagon was tied up to. There was a row of Russian olive bushes behind the chicken coop that ran north all the way back to the big barn thirty yards beyond the coop. The new well, which the Bucklins used every day, sat right in the middle of the barnyard and was guarded by two tall cottonwood trees, their leaves turning fall yellow. The coop, the house, the corral, and the barn sat around the well in a north-south east-west relationship. The barn was straight north and the house straight south.

Once we passed the new well, we had to run to our right to go around the big barn. There was an old but distinct wagon trail that started at the barn and ran to the old well, which was our finish line. When we rounded the east side of the barn, we would be able to see the upper half of the large cottonwoods. .

It seemed like a long way to run, but Jamie and I had done it before. Many times we had to slow down and walk in order to catch our breath, but there were occasions when we were able to make it all the way from the barn to the well without stopping. But this was our longest race. We had never run from the front of the house to the well.

I reached the crest of the hill first and stopped to catch my breath. Jamie was about forty yards behind me, so I figured I had time enough to do so. I was pretty sure he would have to stop also. I looked down at the old well. The sides of it were wood, and it had two posts that ran up from the ground about six or seven feet high. A rod about five feet long connected the two posts and served as a handle to use as a crank to raise and lower a water bucket. A small roof was built over the entire structure and was fastened to the two posts. About ten yards to the east of the well was a water trough about eight feet long and three feet high. When it was extremely dry, it was Jamie's responsibility to see that there was always some water in the trough for the livestock. Many times Jody or I would help him; we were out here often.

A big cottonwood stood directly behind the well about forty feet away. There were boards nailed to the tree so that we could climb up into it and sit or climb among the huge limbs. From a giant limb protruding from the right side of the tree twenty feet off the ground hung a swing. We could really go high in that swing. The tree loomed like a giant shadow under the dark, overcast sky. From the top of the hill, I could not tell that the leaves were turning a golden yellow. But it was easy to see that the great tree was full of life from the large cloud-like shadow it cast against the horizon.

I had heard Jamie's father say that many years ago there had been a homestead on this location, and the people had been wiped out by the Sioux Indians. What was left of their buildings had been torn down and used for part of the buildings on the Bucklin place. Sometimes, when we played here into the darkening hours, we would get shivers down our spines when we heard a coyote. We weren't so sure that they might not be Indians, and we would head back to the Bucklins' on the double. There was even an imprint on the ground that was still plain as to where the house had stood. There were some potholes that we figured were the corners of a barn or large building. Not too far from where the house sat was a pit about six or seven feet long and three or four feet wide. It was obvious that at one time it had been a storm cellar or shelter, and the years had taken their toll of the timbers and rotted them away, collapsing the structure.

Sometimes, when we were out here we would look for arrowheads or guns or something that would give us a clue as to what had really happened to those settlers. It was exciting and mysterious. One time, we even acted out what we thought had happened, with my older brothers and sisters being the Indians and we younger children being the settlers. It was fun.

Running the remaining distance to the well was easy since it was all downhill. Jamie stopped to rest when he reached the crest. When he stopped, I took off for the well.

"Wait, Ralphie, I give up. I am too tired to run the rest of the way. You win."

"Okay, I'll wait," I returned, more glad of the fact that I did not have to run the rest of the way than I was of winning. I waited until Jamie caught up to me, and we both walked the remaining distance to the well. When we arrived, we went to the well and lowered the bucket. We could hear it hit the water with an echoing splash in the well thirty feet below us. We waited until we figured the bucket was half full and began to crank the handle to raise the bucket. It was heavier than we had anticipated, and we struggled to turn the handle when it reached its peak. Eventually, the bucket appeared out of the darkness of the well. Closer and closer it came to the top until it was within reaching distance.

"I'll hold the handle, Jamie, and you grab the bucket. Be careful so you don't fall in."

Jamie let loose of the handle, and I braced myself for the additional pressure from the weight of the bucket of water. He leaned over the side of the well and stretched for the handle. He could not quite reach it. He raised himself up with his arms, placing his belly on top of the side of the wall. He reached again, and his feet lifted off of the ground. He teetered on the well wall. I wondered if he would fall forward into the well or backward onto the ground. In this position, he was able to reach out far enough to grab the handle. Slowly he pulled himself back with the help of the wall and brought the bucket with him. When he got both feet on the ground, he grabbed the bucket with both hands and lifted it high enough to set it on the edge of the wall. I let loose of the handle and grabbed the tin cup that hung on a nail by the handle. The cup was rusted in spots but no one ever seemed to mind. I dipped the cup in and took a drink. The water was cool and tasted of iron. I could see little red flakes floating around in the water as I sipped slowly, trying to avoid swallowing any of the little particles if possible.

When I had finished, I tossed out the water that remained containing the red flakes and handed the cup to Jamie. He proceeded to take a drink. He slurped noisily as he too tried to sip the water off the top, trying to avoid the little red particles. Likewise, he left a little water in the bottom and tossed it to the ground. We dumped the bucket of water back into the well and hung the cup back on the nail.

Just then, we could see the others appearing over the hill. John Northfield and Chris Jennings were on horseback, along with the preacher who had come over from Selby. Dad had unhitched the wagon and had brought a wagonload of the women. Some of the older ladies were in the wagon, along with my sisters Elsie and Lydia. One of the other men also brought a wagon, and this was filled mostly with men. Artie and Eddie were in that wagon. Shortly, everyone had arrived with the exception of Jody and Mr. Bucklin. Some people watched the hill, waiting for the wagon they were coming in to appear. Others were looking up into the sky and pointing out how very dark it was in the west. There was very little breeze.

Suddenly a movement appeared on the south hill, and two heads bobbed up and down as they grew on the horizon. It was the wagon with Jody and Mr. Bucklin. The horses were in a brisk walk as they came toward us down the hill. When they arrived, Mr. Bucklin got out and tied the team to the well post that held the other two teams. He went back to the wagon and extended his hand up to Jody. She grabbed his hand and stood up in the wagon. She slowly lifted one leg over the side and placed her foot on top of the wheel. She reached for her father's broad shoulders, and he quickly supported her weight and lifted her down with his hands placed around her waist. The ceremony was about to begin.

Everyone lined up in two lines, forming an aisle leading to the giant cottonwood. At the end of the line stood the preacher, right under that big old tree. Jody took her father's arm, and they started to walk toward the preacher. She had on a pink dress with white lace about the shoulders. A little pink hat was tied with a white ribbon around her neck. A gold locket hung almost down to her waist. I had seen Mrs. Bucklin wear it many times before, but it was the first time I had ever seen Jody wear it.

Her hair was straight and long, hanging down to the middle of her back. It looked almost brown under the cloudy sky, but when the sun fell upon it, it was a fiery, deep, red-brown color. Can't say as I had ever seen that color hair anywhere before. She walked expressionless, her dark green eyes gazing straight ahead. She had a small nose and lips that were light purple in color. Her skin was light pink and looked very soft to me. She was small, like her mother.

When they reached the preacher, everyone closed in, forming a half circle around them. Mr. Bucklin turned to his daughter and gave Jody a light kiss on her left cheek. After he had done so, he backed up several paces and joined Mrs. Bucklin. They were standing right in front of Jamie and me, so we moved to our left so we could see what was going on. We were now in a good position to see everything that was about to happen. We could see the side of the preacher's face and Jody's face. We could see just about all of John Northfield's face and also of Chris

Jennings', who was standing right beside him. A gentle breeze began to blow as the preacher spoke.

"Dearly beloved," he began.

As the preacher continued, I watched John Northfield. He kept looking at Jody. He seemed as though he did not hear a word the preacher was saying. He was a rather tall man but not as tall as Mr. Bucklin. He was of medium build. He had black wavy hair that came down over his ears. His hair came down over the top of his shirt collar. He had brown eyes and heavy black eyebrows that grew together over his nose. He also had a heavy black mustache that ran down past the corners of his mouth. I could see a small scar that started at the left corner of his chin along his jaw bone for about an inch. He looked rugged and villainous at the same time. He had on a dark brown suit with a white shirt. A thin narrow black tie tied in a bow strained to keep his collar from opening. His dark brown boots were polished to a shine. Northfield's appearance was neat, but he did appear rather uncomfortable.

"Could I have the ring?" the preacher asked of Chris Jennings.

Jennings lifted his left hand to his left vest pocket. With thumb and forefinger he searched for the ring. His hands were big and strong looking. Blonde hair covered the back of his hand. He was several inches taller than Northfield. He had a larger frame too. His hair was long and straight and blondish yellow. It was very neatly combed except for a few strands that fell over his forehead toward his right eye. He had the lightest blue eyes I had ever seen. I was very envious of them and wished that my eyes were the same. He was clean shaven and had no mustache. Bushy sideburns came down past the bottom of his ears.

He had on a black suit and vest with a white shirt on underneath. However, he had no tie. His boots were shined just as bright as Northfield's and were black in color. I envied his appearance with the dark suit, blonde hair, blue eyes, and light skin. I wished then and there that I could look like him when I grew up.

Jennings found the ring and handed it to Northfield. The preacher continued to speak and Northfield placed the ring on Jody's third finger. A low rumble of thunder was heard overhead. I looked back over my left shoulder and could see it was very dark in the west; a storm would be upon us soon.

"I now pronounce you man and wife," announced the preacher, closing his Bible.

John and Jody faced each other now. He lifted his arms around her and brought her to him. He lowered his head down to her. She raised her head toward his and leaned forward on her tip toes. She had on brown high-button shoes. They closed their eyes, and their lips met. They kissed for a long moment. I turned away, feeling uncomfortable and embarrassed watching them.

I heard someone call, "Congratulations," and looked to see Jennings with his right hand extended toward Northfield. Northfield kept his left arm around Jody as he shook Jennings' hand with the other hand. Other people huddled around calling "Congratulations" and "Good luck." The wind began to pick up.

"Let's all go back to the house where we can have something to eat and drink and not get wet," shouted Mr. Bucklin, "Everyone can see them there."

I watched Jennings whisper something into John Northfield's ear. When he finished, Northfield shook his head up and down in agreement. Jennings put his black cowboy hat on and walked over to me and Jamie. He bent over and said, "How would you like to ride my horse back to your house, Jamie?"

Jamie's mouth dropped open. He was at a loss for words.

"In fact, I think there might even be room for your friend on my horse, too," Jennings continued.

Jamie regained his composure and replied, "But what are you going to ride back to the house?"

"I'm going to ride John's horse back. In fact, when they leave your house, they are going to go to Selby and spend the night. The next morning they are going to leave on the train for Isabel. I'm going to take his horse back with me when I leave this afternoon. That is, unless it is raining real bad, then I'll probably stay the night and leave in the morning. What do you say, Jamie; do you and your friend want to ride him back?"

Jamie looked at me and we both grinned. Did we ever want to ride his horse! It was black and white, unlike most of the horses around. It was an Appaloosa, Chris told us, and his name was Paint. Chris lifted up Jamie onto the saddle and told him to hold onto the saddle horn. His big strong hands grabbed me under my arms and lifted me up behind Jamie. I put my arms around Jamie's waist. Chris hung onto the reins as he mounted Northfield's horse. It was a black male with two white front feet and a white diamond on his forehead. His black coat shone.

"Okay, boys, hang on," he said as he began to lead us off, still holding Paint's reins. We began to trot and eventually went into a slow gallop that had Jamie and me bouncing all over Paint's back. We headed up the hill and passed the other three wagons that were fully loaded with the rest of the people. Dust began to rise from the old trail as the horses' hooves kicked the dust. It was quite windy now.

We were the first to reach the house, and Chris tied the horses to the back porch rail and lifted us down. We stood on the back porch and watched the three wagons race home down the hill. It wasn't a race against each other but a race against the rain that was fast approaching from the west. When the wagons rounded the barn, several big rain drops struck the porch at our feet. Everyone hurried across the barnyard to the back porch where we stood. John Northfield and Jody arrived first, followed by my dad with the women. Third, was the wagon with the men. Mother was griping at Father about going so fast when he stopped the wagon at the porch. He tried to explain that he had to go fast to keep everyone from getting wet. She seemed unhappy with his explanation even though it was raining harder now.

The rain subsided nearly as quickly as it started, heavy at first and after about thirty minutes slowing to a drizzle. About one thirty in the afternoon, the rain stopped completely. Off in the west, a brilliant rainbow appeared across the sky. I would have guessed that one end of it would be right in the middle of the Missouri River. It was beautiful.

John and Jody decided they would be on their way to Selby. They were going to take a buckboard to town with a few things. Mrs. Bucklin would go in the morning to Selby and bring some of Jody's things for her new home. Some of the men, including Chris Jennings and my dad, would help Mr. Bucklin load the wagon.

Everyone stood on the front porch as Mr. Bucklin went to get the buckboard from the barn. Shortly he returned and drew the buckboard up close to the porch. He got out and came up on the porch to John and Jody.

"You take good care of her, John. She's a good girl, and she needs love and understanding to be a good wife, just like any woman. And you, Jody Bucklin, you be a good wife to him. Take good care of him and be strong. We will try to see you when we can."

Mrs. Bucklin was crying, as were my older sisters and Mother. Everyone seemed sad when ten minutes ago everyone was happy. I thought it was kinda ridiculous since the Bucklins would see them again in the morning. Mr. Bucklin shook Northfield's hand again and then kissed Jody. Mrs. Bucklin kissed Jody and then shook Northfield's hand. It looked silly to me. As they turned to leave, Northfield came over to where Jamie and I were standing.

"You come out and see us sometime, boy. I got a real nice ranch out there and lots of good hunting. Hear?"

"Yes, sir," Jamie returned, his heart not in it.

Northfield returned to Jody and lifted her into his arms. He stepped off the porch into the mud and carried Jody the short distance to the buckboard. The people laughed and waved as Jody pretended to fight and kick. Once in the buckboard, they turned to everyone and waved. Northfield snapped the reins, and the horse started off down the lane. When they reached the road, they turned left and headed for Selby. Everyone waved and called good luck. Some of the women and girls continued to cry.

As for me, I was just a bystander, not realizing what everything meant. I had no idea that it would be fifteen months before I would be seeing them again in Red Elm.

Chapter

4

All of us were sitting around the kitchen table having coffee and cake. It was mid-morning, and most of us had finished our chores. I was in a very happy mood. I had received my shotgun as promised on my twelfth birthday a month earlier. Not only had I gotten my first gun, but it was only twelve days until Christmas, and I was looking forward to the school vacation so that I could go hunting with my brothers and Jamie. I wasn't a very good shot yet, but father and Artie helped me when they could, teaching me the proper way to handle the gun.

We would be getting out of school in one week, and we would have two weeks of vacation. I was excited about all the hunting that I would be able to do. I hadn't shot anything but tin cans yet, but I was confident that it would not be long before I would bag my first pheasant or rabbit.

"Come on, Artie, won't you go hunting with me?" I pleaded.

"I haven't finished my chores yet, Ralph. Dad wants me to go to town to the depot to pick up a package that he ordered. Besides, don't you think maybe it's a little too cold to go? We might catch cold."

I gave him a look of dissatisfaction with his reply. I eagerly wanted to go hunting. However, Father had temporarily given me strict instructions that I could not go hunting alone. I had to go with an older brother or Dad at least. Unfortunately, Frankie and Eddie were both upstairs, sick as dogs with bad colds. That left only Artie or Dad to be my hunting companion for the day. But as luck would have it, Father had left early in the morning the day before with several of the neighbors to go to the river for wood. Father did this at least once every year in the winter. The men combined a little deer hunting along with the job of cutting firewood for the winter.

Father's return was always a cause for great excitement around the house. The first person to spot him coming down the road would call out to the rest of us. We would run to the front porch and strain our eyes to see if there was a buck tied over the firewood in the back of the wagon. Fresh venison was a great treat for us. I particularly liked the jerky that Father would make in the smokehouse. I would take it to school and eat a strip of it during recess. It was tough to chew.

"Dad won't be home until tomorrow evening, Artie. How can I learn to use my gun if I can't get anyone to go hunting with me? Couldn't I maybe, just this time, go out by myself?"

"No, sirree, Ralph. Dad said you couldn't, and I ain't gonna have him mad at me, even if he can't switch me."

I looked at Mother for any sign of encouragement that I thought might allow me to go hunting on my own. I found none.

"I'll tell you what, Ralph. If it is okay with Mom, I'll take you to town with me, and I don't really see any reason why we couldn't take our shotguns along. And just maybe, on the way back, we'll have time to go through some of the draws and kick out a pheasant or rabbit or two. How 'bout that?"

"Yippee," I shouted, throwing my arms into the air. "When do we leave?"

"We'll leave right after lunch. That will give me time to fix the harness on the buckboard. We'll take it to town so we'll have a little protection from the cold wind, but first of all, you gotta get Mom's approval."

I had almost forgotten. I was kind of afraid to ask, because I maybe would be turned down; more than anything, I wanted a chance to go hunting. I looked at Mother and tried to read her face for the answer. It was blank; nowhere in her brown eyes could I foresee an answer. I looked for the slightest quiver in her light pink lips that would give me an inkling of a smile. I knew if she smiled I could go. That was the way she said yes. But she just sat there, blank as a piece of paper.

"Mom, can I go to town with Artie this afternoon?" I said, trying to look as glum as possible. Mother stood up and stared down at me from across the table. She leaned over the table toward me and supported herself with both hands on the table. Slowly she opened her mouth and whispered, "Yes."

"Yippee," I shouted again, jumping up out of my chair. I banged both fists on top of the table because of my happiness.

"Be quiet, Ralph. You'll wake or disturb Ed and Frank, and they need all the rest they can get. If you don't hush up, I won't let you go."

I quickly quieted my voice but continued to wave my arms wildly above my head. I was very happy. Shortly, I calmed down enough to return to my chair and finish my cake. As I was about to sit down, there was a loud knock at the kitchen door that startled all of us in the room. In my excitement, I had not noticed anyone coming up to the door. I guessed that Mother and Artie had been paying attention to me, as they jumped at the sound of the knock also. Mother was closest to the door, so she went over and peeked through the curtains to see who was there.

"It's Jamie," she said, not turning her head away from the door. She closed the curtains and grabbed the door handle. When she opened the door, the cold wind rushed into the room sending shivers down me and raising little bumps on my arms.

"Come in, Jamie; you must be freezing," Mother said.

"Thanks, Mrs. Thomas," Jamie returned as he quickly slipped through the door into the kitchen. Jamie's cheeks were very red from the cold. His nose was red also, and there was a little drop of moisture on the end of it. Quickly, he erased it with his left coat sleeve and sniffed several times to clear his nose. He looked as if he was frozen stiff. He had a red stocking cap on his head and a red scarf wrapped around his neck and up over his mouth. His coat was black and bulky. He held both arms straight down to his sides. His sleeves were a little too long, and you could only see the tips of his red gloves popping out the bottom of the sleeves. His boots flopped noisily on the kitchen floor as they were a little too big for his feet. And, wouldn't you know it, his boots were on the wrong feet.

"Jamie," I laughed, pointing down, "you have your boots on the wrong feet."

Jamie looked down, and his nose and eyes disappeared behind the red scarf. He bent over slightly and slowly his right arm bent up toward his face. As his arm bent, his red gloves appeared to grow up out of his sleeve. He grabbed the scarf in front of his nose and pulled it down so that he could see if I was telling the truth.

"So they are," he said, not seeming too surprised. "But I was in a hurry to get down here."

"Well, come over by the stove and take your boots off so you don't track snow all over the kitchen," replied Mother.

"What were you in such a hurry about, Jamie?" I questioned as I lifted my fork to take a bite of chocolate cake. Jamie ignored or forgot my question. His eyes followed my fork as I lifted it to take another bite of cake. He said nothing.

"Come sit down, Jamie, and I'll get you a piece of cake," Mother said as she observed Jamie staring at me. She helped him off with his winter clothes and directed him to the table. "Tell us why you came all the way down here in the nasty cold."

"Oh, yeah," Jamie replied as he came out of his trance and proceeded to sit down at the table across from me.

"Well, Father got a telegram when he went into town yesterday. It was from Jody. She had been planning to come back for Christmas with John, but it seems as though there are too many things to do out at the ranch. So they won't be coming for Christmas."

Jamie looked dejected at the thought of not seeing his sister for Christmas. Mother came over and put her hands on Jamie's shoulders.

"Well, I'm sure that they wanted to be here very much, Jamie. I'm sure that they will try to get out to see you and your folks as soon as they can."

"Well," said Jamie, seeming to cheer up quickly. "That's why I'm here."

We all looked at Jamie, rather puzzled by his statement.

"You see," he continued, "Jody has asked me to come out and see her over Christmas." Jamie was grinning from ear to ear. "And you haven't heard the best part. The best part is that I get to ride the train if I do get to go." Jamie's eyes were wild with excitement as he leaned over the table to tell me this.

"That's wonderful, Jamie," Mother replied as she placed a piece of cake in front of him and sat down beside him. While Mother did this, Artie pulled up a chair and sat down beside me.

"Are you going to get to go? Have your folks said?" continued Mother.

"Well, they haven't said yes and they haven't said no yet; you know how it is. They said that they think maybe I'm too little to go all by myself. That's why I'm here. Jody asked me to bring Ralphie with me."

I opened my mouth in shock, dropping a piece of cake from it back onto my plate.

"Are you kidding, Jamie? You mean she wants me to go? Mom, can I go? I haven't ever ridden the train before. You'll let me go, won't you?" I fired questions at her rapidly.

"Now, wait a minute, Ralph. Going to Selby is one thing, but going all the way to Red Elm on a train is another. You will have to have your father's permission for that. I won't give it to you."

"When would we leave?" I asked of Jamie, not really listening to Mother and assuming I could go.

"We would leave next Saturday," Jamie continued. "Father says that I can go if you go along too. Otherwise, he is not sure if he will let me go alone. Since Mother has been feeling poorly lately, he thinks it might be easier on her if she don't have to look after me all the time. Dad also said that I should tell you to bring your shotgun if you can go. John and Chris Jennings would take us hunting while we are there."

I was thrilled. The thought of taking a train ride and going on a trip and going hunting was just too much to believe. I couldn't have been more excited if I had gotten two shotguns for Christmas.

"You'll tell Dad that it is okay with you if I go, won't you, Mom?" I asked, looking for encouragement from her.

"We'll just have to talk it over with your father when he returns and see what he says, that's all."

"I sure hope he lets me go."

"Well, I have to get home. I won't have time to eat this cake, Mrs. Thomas. My dad says I'll have to do a lot of work around our place if he does let me go."

With that, Jamie got up and moved to the stove where his boots were drying. He balanced himself on his right foot as he lifted his left leg to put on his boot. This time he got the correct boot on his foot. He quickly slipped the right boot on and slipped his arm into his coat that Mother was holding for him. Mother helped Jamie adjust his cap on top of his head and tied the red scarf around his neck and then adjusted it to cover his mouth and nose. Jamie raised his arms one at a time and charged forward thrusting each hand into the red gloves that Mother held up to him. At last he was ready for his return trip home. He and Mother proceeded to the back door of the kitchen. Mother grabbed the handle and prepared to open the door.

"I sure hope you can go, Ralphie," Jamie said, turning and looking first at me and then up at my mother. "Good-bye, see you later."

Mother opened the door. Once again the cold wind blew into the room. Jamie gave us all a quick little wave good-bye. He turned and slipped through the doorway out of the kitchen. Mother closed the door behind him.

"I sure hope I can go too," I said to myself, out loud so that Mother could hear me. "I sure hope so."

"Let's go, Ralph, or we won't have any time to go hunting," Artie called to me.

I was standing on the back porch, waiting for Artie to check the cinches on the harness of the buckboard. The wind had stopped blowing, and the sky was gray and overcast. It was snowing, white flakes drifted lazily down to the ground adding a fluffy white covering over the two or three inches of snow that already lay on the ground. Everything was peaceful and quiet. I thought how beautiful everything was going to be for Christmas.

"Okay, I'm coming."

I was bundled up warmly since it would take us more than an hour to get to town. I had on flannel underwear under my denim pants. Besides them, I had on a red flannel shirt that was very soft and was wearing thin at the elbows. It was very comfortable and very warm. It was my favorite shirt. Over my shirt, I had on a gray wool sweater to help keep me warm. I had on a blue denim coat that had a wool lining in it. On my head was a yellow stocking cap. I had on my canvas gloves instead of the fur gloves that we normally wore when we went to town. The canvas gloves we used when we were working or hunting. On my feet I had my boots, which had rubber soles but cloth leggings. At least, for the moment, I was warm and dry.

I held four wool blankets in my arms. We would put one or two of them on the seat of the buckboard. Wrapped like this, the wind would not blow directly on our legs, and we would not be so cold. Since the wind was not blowing now, the trip to town would not be too bad. We did not even bother to bring our foot warmer. Since we would be doing some hunting, Artie figured we wouldn't get much benefit out of it; it would probably cool off quickly.

I jumped off the porch and brought Artie the blankets. He spread two of them out on the seat, allowing one to hang over the front of the seat and touch the floor.

"Go get our guns, and don't forget the shells," Artie ordered.

I went back to the porch and through the door into the kitchen. Leaning against the wall behind the door were Artie's and my shotguns. On the floor beside them sat two boxes of 12-gauge shotgun shells. Artie's shotgun was a 12-gauge, double-barrel shotgun that had nicks and scratches in the stock from years of use. There wasn't much finish left on the walnut stock. There were little specks of rust on the barrel.

In contrast, my shotgun sparkled. The stock was polished and shiny. There were no scratches or nicks anywhere. The single barrel was black, containing no rust spots, and it also shined. I was very proud of it.

I grabbed Artie's shotgun, placed the stock under my left arm, and dropped it over my left forearm, allowing my left hand to remain free. I picked up my gun with my right hand and carefully shifted it to my left hand. I rested the butt on the floor as I bent over and stacked one box of shells on top of the other. I grabbed the lower box and slowly straightened up, balancing the one box on top of the other box. I lowered my left hand on the barrel of my gun so that I could lift it off of the floor easier. With my backside, I pushed open the storm door to the back porch. Halfway through the door, I turned and hit the barrel of Artie's gun against the door frame.

"Hey," called Artie, hearing the noise and seeing his gun entangled in the doorway. "Be careful with my gun."

From the sound of his voice and the look on his face, one would have thought that he had the new gun and not me. I managed to get through the doorway without any further damage. I was surprised and proud of the fact that I had not dropped and spilled the box of shotgun shells that I balanced in my right hand.

I made it to the wagon, where Artie grabbed his shotgun out from under my arm. He examined the barrel carefully as if expecting to find a dent in it.

"Huh," he grunted to himself in the apparent satisfaction that he could find no dent when he surely expected to find one. He laid his shotgun under the buckboard seat. He took both boxes of shotgun shells from my right hand and set them under the seat beside his gun. "Put your gun under the seat, and then go get something to cover them up with. Ain't no point in letting your gun get all wet and messed up. In fact, there's an old saddle blanket in the barn hanging over one of the stalls. Go get it."

I carefully set my gun down with both hands. I pulled Artie's gun out a little bit when he wasn't looking so that I could make room to get my gun up next to the blanket out of the wet snow. I ran to the barn and found the blanket Artie mentioned. When I returned to the wagon, Artie was already seated and had one blanket over his legs. I leaned over his side and spread the blanket over the stocks of the guns. I ran around to the other side and placed the remainder of the blanket over the barrels. I grabbed the arm rail of the seat, put my left foot onto a spoke of the wheel, and swung myself up into the seat beside Artie.

"Pull the blanket behind you up over your shoulders," Artie commanded. I did as he said. Artie did the same and shortly both of us were bundled under the same blanket. Artie took the blanket spread over his legs and unfolded it so that it covered my legs also. We tucked the blankets in under our seats so that they would not come loose. For the moment, we were snug and warm.

Artie grabbed the reins and snapped them sharply so that they stung the rump of our old gray horse, Duke. He started off with a quick jerk, as if he had suddenly been stung by a bee while asleep. Duke broke into a trot as we headed off down our lane to the road. We turned left and headed east down the road to Selby. It was still snowing, the big white flakes slowly drifting down to the ground. I looked back over my left shoulder to our house. It looked peaceful, warm, and inviting. There was a small trail of black smoke that lifted up from the kitchen chimney and floated lazily off into the sky. It was very beautiful, I thought.

Shortly, we were in front of Jamie's house. We looked for any activity, but we could find none—although we were sure someone was home. The only indication of life was the smoke that rose from their kitchen chimney that was hidden behind the peak of the roof of the house.

Old Duke trotted on. As we went down the road, Artie surveyed the countryside, looking for ditches or sloughs where he figured we would find rabbits and pheasants. Since most of the land was used for raising cattle, a lot of land did not offer any cover for the game. Occasionally, there would be a cornfield that had been shucked. The stalks offered good cover and normally there would be some corn that the pheasants could find. The wheat would have long been threshed and harvested, so it was pretty easy to find where the cover would be.

Artie told me that the hunting might not be good since it was snowing. Normally, the game would sit very tight in the cover; it would be hard to flush the rabbits and pheasants out. He explained how we would have to walk slower through the cover than usual. This apparently was a tactic that made the game nervous. As a result, they would flush from their hiding place and would allow us a shot at them.

It continued to snow, but since there was no wind we were not cold or uncomfortable as we rode along the country road. Everything was peaceful and quiet. A thick blanket of snow covered the ground, and although I had seen snow in previous winters, I couldn't remember seeing one that was so beautiful.

"There's town," Artie said, elbowing me in the ribs. I must have been daydreaming. I hadn't realized that we had come that far, but there was Selby, sitting almost directly north of us. I could make out the outlines of buildings off in the distance. They appeared to be gray and cold. They did not have a friendly, cheerful look to them like my house did. I felt a strange nervousness that I could not explain. I had been to Selby many times, in both the winter and the summer, and I had never had this feeling before. Having Artie sitting beside me made me feel better. I felt as though I needed his protection from those buildings off in the distance.

Selby was a small town. By coming in on the south road, the first building we would come to would be the train depot. It sat on the southern edge of the town, and after you crossed the tracks you would be on the main street of Selby. The street was very wide and maybe three-quarters of a mile long. At the end of the street sat the schoolhouse. I knew it was there even though I could not see it through the snow.

Each side of the street would be lined with stores. Every so often there would be a vacant space between some of the buildings. From memory, I knew that there were three hotels, two saloons, and two general stores. There was also a livery stable, a blacksmith shop, and two general stores. In the center of the middle block was the opera house. People still talked about a famous English lady who sang there many years before. I tried to remember her name but couldn't.

There were several other buildings that had different things to offer, but I never paid much attention to what they were. I was most fond of the Bates General Store since they had something new to see every time we came to town. I liked to look in at the candy counter most of all. Licorice sticks and jelly beans were my favorites. Sometimes the owner of Bates General Store would give me a licorice stick. My other favorite place to go was to the blacksmith shop. The man who owned the shop was named Gus, and he was a very big man. He had huge shoulders and a very thick black mustache that covered his mouth. When he talked, his voice boomed throughout his shop. When he laughed, he shook the ground beneath my feet. In the summer time when it was hot, he would work with no shirt, covering his chest with a leather apron that hung down to his knees. His shoulders and chest were covered with thick, black, curly hair that shone brightly over his dark skin when he would sweat. He had black curly hair that came down to his shoulders. The top of his head was bald. He had brown eyes that were small compared to his nose. Gus was a nice man who was always happy. I liked to watch him swing his hammer against the red-hot iron that he was making into a horseshoe or wheel.

"Well, are you going to sit out here in the cold?" Artie said, poking me in the ribs with his elbow. I hadn't realized that we were at the depot. Quickly, I looked around for an "iron horse"—that was what the Indians had called them when they first saw them. I had seen them, but I had never ridden on one. I thought it would be fun.

I pulled the blanket from my shoulders and jumped out of the buckboard. I checked to see if my gun was still dry. I was satisfied that it was and followed Artie into the east door of the depot.

No one was in the station other than the man who sold the tickets. There were a few benches in the center of the room. Along one wall were some boxes and wooden crates. We crossed the room to the west wall that had a window in it with an iron bar across it. It was through that window that I could see the station manager when he entered the room.

"Do you have a package for Dad?" Artie asked the man. The man looked up from some papers on his desk.

"Hi, Art," he said. "Sure do. Those two boxes against the south wall are for you. They came in yesterday."

"Thanks," Artie replied, turning toward the boxes.

Artie walked to the boxes and looked at the labels on each box.

"Those two are ours," he said, pointing to two boxes standing one on top of the other in the middle of the other boxes. "You hold the door, Ralph, and I'll carry them out."

I turned and went back to the east door. Artie grabbed the top box and picked it up. It was about two feet high and two feet across. I opened the door as Artie reached it. I stood there holding the door open as Artie passed through and went to the back of the buckboard.

"Hey, boy," called the station man, "close the door; it's cold outside."

I quickly obeyed and shut the door. I looked through the window, watching Artie put the box down in the back of the wagon. After he had done that, I opened the door so Artie could pass through to get the other box. Artie went to the other box and bent over to pick it up. With a low grunt, Artie lifted the box from the floor. Struggling a bit, he carried it back to the door I held open. Artie passed through and, remembering what the station man had said, I closed the door after stepping outside.

I followed Artie to the wagon. He set the box down beside the other and motioned to me.

"Come on, Ralph. Get in the wagon if you want to go hunting," he said.

Eagerly, I climbed into the wagon and pulled one of the blankets around me. Artie climbed in beside me and lifted the blanket I had over me around his shoulders. Artie picked up the reins and, with a flick of his wrist, snapped the reins over Duke's hind end; off he went in a trot.

"We won't go into town since it will be getting dark soon with this snow," Artie commented.

I listened, but said nothing, anxiously awaiting the moment that Artie would stop the buckboard and tell me to get my gun. It was still snowing those big, beautiful white flakes as we headed south back toward home.

As we rode along the quiet countryside, Artie looked over possible hunting areas. We passed creeks that I thought had good cover. Still, Artie did not stop the wagon.

"Let's see what kind of cover the Bliss farm has," Artie said.

When we approached the edge of the ranch, Artie stopped the wagon.

"See that ditch over there," Artie said, pointing to a small clump of trees to his left. "I'll tie Duke up to a fence, and we'll hunt that ditch. Get your gun, Ralph."

I jumped out of the right side of the wagon and pushed one of the blankets away from the guns under the seat. I grabbed my shotgun. It felt good in my hands. Artie jumped out of the left side of the buckboard and pulled out his old shotgun.

"Load your gun, Ralph, and head down to the end of the ditch. I'll stay up at this end of the ditch. Walk real slow, very slow. You want any pheasants in there to get real nervous. Just take your time. If you get a pheasant or rabbit up, don't get excited; just slowly raise your gun and fire. Understand? And for heaven's sake, don't fire if you see me. I don't want to get shot. Got that?"

Artie gave me a stern look as I bent over and opened a box of shotgun shells. I grabbed as many as I could in one hand and shoved them into my right-hand coat pocket. I grabbed a few more and did the same as before. I pulled back the bolt on the gun and shoved a shell into the barrel. I pushed the bolt forward to close the chamber. I checked the safety to be sure it was on. I was all set to go with my new 12-gauge, bolt-action, Remington shotgun.

Artie's was a double-barrel, 12-gauge. Once again, he inspected the gun to see if there was a dent from my hitting it in the doorway at home. Satisfied, he flipped the lever that broke open the gun and placed a shell in each barrel. He snapped the gun shut and clicked the safety. He grabbed a handful of shells and shoved them into his pocket.

"All set?" he said, looking at me.

"Yeah," I returned excitedly.

"Okay, head down to the end, like I told you, and head slowly back up toward me."

I headed off down to the end of the ditch, making sure to stay away from the ditch so that I didn't scare the game I expected to find there.

When I reached the end, I turned and saw Artie already standing in the center of the ditch at the other end. He motioned with his arm that he was ready and that I should start toward him through the ditch. Once again, I checked my safety on my gun. It was on.

Slowly, I started through the ditch as Artie had told me. Much of the grass was bent over from the weight of the snow. It looked like good cover for a rabbit or pheasant to hide in. Up ahead, I could see a pile of brush. Just the sight of it excited me since I knew that there was a good chance of seeing a rabbit there. I got more excited with every step I took. I fingered the safety on my gun, hoping I could click it off at any moment.

On I walked, looking for game or a track in the snow that would lead me to game. Still, I saw nothing. I kicked at clumps of grass, hoping that something would jump out. I was now almost to the brush pile. I stopped when I was a few feet from it. I looked into the pile, hoping to find a bundle of fur that would mean a rabbit. Not seeing anything, I kicked at the pile. The dead limbs cracked, and the snow fell from them from the force of my kick. Still, nothing jumped out of the pile for me to shoot at.

Slowly, I started around the right side of the brush pile. I kept kicking the pile. When I got to the other side, I was satisfied that there was nothing there. I turned toward Artie to continue up the ditch. That's when I saw him; there he was—a rabbit under a clump of grass that was covered with snow. He looked like a clod of black dirt against the white snow. Quickly, I raised the gun and fired.

Bang!

The sound exploded from the gun. The gun darn near broke my shoulder from the force of the shot. The force of the shot even moved me back a step or two. I looked at the rabbit. Sure enough, there he was, deader than heck.

"Hey, Artie," I yelled at the top of my lungs. "I got one, Artie. I got one."

I stood there proudly surveying the first kill of my life.

"Come here, Artie, come here," I yelled.

Artie reached me in a few minutes and looked down at my rabbit.

"What the hell you doing, Ralph? Are you crazy?"

"Why?" I asked, wondering what I had done wrong.

"You don't ever shoot a rabbit sitting still, Ralph. That's the dumbest thing you can do."

"Why, Artie?" I asked, not understanding.

"Because," Artie continued, "first of all, some rabbits may be sick. If they are, they're not gonna run even when you are up close to them. And, secondly, you'll blow them all to pieces at close range. Just look at your rabbit!"

Artie pointed to the rabbit on the ground. I moved closer to see. There was fur all over the ground that had been blown off the rabbit from the buckshot. I could see half his guts on the ground.

"Yes, sirree, Artie. I sure did get him, didn't I?"

"Hellfire, Ralph," Artie said, starting to chuckle, "you shot him up so bad even the back legs are no good. May as well leave him to the foxes or coyotes. He ain't no good to us that way. Let's walk back up the ditch; maybe there's something still in there, and we can flush it out."

I looked down at my first kill. I felt terrible. The first thing I ever got in my whole life, and I couldn't even take it home. I was sad to leave that poor bunny laying there dead in the snow. I promised myself I'd never do that again and that I would remember what Artie said. Still, I felt a touch of sadness for what I had just done.

"Hey, Ralph," Artie called back to me, "don't feel bad, little brother. I did the same darn thing. Besides, he won't go to waste; some coyote or fox will find him and eat him. He'd probably got caught by one anyway. Check your gun to see if it's loaded, and check your safety.

Artie's words made me feel a little better. I checked my gun and checked the safety. I was ready to get a chance to correct the mistake I had made a few minutes before. Slowly, Artie and I headed back up the ditch Artie had just come through. I was on the left side of him. He told me, once again, that I should go real slow.

We got to the end of the ditch, but we didn't kick up anything else. The only thing we saw was a pheasant track. Artie explained to me that the pheasant had probably been sitting real tight in the grass and that when he came down to me after I had shot, that the pheasant had circled behind him. We followed the track in the snow for a short ways. It led out into the clearing beside the ditch. We could still see the wing tip impressions in the snow where he had started to fly off.

"It is starting to get late, Ralph, so let's hurry back to the wagon. We'll see if we can find another ditch back toward the house to hunt before it gets dark," said Artie.

We hurried back to the wagon and got in. We didn't bother to put our guns in the back of the wagon. After unloading our guns, we rested them against the front seat of the buckboard so we would not waste much time if we stopped again.

It was still snowing when we stopped the buckboard a half a mile or so down the road. I could see a small ditch off to the right about fifty or sixty yards.

"Let's hunt this," Artie said. "It doesn't look too good, but it will be dark in another fifteen minutes or so. We'll both start at the same end and just walk to the other. Hurry up."

Artie was out of the buckboard and had his gun loaded before I hardly had the blanket off me. He tied old Duke up to the fence as I jumped out of the wagon. I landed on both feet, and the force of my feet against the ground caused the snow to be pushed away, making my footprints look two inches bigger than they really were.

I loaded my gun and put the safety on. Artie waited for me by the fence. He took my gun and held it for me while I crawled under the fence in the snow. I got up quickly and brushed the snow off me as best I could. Artie handed me his gun and mine over the fence. He put his right foot on the lower barbwire and, while supporting his weight with his hands on the fence post, swung his left leg over the fence.

"Darn near hooked my pants," Artie said, after clearing the fence. "Come on, let's go."

We took off to the ditch in a slow trot. It was hard to move too fast in the snow with all the clothes we had on. We reached the ditch and slowly we started through. There wasn't any timber or any brush piles in this ditch. What was long grass was bent over by the snow, the same as in the last ditch. The cover did not look very good to me, and it wasn't.

We reached the other end of the ditch and never saw a thing, not even a track. I would have to wait until another time to get a chance for another kill. I was disappointed that we were going home without any game. We turned and headed back to the road. The snow was starting to let up, and it was beginning to get colder as we walked. By the time we reached the wagon, my toes seemed half frozen. I wondered if they would have seemed so cold if I had gotten a big fat pheasant.

We laid our guns under the front seat and covered them with the blanket. I climbed into the buckboard then threw one blanket over my legs and the other over my shoulders while Artie untied old Duke. Artie climbed in and pulled the blanket over his legs and the other around his shoulders.

We headed down the road toward home. It was dark now, but with the snow on the ground, it was light enough that we had no trouble seeing the road. Everything was quiet, and the snow was stopping as we moved along. It was getting much, much colder. My toes were freezing. Artie said nothing, and as we rode along in the silent darkness of night, I thought about the rabbit that I had shot. I felt sad and couldn't help thinking of it lying dead in the cold snow.

I wondered if a fox or coyote would find it. I hoped so. I didn't want it to be wasted.

I wondered when I would get my first pheasant. Maybe it would be tomorrow. I cheered quietly at the thought of that. I looked forward to sitting down to a nice, warm meal that I knew my mother and sisters would have prepared for us. And, in the cold night air, I knew how wonderful it would be to lie down in my feather bed and pull the heavy quilts up to my chin. I was tired, and I knew I would sleep.well.

I thought about Father coming home tomorrow from the river, and I wondered if he had gotten a deer. These last thoughts made me happy and excited, and I looked forward to all of them. And Jamie, what about Jamie, I wondered. Would Father let me go with Jamie to see his sister in Isabel? I had forgotten about that during the day. But now I got excited at the thought of a train ride. He had to let me go, he just had to, I thought, but I wondered if he would.

Chapter

5

"Hey, everybody, here comes Dad! Here comes Dad!" It was Eddie yelling from the girls' upstairs bedroom. I jumped up from the kitchen chair I was sitting on and ran to the front porch door. My sisters, who were in the kitchen helping Mother fix supper, followed me. As I stood looking through the front door, I heard Mother behind me calling up to Eddie to get back in bed.

Eddie whined a complaint at Mother's words and insisted that he would do so as soon as Father arrived. All he wanted to know was if Dad had gotten a deer. I guess Frankie was still too sick or just asleep because I couldn't hear him upstairs with Eddie. Frankie was having a terrible time recovering, while Eddie would be up and around again in a day or so.

Through the front door, I could see a couple of wagons coming down the road from the west. It was getting dark, and from where I was I could not tell which wagon was ours. My sisters were in the parlor looking out the south and west windows. I was satisfied to be where I was because I knew I would be the first one out the door to see and touch the deer that I hoped would be on the wagon. Mother leaned over me and looked out the door window also.

It had been a very cold but sunny day. Artie had been too tired from doing all the chores to take me hunting. As much as I wanted to bag a pheasant, I was almost glad we didn't go since it was so cold. Mother left my side and said she was going to put some coffee on now so it would be ready for Father when he arrived.

The wagons grew bigger as they came down the road, and I could hear my sisters arguing as to who was in the lead wagon. From where I was I could see that it was Mr. Bliss in the lead wagon with Dad following.

Suddenly, out from the east side of the house trotted Artie riding bareback on Duke. He was heading up the lane to the road to go out and meet the wagons.

Darn him, I thought to myself. *I wanted to be the first to see what's happening.* I guess Artie had spotted the wagons from out back while he was doing chores.

Artie was out to the road now, and he turned right and headed west down the road to the two approaching wagons. They were only a couple of hundred yards apart now. It was still hard to see which wagon was ours in the dusk. As Artie approached the wagons I watched him for any clue that would tell me who was who and if anyone had gotten any deer.

I could see Artie wave to the first wagon when they were a few yards apart. I was mad at the thought of not being out there. I wanted to know what was happening. Artie turned Duke around and walked him slowly beside the wagon while he talked to the driver. I figured it was Dad's wagon. Then, quickly, Artie turned Duke around and headed him to the second wagon. I could see Artie wave again. He stopped short of the second wagon and waited for its arrival. When the wagon passed, Artie turned Duke and followed at the rear end of the wagon.

Artie was bending over now, lifting the cover over the back of the second wagon. He was looking at or for something, I couldn't tell which. I was mad at him for snitching and peeking before I had a chance to. My sisters had seen everything I had, and I could hear them making all kinds of guesses and remarks about what they had observed.

Both wagons were entering our lane by this time, and I could see that Father's wagon was in the rear. I started to open the front door of the house.

"No you don't, Ralph," Mother said from behind me, grabbing me by the right shoulder. "You're not going outside without a coat and hat on. If you have to get out there, go put them on first."

She lifted her left arm and pointed toward the kitchen and released her grip on my right shoulder. I must have been so shook up about Artie being out there that I had not heard Mother return from the kitchen. I took off on a run to the kitchen. From behind me, I could hear Mother giving the same instructions to any of my sisters who also wanted to go outside. I grabbed my coat from the peg on the west wall of the kitchen. Underneath it was my yellow stocking cap. I pulled it down on my head and over my ears while I held my coat between my legs. Once this was done, I grabbed my coat and put it on and ran back to the front door. I bumped into my sisters in the hallway. They were on their way to the kitchen for their clothes too. When I reached the front door again, there was Mother, all bundled up and ready to go outside. I hadn't noticed that she was dressed that way before, and I tried to recall if she had put on her winter clothing before or after I had gone to get mine. Both wagons were only thirty or forty yards from the house now. I quickly buttoned my coat and pulled the gloves from the pockets.

As soon as my gloves were on, I gently but firmly pushed Mother aside and grabbed the door handle. I quickly turned the knob and with my left hand pulled the door back rapidly. I stepped through the doorway out onto the porch. It was very cold, and the wind was blowing so hard into my face that my eyes watered. I wiped the tears from the corners of my eyes so I could see once again.

My sisters and Mother quickly joined me on the porch. Mr. Bliss's wagon was only a few yards from the porch now. I looked beyond his wagon and could see Father.

"Did you get one, Dad?" Did you get one?" I yelled excitedly, wanting to know if he had gotten a deer.

"Come see for yourself, son," Father returned, bringing his wagon to a halt.

I leaped from the porch and ran to the wagon a few yards away. I ran to the back of the wagon and jumped up to reach the top of the tailgate to pull myself up so I could look under the cover. I was so heavily dressed that I couldn't get my arms up to reach the top. I jumped again and was able to grab the top of the wagon. I lifted my right foot to find a place that would allow me to stand up. My heart was pounding as I couldn't wait to see what was on the other side of the tailgate I was holding on to.

I found room enough for my foot at the floor level of the wagon; quickly, I pulled myself up so that I was standing on both feet with my stomach on the top of the tailgate. I pulled wildly at the cover to see what was underneath. There it was, lying there in the fading light of dusk—a beautiful buck deer. His head lay at my feet, and I could count three points on each side of his head. I had seen more points on deer before, and I knew that this was not as big as some I had seen, but I knew it was the best one Father had ever brought home.

I looked for the bullet hole but was unable to find it. I wanted to see where Father had shot him, and I wanted to try to picture in my mind how he got him.

"It has six points," I shouted, having forgotten that no one had made it known to the other. "He's a real beauty, Dad; where did you shoot him? Where did the bullet go? When did you get him?"

I fired question after question at him but never got an answer. I looked up only to find Father on the front porch hugging Mother and my sisters. He hadn't even heard me. He was going to tell the others, and I wouldn't be in there to hear it. I had to hear what happened, I thought. I jumped from the wagon and ran to the porch. When I reached it, Father turned and stopped me.

"You go with Artie and tie the deer up in the barn. Let me—"

But, gee, Dad," I cut in.

"Let me take Robert inside to have a cup of coffee and to warm ourselves a bit. Don't worry. I'll wait till you get back to tell you all about it. I promise."

"Come on, Artie. Let's go. I don't want to miss a thing."

I turned and ran back to the wagon and climbed into the seat waiting for Artie. Artie tied old Duke to the back end of the wagon and climbed in beside me. He snapped the reins, and we headed back to the barn. When we reached the barn, Artie stopped the wagon so I could get out and pull one of the doors open. After I had done so, Artie drove the wagon inside. I pulled the door shut behind him.

It was dark in the barn, and when Artie got out of the wagon, he grabbed a kerosene lantern off of a barrel and lit it with a match. The warm glow of light began to fill the barn, casting eerie shadows against the walls. I was glad Artie was with me, because it was kinda spooky. He hung the lantern on a barn post nail near the back end of the wagon.

I waited anxiously for him to untie the covers of the tailgate so that we could let it down and I could see the beautiful buck again. We let the gate hang down to the floor, and I could see the deer. It looked bigger than before, and I bent over to inspect the head. I could see that his mouth was partly open and his tongue was hanging down. His eyes were still open, and they were glassy and foggy brown. It had real pretty, long eyelashes. Artie grabbed one of the antlers and pulled it forward so that its head hung over the back of the wagon. He grabbed a rope and tied it around one antler.

"Let's try to lift him down on the ground and bring him over to that rafter," Artie said, pointing to a rafter to his left. "Climb into the wagon and grab his hind legs. I'll take the front legs. Try not to drop him; we don't want to bruise the meat."

I jumped into the wagon and grabbed the deer's back feet. Artie grabbed the front legs and pulled the deer forward. When he was over halfway out of the wagon, I could begin to feel the deer's weight, and I pulled hard on his legs trying not to drop him. He was heavy, even though I could see that his guts had been removed. Two sticks were stuck inside his ribs to keep his stomach section open. Artie explained that this was done to let the stomach section cool down so it would dry out quickly and not spoil the meat.

When we had him on the ground, we half carried and half dragged him over to the rafter. I had a hard time keeping my end off the ground since his legs were smooth and his weight would make his legs slip through my hands. Artie threw the loose end of rope over the rafter and tightened up the line. We both pulled on the rope. Slowly the big buck rose until finally his hind legs didn't touch the ground. Artie quickly tied up the rope around a beam.

We stood back and admired the buck in the light of the lantern. He cast a giant shadow on the wall. You could see the antlers' shadow on the wall as though it were a giant spider. The buck was a beautiful reddish brown. It had a white spot on its chest as well as one under its chin.

"It's a white tail, and there's where Dad shot, Ralph," Artie said.

"Where?" I said, wanting to see it.

"Right there," Artie said, pointing up to a hole about six inches up from his chest and four inches behind his left front leg. "A perfect shot."

I could see the hole. It was smaller than I expected. For some reason or another I thought the hole would be big. I stood there and looked up at the deer hanging by its antler. I wondered why it didn't break off from the weight of the deer. I tried to imagine it running through fields and fighting with other bucks, locked horn and horn. Somehow, looking at the buck, I thought maybe the stories of buck fighting each other were not true. The deer was just too pretty to fight with anything. I wondered if I could bring myself to kill such a beautiful animal.

I blinked my eyes and cleared the thoughts from my mind. I realized that I was cold, even in the barn. I started stomping my feet and blowing on my fingers to keep warm. It would be bitter cold tonight for sure. Artie had unhitched the team and put them in their stalls. He broke a bale of hay and gave a quarter of the bale to each horse. Satisfied that they would be all right, he went to the beam and lifted the lantern.

"Come on, Ralph. Let's get back to the house," he said.

We walked to the barn door together and slowly he pushed open the door. We turned and looked back at the buck hanging from the rafter. Slowly Artie turned the knob to shorten the wick. The light dimmed on the red hair of the buck. I wondered if it was better that the buck was dead—would it have suffered more in the cold nights of winter? I wondered..

The last ray of light flickered in the lantern. I was blinded by the sudden darkness. Artie set the lantern inside and closed the door. It creaked loudly in the night.

Back at the house, we found everyone sitting around the kitchen table. Father was the center of attention. Eddie and Frankie were over in the corner by the hallway door. I guessed that Mother wouldn't allow them too close to the others since they were still sick. Mother was fussing over a pot of coffee at the stove. Artie and I took off our winter coats, boots, and hats and hung them on the pegs on the wall to our right.

"Well, I better be running along, folks," said Mr. Bliss, standing up. "It is getting late, and Ann will have dinner waiting. I don't want to worry her or the kids none since it's dark now."

"Sure you won't stay and have a bite to eat?" asked Mother.

"No, I'd like to, but it will have to be some other time. I been gone long enough from the place now; I better be getting back," he replied.

Mr. Bliss turned and headed toward the hallway leading to the front door. We all got up and followed him. We stood in the doorway and watched him climb into his wagon. He snapped the reins over his team and slowly they turned in a half circle away from the porch. He had only traveled a few yards when he disappeared into the night. We could hear his wagon creaking even though we could not see him in the darkness.

Father closed the door and told all of us to tend to our duties and he would tell us about his trip over our dinner. My sisters and Mother tended to dinner. Frankie and Eddie went back upstairs under Mother's orders, even though they were squawking about it. Artie and I just sat in the kitchen and listened to the gab of my sisters, Mother, and Father. He asked how Eddie and Frankie were doing, if all of we children had been good, if Artie had picked up the packages in town, and things like that. I sat impatiently waiting for dinner. I wanted to hear how Dad got his buck.

We all sat quietly as Father started his story of the trip to the river. He explained how he and Mr. Bliss met the other men at the Powell ranch on Friday morning. From there, they traveled in a line down to the river about three or four miles away. When they reached the river, they set up camp and proceeded to cut firewood during the middle and early afternoon hours. They quit along about three in the afternoon and spread out along the river, hoping to bag a deer.

The first day, no one got a deer, but apparently the men had seen plenty of tracks. Dad explained how they had gone to bed early that night so they could get up early Saturday morning to hunt, sure that the deer would be moving around before they bedded down during the daylight hours. They had pitched two tents, and there were three men in each tent. I imagine that they froze in the cold that night, but Dad said everyone was quite comfortable, and no one complained of being cold.

Saturday morning, the men were up before dawn to go out to hunt. Dad said he headed down the east side of the river about two miles from camp. Three of the men went across the river to hunt on the west side. The other two headed north of camp on the same side as Dad. Dad told how he headed south until he found a steep bluff on the edge of the river. A small draw lay directly east of the bluff. Dad said he knew that a deer moving along the river would go through the draw east of the bluff rather than stay along the river and go west of the bluff and into the water. He mentioned that it was snowing and that he had no sooner set down when he saw a buck heading north through the draw in a slow trot. Dad said he lowered his gun and aimed for a spot behind the left front shoulder and fired. The buck went down not more than fifty yards from him. He had made a clean kill. I closed my eyes and tried to picture exactly what happened as Dad had just described.

Dad continued, telling how he got up and headed for the buck. He got his knife out and rolled the buck on its back and started to slit his belly to gut the deer.

"There I was, working on the deer, when all of a sudden I hear a snort behind me. I turned around and damned if there weren't three Sioux Indian men sitting on their horses not thirty yards from me. Sure as hell, I knew they were off the reservation and weren't supposed to be—"

"Honey, don't swear in front of the children," Mother scolded.

"They never said a word. I figured they were the reason the buck had been moving in a trot. Deer will walk when they are not being pushed. Anyway, there they sat just looking at me. They were all in their late thirties, I guessed. Even in the winter, their skin was dark red and their eyes were black as coal. They had on broad-rimmed hats with eagle or hawk feathers sticking out of the bands. Each one was wrapped in a brightly colored blanket. I couldn't figure out why they would have those blankets on if they were hunting. Maybe they weren't hunting though, I thought.

"Anyway, they never said a word. I tried to show no fear and turned back to clean the deer. I listened carefully for any sound from the three men behind me. I rolled the buck on his side and started pulling the guts out. When I finished, I looked up at the Indians. They were gone! Just like that—disappeared in the snow! Couldn't believe it. I never was so happy to see those tents in all my life. I wasn't even tired from dragging that buck back. I was so excited and nervous."

Dad related to the other men what had happened when they returned. They agreed to stay together when they went out in the afternoon. He told how they worked during the midday Saturday cutting wood in the snow. About two thirty they quit working and went hunting. Mr. Bliss had gotten a fine twelve-point buck, and Mr. Ebling shot a doe that afternoon, even though it had been snowing quite heavily. None of the men saw the Indians Dad had seen in the morning.

The next morning, the men only hunted for a couple of hours or so because of the bitter cold. No one got a deer, he related. They hunted until about eleven in the morning, when they broke for lunch. After lunch, they broke camp and headed for home. Dad mentioned that they saw three sets of horses' tracks about a mile north of their camp, but, once again, they didn't see the three Indians that Dad had seen Saturday morning.

"Well, that's about it," Dad said, pulling a small gold watch from his right pants pocket. He checked the time and placed the watch back in his pocket. "Okay, kids, let's clean up the kitchen, and off to bed with you. You still have school for another week before Christmas vacation."

We all grumbled softly at the thought of another week of school. Frankie and Eddie were rushed off to bed while my sisters started cleaning off the table. I sat on my chair motionless, trying to imagine everything that had happened to Dad just as he had told it.

A cold chill went up my spine and goose bumps popped out on my arms as I thought about the Indians. I wondered what I would have done if they had come up to me. I wondered what they were doing.

"Ralph, up to bed with you," said Dad as he tapped me on the shoulder. "You have school too, ya know."

I got out of my chair and headed for the hall. Just as I reached the doorway, I bumped into Mother returning to the kitchen.

"Well, did you ask your father? What did he say?" Mother asked me.

"What are you talking about?" I asked, still thinking about the Indians.

"Don't you remember?"

"Remember what?"

"About your friend, Jamie. Remember, now?"

"Jamie, Jamie," I mulled over to myself, holding my chin in my right hand while staring at the floor. "Oh yeah. Gee whiz, how could I have forgotten? Oh, Dad, you gotta let me go, you just gotta."

I turned toward Dad, waiting for him to give me his approval.

"Go where, Ralph? What are you talking about?"

"Jamie wants me to go to Red Elm next Saturday on the train to see his sister, since Mrs. Bucklin has been ill. Can I go, Dad, can I go?"

"Now, now, Ralph, that's a long trip for two small young boys. I don't—"

"Small, I'm not that small," I said, trying to stand as straight as possible. "I'm twelve years old, Dad. I'm not small—look."

"Well, what do you think, Mother? Think our youngest child is big enough to go on a train ride with Jamie?" Dad said, looking at Mother.

"Now, wait a minute; you're not getting me into this. I'm not taking any sides. You and Ralph discuss it between yourselves," Mother replied.

"What do you think, girls?" Father asked of my sisters. "Think we should let him go?"

"I'd be glad to see him go," said Lottie. "Maybe he won't come back; we'd be rid of him."

Everyone in the room laughed, except me. I was really mad about what she had said, and I made a fist with my right hand and waved it at her.

"You would miss having Christmas with us," Dad said to me. "You would have to open your presents either before you left or after you got back."

"Aw, I'd be glad to miss Christmas just to get away from them," I said, pointing to my sisters. "They have their stuff all over the place anyway on Christmas morning. Who wants to see dresses and other girls' stuff? Maybe I wouldn't come back."

I crossed my arms and cocked my head, satisfied that at any moment my sisters would beg me to stay.

"Well, I'll tell you what, Ralph. I'll discuss it with Mr. Bucklin, and if he thinks it's okay, and if Mother thinks it's okay, you can go. But you got to do extra good this week or you're not going."

"Oh boy," I yelled, throwing my arms around Mother. "I'm going to ride on a train; I'm going to ride on a train," I chanted at my sisters happily. They looked at me with tight lips and mean eyes as I continued to chant. That would fix them, I thought.

"I hope you don't come back," said Lottie.

I let go of Mother and started down the hall to the stairway.

"Thanks, Dad," I called back. "I'm going to bed—got school in the morning, you know."

I headed up the stairs to the bedroom. When I entered the room, Eddie and Frankie wanted to know what I was yelling about. I told them that I was going to Red Elm with Jamie next week. I calmed down a little, not wanting to make them either mad or feel bad because they were sick. I could see they weren't real happy over my good luck, so I didn't say any more.

I pulled my clothes off and jumped into bed. I pulled the thick quilt over me. "Turn the light out, will ya, Eddie?" I called.

Eddie said nothing, but he reached out and turned the handle on the lantern sitting on the chair beside his bed. The room was totally dark now. It took a few moments for my eyes to adjust to the darkness. I could hear Eddie sit up in bed. He pulled the curtains by his bed open and looked out. The moon was beginning to rise in the east. It was almost full, and, with the snow on the ground, it was light enough to see quite clearly outside.

I lay on my back and looked at the light doming through the east window. Eddie was silhouetted in the window. I tried to close my eyes to go to sleep. I wasn't tired at all. I was wide awake. It had been a long weekend, and many things had happened. I began to think of the ride to town with Artie and the poor little rabbit I shot. I wondered if a fox or coyote had found him. I thought of Dad's trip to the river, the deer he shot, and the three mysterious Indians. I thought of Christmas coming up and not being here to share it with my brothers and sisters and Mom and Dad. I wondered about the train. What would it look like? How fast would it go? Would we get any game at Red Elm? I wondered what Red Elm looked like. Many excited thoughts went through my mind about the trip. I was wide awake and excited. I tried to imagine what everything would be like out there. I was a little scared. I remembered Lottie's words. Would I ever get there, and, if I did, would I ever get back? I stared out the window and wondered.

Chapter

6

"Wow, look at that train!" I said, excitedly poking Jamie in the side with my right elbow. "Man, this is gonna be a lot of fun. I just know it."

"Number 51, see it, Ralphie? See it on the side of the engine!" exclaimed Jamie.

We watched the train pull up beside the depot. I could hardly wait to get on it. I had never been on a train, and this was going to be my first train ride. The big, black engine pulled slowly past the depot. The big iron wheels turned slower and slower, finally coming to a halt.

I could see the coal box immediately behind the engine. Father told me that we would have to pick up coal in Mobridge before going on to Red Elm. Behind the coal car was the baggage and mail car. It was black and had two doors that were located near the center of the car. It only had one window to look out of, which was up near the front of the car. It looked as if it was built more solid than the passenger cars that followed it.

There were three passenger cars after the baggage car. There were doors on both ends of those cars with little steps to get into them. There were lots of windows on the cars to look out of. It was in one of these cars that I knew we would ride.

Suddenly I heard a loud hiss and turned my head to see a big cloud of white smoke pouring from the bottom of the engine. It half hid the engine.

"Look at that, Jamie; it's on fire!" I yelled.

"No, no, Ralph, that is just steam," Father said. "The engineer has to release some of the pressure from the boilers, and when the hot air hits this cold air you get steam."

"Can we go out and see the engine?" I asked.

"Okay."

"Come on, Jamie."

We swung the door of the depot open and turned to our right and headed for the engine. Up close it was really big. The big wheels under the round boiler tanks and under the engineer's little room were almost as tall as I was. Big, thick bars connected all three of the big wheels together. We had seen those bars turning the wheels when the train approached. Up at the front of the engine were two smaller wheels that looked like guide wheels for the engine. But the best part of all was the cowcatcher, a piece of metal that reached out ahead of the engine down low, close to the tracks. The bars that ran up and down it almost made it look like a cage.

I had heard of these cowcatchers and how they protected the engine from things that got on the track. I wondered if this train had been saved from hitting buffalo, cattle, boulders, and blockades from train robbers by its cowcatcher. Number 51 was painted right on the nose of the train. Above it was a big light that was not on but probably was used at night. Right behind it was a round smokestack about three feet high. Yes, sir, that train was neat, I thought. I wondered what it would be like to be an engineer.

"All aboard," came a shout from far down the track.

"Come on, Ralphie. Let's go. We're gonna miss the train," Jamie said, grabbing my right arm.

"Right," I replied, taking off on a run down the side of the train to the passenger cars. It was hard to run in our heavy winter clothes, but soon we were standing beside the first passenger car.

"Where you boys been?" questioned Mr. Bucklin.

"Looking at the engine," replied Jamie.

"Don't you boys think you forgot something?" asked my father.

"What?" I asked.

"How about your guns and clothes? Are you gonna take them with you?" he replied.

"Gee whiz, Jamie. Let's go," I said, heading for the depot.

"Wait a minute, boys," said Mr. Bucklin. "We already loaded your things on the baggage car. But you are going to have to remember to look after your things. Now, we gave the conductor your tickets, and he will see that you get off at Red Elm. You understand?"

"And you listen to what he tells you," Father cut in. "And don't get off the train less he tells you to. Ya hear?"

Jamie and I both shook our heads yes.

"Okay. Then get on the train and don't run round while the train's moving. You'd more likely fall off for sure," said Father, helping me up the first step of the passenger car. I climbed three steps to the door of the car and pushed the door open. Jamie followed behind me.

I stepped inside and found myself in a narrow little hallway that led to the seats. There was a door on each side. On one door was painted in white MEN, on the other door WOMEN.

"Hey, Jamie, look at that. I didn't know trains had toilets," I said, pointing to the door that said MEN. "We'll have to try that when the train is moving."

Jamie nodded in agreement. I headed on down the aisle. It was narrow. About ten seats were on each side of the aisle. Each seat was big enough for two people to sit. Above the seats was a long metal rack. There were a few suitcases up on the rack. The people that owned them sat directly underneath them. I wondered if they ever bounced out and hit them on the head. There were only five other people in the car— three men, who all sat in separate seats, and a man and a woman who were sitting together. They were all near the other end of the car. Near the door at the other end of the car was a big jug with water in it for the passengers. Two cups hung on nails next to it. The jug was upside down.

I sat down in the first seat after the toilets. I wanted to be close by to see what a toilet on a train was like. Jamie got in the seat behind me. I guessed he wanted to see out of the window like I did. We waved at our fathers through the windows.

It made me nervous to think that for the very first time I was going off on my own without any of my family. My stomach was upset, and my hands got sweaty. *I'm going away*, I thought to myself. *Who knows what will happen to me, or the train. Maybe we'll wreck; maybe I'll never see home again.*

I looked at Jamie. He seemed alright. He was still looking out the window. He didn't seem nervous to me. I wondered if he was scared about going away.

"Isn't this great, Ralphie?" Jamie said, when he noticed me looking at him.

"Sure is," I replied softly.

"Just think, Ralphie. We're going on a train ride for the first time in our lives—just you and me, Ralphie. Nobody else. We're men now, aren't we, Ralphie? Just me and you and old Number 51 going to Red Elm to see my sister."

"And just think, no school for two weeks, and getting to go hunting," I said, picking up confidence and encouragement from Jamie's words. "And it's Christmas time too. What a trip this is gonna be."

A sudden jolt shook the car, knocking me back into the seat. Slowly the train started to move past the depot. We looked back at our fathers and waved through the windows. The train slowly picked up speed as we looked back at Selby from our windows.

"Isn't this great, Ralphie?" Jamie exclaimed.

I didn't say anything as I watched the buildings get smaller. I was sad to be leaving Selby, and I was kinda scared to be going to a strange place by myself. I sat down in my seat and looked out the window at the countryside. Everything looked cold and cruel, I thought. With the white snow on the ground and the trees bare of leaves, nothing looked very friendly. Every once in a while I would see a hawk swirling in the sky over a field. I hoped that one would dive down to catch a rabbit or mouse so that I could see it. Jamie said nothing to me, and I said nothing to him. I guessed that he was looking out the window in the seat behind me. I wondered how fast we were going.

"Hi, boys. Everything okay?" I turned to see the conductor standing in the aisle by our seats.

"Yes, sir," I replied.

"Well, I'll look after you for your folks. Your dads gave me your tickets, and I took care of your luggage, so we shouldn't have any problems. Just don't get off the train unless I say it's okay. We will be coming into Mobridge soon, and we will stop for a few minutes. But I don't want you getting off the train. Too many Indians will be around the station. They might give you boys some trouble if they see you by yourselves. Understand?"

"Yes, sir," Jamie and I said together.

"Got any questions?" the conductor returned.

"Just one, sir. Are those really toilets?" I asked, pointing to the doors in front of me.

"Sure are, son," he replied, smiling.

"Are they hard to use, or do you not use them when the train is moving or what?" I asked.

"You can use them anytime," the conductor replied. "Just don't flush them when the train is in or going through a town. Okay?"

"Okay," I replied.

"Incidentally, you boys forgot this," the conductor said, handing me a brown paper bag. "You forgot your lunch."

"Thanks," I said, grabbing the sack. "One more question, sir. How long will it take to get to Red Elm?"

"Oh, about three and a half hours," he said, lifting his little blue cap off his head with his thumb and first finger and scratching his head with his little finger. "We have to stop at Mobridge, Parade, and Lantry before we get to Red Elm. We ought to get there about two thirty or so if we don't have any delays."

"Thanks, Mister," I replied.

The conductor put his hat back on and headed back down the aisle. Gosh, I had forgotten to ask how fast we were going. I was mad at myself for not remembering. I set the sack down beside me and looked out the window.

The countryside was much more hilly now. I figured that we were getting closer to Mobridge now. I knew it would be hilly with a lot more trees when we got closer to Mobridge. I knew the town sat down right near the Missouri River. Dad told me we would go over a long bridge over the river. He assured me the bridge would not collapse.

"Look up ahead!" Jamie said, leaning over the back of my seat and pointing at the window.

Sure enough, there was Mobridge. I could see practically the whole town sitting down low in a valley before me. Buildings popped out in the clearing between the trees. Although I couldn't see the river, I knew it would lie just beyond the west end of town. Mobridge sure looked a lot bigger than Selby.

Chapter

7

"**M**an, look at all those Indians!" exclaimed Jamie.

"Sh," I hissed at Jamie, giving him a scowl. "You don't say stuff like that. What if they heard you? They would come on this car and scalp us. You heard what the conductor said."

I looked back out the window at the Indians at the depot. There were four of them that were loading and unloading boxes on the baggage car in front of us. I had never seen Indians close up before. I couldn't believe how dark they were. Even in the winter time they were still a dark red. None of them were tall, but they all were barrel-chested with big shoulders. I wondered why people were so afraid of Indians. They had on clothes just like mine, my brothers, and my father. About the only difference I could see was in the hats they had on. And really all they were were ten gallon hats rounded off on top. Each had a brightly colored wide band and at least one feather sticking out of the band. Each Indian had his hat pulled down low over his eyes. It was hard to see their faces. Jamie and I sat there with our noses to the window, watching every move they made.

"*Yeeeiiii*," came a wild scream as an Indian suddenly appeared a foot in front of our noses outside our car. Jamie and I jumped back from the window and scrambled backward to the aisle, not taking our eyes off the wild Indian in the window.

He just stood there with his arms up, his brown eyes bulging. He gritted his big yellow teeth and wrinkled his wide flat nose. He had a long scar from his left cheek bone to the left corner of his mouth.

Long, straight black hair hung from under a dark brown Stetson. A red and yellow band circled the hat, with one big, black and white feather sticking in the band. He did nothing but look at us. Jamie and I stood side by side in the aisle, trying not to show any fear. My heart was pounding wildly. Had he heard Jamie, I wondered?

As quickly as he appeared, he disappeared. Jamie and I stood there and looked at the bare window.

"Whew! That was close," exclaimed Jamie, still looking at the window. "Did you see how ugly he was? Wonder where he got that scar? Fighting Custer I bet."

Bang! I jumped nearly two feet off the ground at the loud noise to my left. Jamie and I turned to see that crazy Indian standing in the doorway of the train car only a few feet away. He was crouched low with his arms spread apart. He had a wild look on his face. Jamie and I hung on to each other.

"No see Injun before?" the wild Indian spoke. "You say me ugly? Huh? Answer!"

We said nothing but shook our heads no.

He's gonna scalp us, I thought. *Why did Jamie open his big mouth?*

"Well, you never forget me. I teach you. I give you both scars just like mine. Okay?" the Indian said, pulling a big knife from a sheath on his belt.

"What in the hell are you doing, Joe?"

It was the conductor who suddenly appeared behind the crazy Indian.

"Be careful, Mister! He's got a knife," yelled Jamie.

"Oh, it's okay, boys. He does this all the time. He's known as Crazy Head Joe around here. He sits and watches the trains come in and then tries to scare the people, especially the kids, on the train. Really, he's harmless; aren't you, Joe?"

The Indian straightened up. Slowly his gritted teeth in anger changed to a big grin.

"I fool you." He broke into a hearty laugh. "I scare you, ha, ha, ha!"

I couldn't believe it. I didn't trust that Indian, not for a minute. I didn't care what the conductor said.

"You boys can sit down now," announced the conductor. "If you use the toilet, Joe, remember, no flush in town! He likes to use it, too."

The conductor winked at us and disappeared. Crazy Head Joe opened the toilet door and went in. Jamie and I sat down in the seat Jamie had been sitting in. I sat down next to the window so that if that Indian came back he would get Jamie first. I was still scared half to death. Within a few moments, Crazy Head Joe appeared from the toilet. He stepped into the aisle and looked at us.

"I like to use train pot. No flush. Conductor always let me use it when train stop. You boys have safe trip, now." Joe flashed a big toothy grin at us and slipped out the passenger car door.

"All aboard," I could hear the conductor shout from behind me. Slowly the train began to move out of the Mobridge station. Buildings and houses passed by before my eyes as we headed west out of town. When we saw the last buildings of town, the train swung to the right and headed north. I could still see Mobridge to the right behind me.

"Look, Ralphie, the river!" exclaimed Jamie, grabbing my left arm. I looked to my left and sure enough, there was the Missouri River through the trees.

"Wow," I said in a long, low breath. "Look how wide it is. How could they ever build a bridge across that thing?"

"I don't know, Ralphie, but I can see it up ahead of us over there," Jamie said, pointing to the left front window of the passenger car. I couldn't see it because of the wall of the toilet, but I figured Jamie was right. Slowly the train turned back to the left and headed west again. I looked out my window straight ahead as much as possible. I could see the river in the distance. I knew we would be on the bridge in a moment. I could hardly wait. Trees flashed before me going by so fast I could hardly focus my eyes on them. Then, boom, no trees. I looked down, and there was water. I knew we were on the bridge. The other side of the river seemed miles away. I held my breath that we would make it. I closed my eyes.

"We made it," yelled Jamie. "We made it!"

"That bridge was really something, wasn't it?" I returned to Jamie. After crossing the long, wooden bridge and opening my eyes, I could feel my heart in my throat.

"It sure was," Jamie replied. "I don't see how it managed to stay up. I thought sure it would collapse as soon as we got in the middle."

The bridge had been everything Dad said it would be. It just went straight across that old river. We had been about forty feet above the water, and I saw a long ways up and down the river until I closed my eyes. I admitted to myself that I had sure thought we would never reach the other side.

"Come on, Jamie. Let's have a sandwich," I said, reaching for the bag the conductor had given us. I opened the sack and pulled out two sandwiches. I handed one to Jamie, which he unwrapped. A thick slice of ham had been placed between two thick slices of homemade bread. It looked very good. I opened my sandwich, which was the same as Jamie's, and took a big bite. It tasted great—just what I needed to end the hunger pains that the train ride had worked up. After finishing the sandwich, I headed down to the back of the passenger car for a drink of water.

I stumbled and bounced down the aisle as the train rolled along. I reached the water cooler on the back wall and grabbed the cup from the wall. I held the cup under the faucet and turned the handle. The train made my hand with the cup in it bounce around, and I spilled water on the floor before the small tin cup was half full. When it reached that level, I shut the faucet off, and braced myself against the seat behind me. With two hands, I brought the cup to my mouth and drank the contents quickly. So fast, in fact, that water ran down both sides of my mouth onto my shirt. I placed the cup back on the nail and brushed the water from my shirt with both hands. I was mad at myself for spilling water on me.

I walked back up the aisle to our seat, this time steadying myself with my hands on the seats on each side. I stepped in front of Jamie and sat down in the seat next to the window, which he was nice enough to leave to me. I looked out the window at the South Dakota countryside. The train was rolling up and down hills and through the valleys of the land. It was very pretty all covered with snow. Every so often we would see a ranch in the distance. It would seem so lonely.

Up ahead, I could see gray clouds. I wondered if it was going to snow again. It was sunny but cold when we left Selby. Now it looked like it was going to snow again. I couldn't remember the last time I looked at the sky and wondered if it would snow. All of a sudden, I seemed cold. I leaned forward and grabbed my overcoat from the seat in front of me where I had originally been sitting. I drew the collar of my coat up to my shoulders like a blanket and leaned back in my seat.

Now comfortable and warm, I looked out to see big flakes of snow coming down. The sky was dark gray. With the big flakes coming down it seemed almost like nightfall had come, even though I knew it was only early afternoon. After all, the conductor had said we would get to Red Elm by two thirty or three. I became sleepy from the darkness and tried to fight myself to stay awake. I felt my eyelids get heavier and heavier until I no longer could keep them open.

"Wake up, boys, you're in Red Elm. It's time to get off the train."

"Huh?" I said sleepily as I felt a gentle tug on my left shoulder. "What?"

"I said it's time to get off the train; you're in Red Elm. You boys have been asleep for a long time," said the conductor, standing in the aisle over Jamie and me.

"Gee whiz, you mean we're here already?" exclaimed Jamie, moving about restlessly beside me. I looked at him, and his eyes were still closed. He was still half asleep.

"Come on, Jamie," I said, shaking him with both my hands. "It's time to go. Your sister must be waiting for us outside."

Shaking him worked. He sat straight up and looked at me. He turned and looked the other way up at the conductor. The conductor lifted his right arm and pointed past us out the window. Jamie and I turned our heads and looked out the window. Through the heavy snowflakes that were still coming down, I could see a big black sign with big white letters painted on it that said RED ELM, SOUTH DAKOTA.

"Gee, let's go, Ralphie. We're here," Jamie cried, almost as if I was the one who was still asleep. I quickly put on my coat that had been draped over the front of me. I adjusted my stocking cap and put on my gloves. I stood up and waited for Jamie to put on his coat, hat, and gloves. When that was done, we moved into the aisle and headed for the front door of the passenger car. The conductor stepped back to let us pass.

"Hey, don't forget your lunch sack, boys," the conductor said, pointing to the lunch sack I had placed on the seat in front of ours after we had eaten. Jamie retreated a few steps to the seat and picked up the sack. We headed for the door together. The conductor called after us not to forget our guns and luggage.

I stepped out of the car and headed down the steps. Jamie was right behind me. It was snowing heavily, but it was not too windy or cold.

"Jamie, Jamie, here we are. Over here."

Off to my left thirty feet or so, stood two people on the platform of the depot. It was Jody and her husband.

"Jody, Jody," yelled Jamie, right in my ear from behind me. He ran past me toward the two people. Jody was waving her arms in the air as Jamie ran closer. Jody grabbed Jamie around the shoulders and gave him a big hug. Jamie hugged his sister back, holding her tightly around the waist.

"Come on, Ralphie!" Jamie turned and called to me, still holding on to his sister. I quickly went over to where the three were standing. When I arrived, Jody grabbed me, hugged me, and gave me a kiss on the forehead.

"It's good to have you here, Ralph!" Jody said. I was embarrassed by the kiss and didn't want to look at her.

"Thank you," I said politely.

"Boys, you remember my husband, John, don't you?" asked Jody, turning to him.

"Hello, Mr. Northfield," I said softly. Jamie waved at him but said nothing.

Mr. Northfield looked down with his dark brown eyes sparkling from under his thick, black eyebrows.

"Hi, boys," he returned, flashing a big smile with his white teeth gleaming from under his black, bushy mustache. "We are really glad to have you for Christmas. Jody and I have waited for a long time for visitors from Selby, and you are our first. Jody could hardly wait to see you. We'll have some fun, and tomorrow, if the weather isn't too bad, we'll all go out hunting. Chris Jennings is going to come over in the morning, and the four of us will go. How's that?"

"Oh, boy," exclaimed Jamie, forgetting his quietness to Mr. Northfield. I couldn't help but remember how Jamie said he disliked his brother-in-law last year. Maybe time had changed his mind toward him a little. Or maybe he was excited about seeing Chris Jennings. I really didn't know.

"Come on, boys," Jody spoke up. "Let's get home while we can. It's a long ride, and I still have to get supper ready. We came by horseback and brought a packhorse for your guns and luggage. Ralph, you ride with John on his horse, and Jamie can ride with me."

Mr. Northfield picked up the two suitcases that we had brought with us. He asked Jamie and me to pick up our guns and follow him, which we did. We walked down the platform to the west end of the depot. Mr. Northfield walked in the lead, while Jody walked between me and Jamie; she had one arm draped over each of us. When we rounded the corner, there were three horses tied to a hitching post. One was the beautiful black horse that Mr. Northfield had brought to Jody's wedding.

"This is Midnight," Mr. Northfield said, introducing Jamie and me to his horse. "And this is Tinker. Tinker is Jody's horse, and the packhorse is Sawdust."

Tinker was a small chestnut mare. She was short but very stocky in the body, and she looked very gentle. She had a white spot on her forehead, and all four feet were white. Sawdust looked just like sawdust. He was blondish brown in color, and he had a gray forehead. I couldn't figure out if that gray was from old age or just his natural color. I didn't ask, though, because I didn't want to appear stupid for not knowing.

"Jamie, you climb up behind your sister. Ralph, you can ride with me," said Mr. Northfield.

Jamie went over to Tinker with his sister. Jody climbed up in the saddle and extended an arm down to Jamie. Jamie grabbed his sister's arm, put his left foot in the stirrup, and swung himself up behind her. I patiently waited for Mr. Northfield to load our things on the packhorse. When this was done, Mr. Northfield untied Midnight and effortlessly mounted the beautiful black horse.

"Okay, Ralph," he said, extending his left hand. "Up you go."

I grabbed his hand with my left hand, placed my left foot in the stirrup, and up I went behind Mr. Northfield. We headed south out of town. From what I could see of Red Elm in the snow, the town was a lot like Selby. The station was at the south end of town, and the main part of town was to the north of the station. We traveled straight south for what I thought was a long time. There were no bends in the road, nor did I see any other roads branch off of the one we were on. The countryside was very hilly compared to the land back home.

"Are we near a river?" I asked Mr. Northfield in a low voice.

"No, why do you ask Ralph?" he replied.

"Oh, this hilly country kind of reminds me of the country near the river back home. So I thought that there must be a river around here too, that's all."

"No, we're not near any rivers, Ralph. At least not yet. There is a river that runs through my ranch, but we are not anywhere near it. All the land around here is hilly. There are some small creeks and draws and some patches of timber. There is some real good hunting in these hills. Most of this land out here is strictly for raising cattle. Not many people plant crops in this kind of country."

"Oh," I replied when he finished. "How come I don't see any houses?"

"You won't see too many houses, Ralph," Mr. Northfield said, chuckling. "Most of the ranch houses are back off this road. You'll never see them. All you would see is a lane leading off this road, and you will have a hard time seeing them in this snow. Most of the ranches around here have four to eight thousand acres or more of land. That is fairly big."

"How many do you have?" I asked.

"Oh, my ranch is about ten thousand acres," Mr. Northfield replied.

We rode along in silence for some time. We came to a road that crossed the one we were on. Mr. Northfield turned Midnight left onto the other road.

"We'll go about three miles or so on this road before we will come to my lane," said Mr. Northfield. "Are you cold, Ralph?"

"No, sir," I replied.

"We'll be home soon. It's not much farther," he returned.

The sky was darkening quickly now. The snow continued to come down in big flakes. The air seemed colder since we left town. The wind began to pick up a bit. A chill ran over my body. I could feel the goose bumps grow on my arms. A strange uneasiness came over me. It was something I couldn't explain to myself. Here I was, miles from home, in a strange place, riding a strange horse, with a man I hardly knew.

I looked at Jamie and was comforted by the sight of him hanging on to his sister Jody. I hardly even knew Jody, I thought. Here I had lived in the house next to her ever since I could remember, and yet I really didn't know her. My sisters did, but I didn't. The only person I knew was Jamie.

I loosened my grip on Mr. Northfield. Why should I hold onto him so tightly when I didn't even know him? We weren't going fast. I wasn't going to fall off. My mind was working on me, I thought.

What am I so shook up about? I thought. *I'm a big boy now; there is nothing to worry about.*

I kept telling myself that there was nothing to worry about, but somehow things just didn't seem right. Something was wrong somewhere. I knew it, and it made me nervous.

Chapter

8

"Hey, this is really neat," I exclaimed with my eyes bugged out. I was standing in the living room of Northfield house. It was beautiful. It was a large room, and the walls were logs. I was standing in a real log house. At the east end of the room was a huge fireplace made of stone. In the center of the chimney over the mantle of the fireplace was mounted a beautiful deer head. On each side of the fireplace was a gun rack. Each rack was full of guns. I quickly counted the guns, which totaled sixteen. Over each rack of guns were three pistols of different shapes and sizes. With the shiny brown logs, the red rock fireplace, and the gun display, the room was beautiful.

The south wall of the room had been lined with animal hides. Mr. Northfield pointed out the hides as being deer, bobcat, and mountain lion. On the wall behind us were hides of some deer, buffalo, and elk. In the center of the floor was a big, black bear hide.

"Did you shoot all of these?" I asked excitedly.

"No," Mr. Northfield said, shaking his head. "Some of them were shot by my father; some of them were shot by my brother, and some of them I got."

"Who shot the bear?" Jamie asked.

"Now, hold on boys," Jamie's sister cut in. "We have lots of time for questions. Let's get your heavy clothes off and show you where everything is. John, you get their things. First of all, through this door to your immediate right is the kitchen. It isn't as big as your kitchen back home, but it will do for now. The other door on the right is our bedroom. The stairs directly across from us lead to two more bedrooms that are located right above the kitchen and our bedroom. See? Look up there."

"Hey, that's neat," exclaimed Jamie, looking up at the two doors upstairs. "You have a balcony overlooking the living room. That's neat."

"That door left of the stairway leads to a large storage room. We keep all sorts of things in there. There is a door that leads to the outside from that room. There is also an outside door through the kitchen. Either one will lead you to the outhouse out back and the barns. The house is rather simple, but it is comfortable. It will serve us for now. We can always build on if we have children. Which bedroom do you want, Ralph? You're our guest."

"Oh, I don't know," I replied. "Are Jamie and I going to share a room, or do we each have our own?"

"Whichever you like," replied Jamie's sister.

"Do you want to share a room?" I inquired of Jamie. I was hoping he would since I still had that uneasy feeling I had earlier riding out here.

"Sure, Ralphie, it's fine with me," Jamie replied.

"Okay then, boys, you take the bedroom over the kitchen. It is the warmer of the two," Jamie's sister said. "There is a large double feather bed up there and some heavy quilted blankets to keep you warm."

"Thanks, Mrs. Northfield," I replied.

"Now, now, Ralph, we will have none of that," countered Mr. Northfield, coming through the dining room door with our things. "From now on, both of you are to call us Jody and John. Okay? No more of this Mr. and Mrs. stuff. Right, Jody?"

"Right, John," replied Jody, nodding her head.

"Here, you boys take these bags on up to your room," John said. "I'll put the horses away, and you get some food on, Jody."

Jody took Jamie's and my overcoats, hats, and gloves into the kitchen. I grabbed my suitcase and gun and headed for the stairs. Jamie did the same.

"Leave your guns downstairs, boys," called John from the living room doorway. "We'll put them by the fireplace."

Jamie and I both set our guns down by the stairway. With me in the lead, Jamie and I went up the stairs. I thought it was really neat, because we had to go up five stairs and then turn to the right and go up four more stairs to reach the balcony walkway that led to the bedrooms and overlooked the living room. The living room looked even bigger from upstairs. It was hard to imagine how really big the fireplace was until I stood eight feet off the ground and looked across the room to see that the fireplace ran all the way from the floor to the roof that was still three to four feet over my head.

We walked down the narrow balcony to the door that was located over the kitchen. I grabbed the door knob and swung the bedroom door open. I stepped inside followed by Jamie. The room was dark. To my left was a large brass bed. On the left side of the bed was a small table on which sat a kerosene lamp. I walked over to the lamp and lifted the chimney. I took a match from a small box next to the lamp and struck it on the side of the box. The match burst into flame, and I lit the lamp and replaced the chimney. The room filled with the light from the lamp. On the other side of the bed was a washstand that held a wash basin and pitcher.

Above the bed hung a large picture of a man and a woman. It looked like an old picture to me. On the opposite wall from the door was a window. There was also a window on the right wall from the bedroom door. Between the two windows in the corner was a large dresser with a mirror hanging over it. A small closet was to the right of the window on the right wall. In the center of the floor was a large brightly colored braided rug.

"Hope this room is alright, boys," came a voice from behind, which startled us. It was Jody.

"Sure, this will be fine, Sis," returned Jamie.

"Put your things down, and let's go to the kitchen," she replied.

Jamie and I set our suitcases down and started to follow Jody to the kitchen.

"Blow the lamp out, will you?" Jody called over her shoulder as she walked down the balcony. I quickly returned to the lamp and blew it out. I closed the bedroom door and followed Jamie and his sister down to the kitchen.

The kitchen was the same size as the bedroom above it. A long, large, stove was on the left wall right below where the bed was upstairs. A door leading outside was on the wall opposite where we entered in the corner near the stove. Directly opposite the door we entered were two windows. Beneath them was a wash sink and cabinets for storage.

There was also a window to our right. On each side of the window were two high storage cabinets. In the center of the kitchen was a large round table with six wooden chairs placed around it. Underneath the table was a large round braided rug similar to the one in the bedroom upstairs.

"Sit down at the table, boys. Dinner won't be too long," said Jody. Jamie and I both sat down at the table. I turned and noticed clothes pegs and pots and pans hanging on the wall that had been behind us. The kitchen was warm, and I felt comfortable here. Somehow it reminded me of home. I looked at a clock hanging over the stove. It was six thirty. I did not believe it was right. It had seemed like such a long day with the train ride, the snow, and the ride on horseback. I was sure it had to be later.

"Is that the right time?" I asked of Jody.

"Sure is. Why?" she replied.

"Oh, I don't know, I just thought it was later, that's all," I returned.

"Well, you both have to be tired after your long trip. You will both feel better after you have had supper."

I shook my head in agreement and looked at Jamie. He was asleep. His head was resting on his arms that were crossed in front of him on the table. It made me tired just to look at him.

"Look," I said softly, pointing at Jamie.

Bang! Bang! Bang! came a loud knock on the kitchen door. Jamie half jumped out of his chair. I couldn't help but laugh even though I was startled too. Jamie's sister went to the door and opened it. Mr. Northfield walked in carrying an armload of firewood. He was half covered with snow.

"It's snowing to beat hell out there," he said.

"John! Watch your mouth. Don't forget we have guests," Jody scolded him.

"Whoops! Sorry dear, I forgot," he replied, embarrassed. "This is the last of the firewood. I'll have to go to the river tomorrow to get some more. This ought to last tonight and tomorrow though.

He walked over to the opposite end of the stove and laid the wood down in a wood box that sat there. John took his coat and hat off and hung them on a peg behind the kitchen door. Within minutes, Jody had set the table and was dishing out the food on the plates. It was stew. We must have all been starved. Each of us asked for a second helping.

We ate so much so that when it came time for dessert, which was fresh apple pie, I couldn't eat any. Neither could Jamie.

"Do you boys want to go with me to the river tomorrow?" Mr. Northfield asked. "We can scout around for signs of game on the way. But you will have to help me with the firewood."

"Sure," I said, squirming around in my chair trying to make my stomach feel better.

"Okay," said Jamie, with not much enthusiasm. I think he was more tired than full. I glanced at the clock on the wall. It was seven fifteen.

"What time are we going to leave?" I asked.

"Oh, we won't leave until about nine, I guess. You boys must be tired, and besides, I have chores to do in the morning. You boys can sleep late."

I had to agree that I was tired but did not say so. I looked at Jamie, and he was nearly asleep in his chair again. I wanted to go to sleep also, but I did not want to the first one to admit it.

"Why don't you boys go up to bed?" Jody said, sensing how tired we really were. She gently shook Jamie and gave him a hug. "Come on, Jamie."

Jamie stirred and tried to appear alert. He got up from the table and looked at me.

"You ready to go to bed?" he said. "I'm tired."

"Okay," I returned, trying not to act as tired as Jamie. "You lead the way, I'll follow."

That bed never felt so good. I lay down in that feather bed, and within minutes, I was sound asleep.

"Okay, boys, time to get up," came a call from the bedroom door.

I opened my eyes and stared at the ceiling above me. I turned my head to the left and saw Jamie slowing starting to stir beside me. I looked past him out the window. I could not see any snow coming down. The sky was dark gray with clouds. I wondered what time it was.

"Come on, Jamie. It's time to get up," I said, jabbing him with my right arm.

"It is? What time is it?" he said, with his back to me.

"I don't know," I returned. "But it looks like it is still dark to me."

I got out of bed and grabbed my shirt and pants from a peg on the wall beside me. The room was chilly, so I dressed quickly. I had slept with my socks on. I walked around to the other side of the bed.

"Come on, Jamie. Let's go," I repeated. "We're going to the river, remember?"

"Yeah," he mumbled, still half asleep. Slowly he rolled over on his back and sat up in bed. He threw the covers off his legs and got out of bed. He walked past me around the bed to his clothes, which hung on a peg next to the one mine had been on. I waited as he slowly dressed.

As we entered the kitchen, Jody was putting our breakfast on the table. The kitchen was warm and felt good to my still-chilly body. I walked over to the table. Two plates were filled with scrambled eggs and bacon. There was a plate with thick-crusted homemade bread on it. A large pitcher of milk sat near the middle of the table. In the very center of the table was a kerosene lamp, which was lit. The food smelled good.

"Hurry up and eat, boys," Jody said. "John is outside getting ready to go. We've already eaten."

Jamie and I sat down and dug in. The food tasted as good as it looked. Remembering my parents' instructions, I ate everything on my plate. It was not hard to do. I was drinking my second glass of milk when Mr. Northfield entered the kitchen door. His feet were covered with snow. He stomped his feet in the doorway and stepped in.

"Ready to go, boys," he said. "How did you sleep?"

"Fine, Mr. Northfield—I mean, John," I returned.

"Well, get your boots and coats on; we have a few miles to go to the river," he said.

Jamie and I both got up at the same time and headed for our boots, which sat on the wood box next to the stove. Jody handed each of us two extra pairs of socks and told us to put them on so our feet would be sure to stay warm. We put them on and pulled our boots on over them. We each grabbed our coats and hats from the pegs on the wall and put them on.

"Here is a bag with some sandwiches, in case you get hungry," Jody said, handing Jamie the bag. "Have you both got gloves?"

We both checked our pockets and found them. We put them on and headed for the door. I opened the door and went outside with Jamie trailing behind me. A low, one-story barn was about forty yards away.

It was not nearly as big as the ones we had at home. Tied to a rail in front of the barn were Tinker, Midnight, and Sawdust. Sawdust was harnessed to a sled about five feet long. The wooden sides and end of the sled were about three feet high. I recognized the sled as being used to haul firewood. I had seen them before, although we did not have one.

To my right, I spied the outhouse sitting about twenty feet from the southwest corner of the house. I told Jamie to wait for me and headed for the outhouse. It had been a long time since I had been. I opened the door and went in. Feeling much better afterward, I opened the door to find Jamie wiggling around a few feet away.

"Gee whiz, Ralphie, I thought you'd never come out of there. What kept you?"

I grinned at him and stepped aside. I no sooner was out of the way than Jamie was inside with the door shut. I didn't bother to wait for him. I turned and headed to where the horses were. I kicked up the snow with my feet as I went. I looked at my tracks and thought they looked neat in the half a foot of snow on the ground. About this time, Mr. Northfield came out of the barn and went over to Sawdust. He adjusted some straps on the harness. I stood there and watched, not knowing what to say.

"Can you ride?" he suddenly said, breaking the silence.

"Sure," I returned.

"How about Jamie? Can he ride?"

"Yes, sir," I said.

"Good. Both of you can ride on Tinker them. She's real gentle. You won't have any problems with her."

"Okay."

"Untie her and mount up. You can pick Jamie up over there," Mr. Northfield said, pointing to the outhouse.

I untied Tinker, grabbed the horn of the saddle in my left hand, and lifted my left foot to the stirrup. In my heavy clothes I could just barely get my foot into the saddle. I turned to see Mr. Northfield watching me from the top of Midnight.

"Let's go," he said, giving Midnight a soft kick in the ribs with the heels of his boots. We headed toward the outhouse side by side. Mr. Northfield led Sawdust on a rope behind us. Jamie stepped out almost as we got there. He was holding the bag of sandwiches. Jamie walked over and stood between our two horses. Mr. Northfield reached down and grabbed the bag from Jamie's hands. He put it in a saddle bag behind him.

"Do you want to ride with Ralph or me?" Mr. Northfield said.

"I can ride with Ralph," Jamie returned sharply. Funny I had never heard Jamie call me Ralph before.

"Give me your hand," returned Jamie's brother-in-law. Jamie did as ordered and reached out with his left hand. Quickly Mr. Northfield grabbed Jamie's wrist with his right hand and lifted Jamie effortlessly into the air and put him down behind me on Tinker's back.

"Let's go, boys," he said.

We headed south past the outhouse. I noticed another barn behind and to the left of where the outhouse was. It sat straight south of the house. I wondered to myself why I hadn't seen it when I went to the toilet. The barn was bigger than the other barn. It had a livestock pen attached to it. There were about forty to fifty head of cattle in it. I wondered if that was all the cattle they had. Surely they had more for a ranch of this size.

We headed straight south past the barn, down a long hill and up another. When we reached the top of the first hill I could look out and see rolling hills spreading out in front of me. The land was barren on the top of the hills in the white snow. However, in the draws and small valleys there were trees and brush that looked like good cover for hunting. We went down and up several more hills. I wondered how far we had come. We stopped on top of a hill, and I looked back over my shoulder to see if I could see the ranch house or barns. I couldn't. The only thing I saw was our tracks in the snow on the hillside behind us. Everything looked the same to me once we left the ranch. I wondered what kept anyone from getting lost out here. I surveyed the land before me, not knowing what to look for.

I saw a dark object down in a long, narrow valley that ran off to our right. I studied it for a moment trying to figure out what it was. It could be a ranch house, but I didn't see any smoke. There should be other buildings if it was a ranch house. Maybe it was an old log cabin from early settlers. I got excited at the thought of it. Maybe Indians got them or something. I wanted to explore the cabin.

"What's that down there?" I said excitedly, pointing the building out with my right hand.

"That? Oh, that's a cattle pen and shed," returned Mr. Northfield. "I've got several of them around here. It gives the cattle some protection in the bad storms. They normally find them without any trouble. Makes it easier to round up the cattle also."

Only a cattle pen, I thought to myself. *Doggone, I was hoping for it to be an old cabin.*

We turned to our left and headed east. Mr. Northfield explained to us as we rode along that the cattle pen also served as a marker for direction. He explained that one would go four hills straight south of his house and see the pen we just saw. From the fourth hill, we would turn east and go down the hill and stay in the bottom of the valley until we ran into another fork. In this other fork we would see another cattle pen. We will go straight to this pen, he explained, and then head straight south. When we got to the top of the second hill, we would see the river down below us.

It seemed simple once he explained it to us. It gave Jamie and me something to look forward to, like we knew how to get where we were going. Strange, I suddenly thought, that we would go all this way for firewood when most of the valley and draws had trees and brush in them. I wondered why we would go so far for wood.

"How come you go so far for wood instead of stopping here or there?" I asked, pointing out a couple of draws. "There's lots of wood around there."

"Sure there is, Ralph," he replied. "But most of it is olive. The wood would not make good firewood. More importantly, the cover you see around here is good for both my cattle and the deer and other game. Sure, I could cut it, but it would mean that over the years I would, or my children would, have to go out farther and farther looking for game. When it is cold, and the snow is like, this you don't want to have to go any farther than you have to for game. That's why I go all the way to the river. There's more timber there than I could use up in a lifetime. Look here! See the deer tracks? They head right up into that draw. These tracks are so fresh, I would almost bet he is sitting in there right now. Think he would be there if I cut the timber down?"

"No, sir—er, John," I said, remembering his instructions to call him by name. I understood his answer and wondered why I didn't know that in the first place. What a stupid question I had asked, I thought to myself.

We found the fork, just like Mr. Northfield said we would, with the cattle pen sitting at the end of it. We headed for it, reached it, passed it, and headed south up the hill. There were no cattle in the pen. We finally reached the second hill, and there was the river below us just like we had been told. You could see the river pretty good since there were no leaves on the trees. It wasn't nearly as wide as the Missouri River. I could plainly see that.

"Come on, boys. Let's get this done with so we can get back home," Mr. Northfield said, heading his horse down the hill to the river. Jamie and I headed down the hill after him. My feet seemed warm until Mr. Northfield mentioned the cold. Now I seemed to be a little cold as I rode along. I wanted to get off Tinker and move around a bit to keep warm. However, I realized that within a few minutes we would be chopping firewood, and that would warm us up.

When Mr. Northfield reached the trees that lined the river, he dismounted and tied Midnight to a tree. I pulled Tinker to a stop, and Jamie slid off her rump to get down. As he pushed off her rump, he lost his balance and fell back and into the deep snow. I couldn't help but laugh as Jamie lay flat on his back. Mr. Northfield, who heard me laughing, joined in at the sight of Jamie on the ground. Jamie wasn't so happy though. He got up quickly and started to brush the snow off himself. I grabbed the saddle horn and dismounted. I walked over to Jamie and helped brush the snow from his back. I just grinned, and Jamie said nothing.

"You alright?" Mr. Northfield questioned Jamie.

"Yes, I'm alright."

"Well, tie up your horse while I start a fire. There is no point in freezing while we are getting firewood."

I quickly tied up Tinker to the same tree Midnight was tied to. Jamie and I both watched as Mr. Northfield chipped small dead branches and twigs into kindling for a fire. He pulled some paper from his pocket and placed the kindling on top of it. Quickly, he cleared a small spot on the ground and placed the paper on the ground. He pulled a wood stick match from his right pants pocket, struck it on his thumbnail and lit the paper. Within moments, the kindling was on fire. He quickly placed larger pieces of wood over the kindling, and a warm fire quickly greeted the three of us. We all extended out hands to the flames to warm them. The heat felt good and brightened up the cold, cloudy, winter day.

"Okay, boys, spread out a little and look for dead or fallen trees that are about eight to twelve inches around. They will be about the best for firewood. But, for heaven's sake, be careful. I don't want anyone falling in the river."

Jamie and I headed west along the river, and Mr. Northfield headed east. He had given us a hatchet to cut some wood, and he had taken an ax. There were plenty of trees, however, most of them were either too big around or too small. The ones that had fallen over were way too big to cut. When we found a tree about the size we wanted, Jamie or I would chop into it. But one swing of the hatchet would reveal it to be a live tree, so we would move on. Shortly, Jamie and I came to a small creek that flowed into the river. A crust of ice covered with snow had frozen over the creek.

"Come on, Ralphie. Let's go over!" Jamie said, his eyes flashing.

"I don't know, Jamie," I said. "We have no idea how thick the ice is."

"We won't even walk on it," Jamie returned excitedly. "Look."

He was pointing at a long vine that dangled down from the tree branches overhead. I had seen these vines before, and, although I didn't know what kind it was, I knew that I could swing on them because I had done it before.

"Chop it off down here," Jamie said, pointing to a spot on the vine. I lifted the hatchet and swung, making a notch in the vine. After six or seven more swings, the vine broke in two. Jamie grabbed the vine and pulled with all his strength to test how well secured the vine was above us. He pulled and yanked several times. Each time the branches above pulled the vine back.

"Okay, Ralphie, here I go," announced Jamie. He let the vine hang down at the edge of the bank. Jamie moved back ten feet or so to enable him to get a good, running start. He would need it since it was about twelve to fourteen feet to the other side. Jamie took off as fast as he could in his heavy clothes. As he neared the edge of the bank he reached out for the vine with both hands. He grabbed cleanly and took off through the air. The trees above him bent with his weight. His body dropped toward the ice. It looked as though he wouldn't make it. He would hit the steep part of the bank on the other side. But just as it seemed he would hit the bank, the tree branches above him snapped back upward, lifting him cleanly over the opposite bank and safely to the other side.

"Hey, Ralphie, how about that?" exclaimed Jamie.

"Boy, I didn't know for sure if you were going to make it."

"It was nothing, Ralphie. I cleared it easy. Throw me the hatchet and come on."

I took the hatchet and tossed it over to Jamie. The vine returned to my edge of the bank. I grabbed it and pulled. The tree branches pulled back. Satisfied with its strength, I straightened the vine so I could grab it with both hands. I backed off just like Jamie did.

One, two, three, I counted in my head. I took off on "three." I reached for the rope as I neared it. I grabbed it with both hands and pushed off with my feet. Into the air I sailed. The tree branches gave, just like with Jamie.

Crrrack! Overhead, I heard branches snapping loudly as I headed for the icy creek bottom. I hit the snow and ice heavily. The ice gave way! Into the cold, icy water I went, back first, my feet in the air. I could feel the freezing water go over my face. I held my breath. The icy water seemed to crush my chest. I had difficulty holding my breath. Surely, I was going to drown.

Chapter

9

"*Grab the rope! Grab the rope!*"
I was freezing to death. I could hear the voice yelling. I wildly reached with my arms. My breath was almost gone. I felt something hard tear across my neck. I grabbed for it to move it away before it choked or bit me. It was the rope! I grabbed it with both hands, and I could feel myself being pulled from the icy bottom of the creek.

Air, air, was all I could think. Sunlight. I could see it. I came to the surface, gasping for air.

I coughed and spit water from my mouth. I didn't know what was going on, but I could breathe. The next thing I felt was a strong hand grabbing my left arm and dragging me through the cracking ice. It was Mr. Northfield.

"Jesus Christ, Ralph! Are you all right?" yelled Mr. Northfield.

"I think so," I said, coughing and spitting water.

"God damn, boy, you scared the life out of both of us," Mr. Northfield said, dragging me up on the creek bank.

"Gee," I said, almost laughing, "I sure am glad to see you."

My teeth were chattering as the cold air hit my wet body. I stood up and looked at my wet clothes dripping dirty water into the white snow.

"Come on, boy, we'll get you to the fire," Mr. Northfield yelled, dragging me off. He half carried me and dragged me to the fire. Funny, I could hardly move. He had to pull me along. By the time we reached the fire, my pants and coat were half frozen.

Mr. Northfield sat me down in front of the fire and told me not to move. He was going back to get Jamie. I sat there in the snow shivering.

I could hardly feel the blaze that was burning in front of me. Mr. Northfield grabbed some more logs and threw them on the fire. Ever so slowly, I could feel the warmth. My pants and coat slowly gave up the ice that had formed on them. My teeth clattered more and more. I sneezed once, twice. I was cold.

It seemed like only a few moments before Jamie and Mr. Northfield returned.

"Listen, boy, you wait a few minutes to try to warm up, then you get on Tinker and head back to the house. I'll put a couple of blankets on you to keep you warm. Just follow the tracks, but go as fast as you can. Think you can do it?"

"Yes, sir," I replied, barely being able to move my lips. "I'll go as fast as I can."

"Okay, you let me know when you are ready to go," Mr. Northfield said, "I'm not going to put the blankets on you till you're ready to go."

I sat by the fire, trying to get warm. I was cold, but yet not cold, I thought to myself. It was a strange feeling, one I had never had before. I looked at my legs and boots. They almost looked dry, I thought. I wanted to get back to the house.

"I'm ready, Mr. Northfield," I said. "Okay?"

"Okay, boy. I'll get the blankets. Stay by the fire."

Mr. Northfield went over to his horse and unfastened the blanket from behind his saddle. He left his horse and went over to Tinker. Once again, he removed a blanket from behind the saddle. He quickly returned to me and dropped the blankets over my shoulders. He wrapped me up tightly in them. Without saying a word he picked me up and carried me over to his horse. He lifted me up into the saddle.

"Listen, Ralph, you take Midnight instead. Just tell him to go home. You tell him all the way, hear? He'll take you straight home, okay? Just tell him "Home.""

He handed the reins to me and turned Midnight around.

"Go home, boy, go home."

He slapped the horse on the rear. Midnight bolted off in a gallop, almost throwing me off the back end. Within seconds, the horse was off, running full speed up the first ridge. I hung on to the saddle horn with both hands. The reins were wrapped between my fingers. Midnight went so fast that the cold air seeped through the blankets. My face was growing colder by the minute. I sat stiff in the saddle. I was jostled around on the saddle but was trying to stay on the fast-moving horse. I kept telling myself we would get there, but with every stride I was sure I would pass out and fall off.

"Go home, Midnight, go home," I yelled, more to stay warm than to encourage the horse. Down one ridge, through a valley, up another, the horse kept galloping. I managed to look behind me once. The big horse's hoofs threw the snow wildly behind me. I was getting colder all the time. I sneezed once. Almost as if I had startled the big horse, he ran faster. My frozen hands clung to the saddle horn.

When will we get there? I wondered. *When will we get there? I'm freezing.* But I kept telling myself, *I'll get there, I'll get there.*

And yet, I thought, *Oh, Lord, will I make it?*

My eyes watered as I tried to look off in the distance. *Why didn't they freeze?* I thought to myself. I was so cold. There it was, there it was—the house. I could see it. Tears were in my eyes, but I knew I could see it. The horse seems to be running even faster now. Was it the house or not? I hoped so, because I couldn't hold on much longer. I looked down at my gloves wrapped around the saddle horn. They were solid ice. I couldn't believe it. I tried to move my fingers and couldn't. My gloves were frozen; my hands were so cold.

"Hurry, horse, hurry," I yelled, not being able to remember the horse's name. "Please, horse, please run." I couldn't keep my eyes open. Where was the house? I was freezing to death. When would we get there? I wanted the horse to stop running. I was tired of being bounced around on his back. I wanted to get off and walk around for a bit. That's what I wanted.

I felt a strange feeling of warmth come across my face. Slowly I lifted my head and sleepily started to blink my eyes, trying to get them to focus. Slowly my eyes focused on a building in front of me. I couldn't remember seeing it before. I turned my head and there it was—the house. The sight of the ranch house quickly brought me to my senses. I kicked Midnight in his haunches as best I could. My pants legs were stiff. I knew where I was and what had happened. I had to get into the house. I leaned in the saddle to get Midnight to turn in the direction that I had shifted my weight. The horse turned and headed for the side kitchen door of the house.

I couldn't wait. The gloves were so stiff they didn't want to budge from the saddle horn. I pulled my hands hard trying to free them. It felt as though the skin was being ripped off my bones as my hands came out of the gloves. The gloves flew off the saddle horn stuck together and dangled from the left rein.

I moved my arms wildly, trying to throw the blankets from my shoulders. My whole body seemed as if it was encased in a cast. I could barely move anything, and when I did, it seemed as though the clothes were cracking to give way. I struggled to free myself. I twisted wildly, lost my balance and fell from the walking horse into the snow. I felt a new wetness and coldness come over me as I lay in the snow. The sudden feel of it brought anger and energy into my body. I rolled over and got on my hands and knees. I stood up, forcing my clothes to bend and give way to my cold body inside. I pulled the stiff blankets off me and started running as fast as I could the remaining few yards to the door.

I grabbed the door handle. I could hardly feel the knob. I had to look at my hand turn the knob to actually know that I was doing it. When I turned the knob a half turn, I pulled and the door opened. Quickly, I stepped inside and pulled the door shut. There was no one in the kitchen. I moved ahead a few feet to the stove. I could feel warm heat coming from it. I stretched my frozen fingers out over the stove to get them warm. Never would I thaw out! My fingers were a bright pink. I expected them to be blue.

Slowly, I was able to wiggle my fingers. I lifted the firewood door on the stove. The wood inside was nearly burnt out. I went to the firewood box at the end of the stove, opened it, and grabbed a log. There were only four pieces left. I wondered how much wood Jamie and Mr. Northfield would return with. I returned to the stove and dropped the log in. Some gray and red burning ashes flew into the air. I closed the door and stood by the stove.

My clothes were thawing now, and I could feel the cold, damp clothes on my skin. I got chills over my body. I took my overcoat off and dropped it on the floor beside the stove. I grabbed a chair from the kitchen table and pulled it up to the stove. I sat down on it and started to take my boots off. The laces were still frozen. My stiff fingers tugged on the strings, but I just didn't have any strength in my fingers to pull them free. Instead, I started unbuttoning my shirt. I took it off and dropped it on the floor beside my coat. I took my undershirt off too. I rechecked my boot strings. They had thawed to a point where I could work the strings with my numb fingers. I quickly loosened my left boot and kicked at it with my other, trying to get it off my foot. When it did come off, my socks came off with it, all three pair. My foot was white—about as white as I'd ever seen it. I tried to wiggle my toes. The big toe moved first. It went down toward the floor. It pulled the other four with it.

Satisfied that my toes moved, I unfastened my right boot. I kicked the heel on the floor trying to pull my foot free of the wet boot. I hadn't loosened the strings enough. I couldn't get it off. Quickly, I loosened the bindings some more and banged my right foot on the floor. My boot finally came off. My socks were pulled halfway off my foot by the boot, so I kicked them off the rest of the way with my left foot. I stood up and loosened the belt buckle on my pants.

"Ralph, what are you doing?" Jody said, entering the kitchen door behind me. She had startled me and caught me with my pants down to my knees.

"T-t-t-taking my, my pants off," I stuttered with clattering teeth. "I fell in the river and h-h-h-had to ride back in th-th-the cold. I'm sorry, b-b-but I'm cold and wet."

Jody walked over toward me. As she did, I watched her tie her bedroom robe around her. Funny, but when we had left in the morning, I was sure that she had been dressed. Well, maybe I was wrong. She picked up my wet clothes on the floor and put them over by the wood box.

"Stay by the stove, Ralph. I'll run and get you a blanket," Jody called, going out the kitchen door.

I sat down on the chair and kicked my pants off. There I was sitting in my underpants with my arms wrapped around myself trying to get warm. It seemed like forever before Jody returned with a blanket. I could hear her coming down the stairs back to the kitchen. Within a few seconds, she entered the kitchen carrying a blue blanket. She came over to me and dropped it over my shoulders and wrapped me up in it. It felt nice and warm.

She grabbed a large pan from a hook on the wall and started pumping the water handle at the sink. After a few pumps, water started to flow out of the spout into the pan. When the pan was half full she stopped pumping, lifted the pan in both hands and carried it over to me. She set it on the floor in front of me.

"Put your feet in the pan," she said.

"Aren't you going to warm the water?" I asked.

"No, Ralph, you never put cold feet in hot water," she returned. "Your feet will seem like they are in hot water when you put them in."

I put my feet in the pan of water. I could not believe it, but almost immediately my feet felt warm. I was amazed. I looked up at Jody to speak, but I didn't get a word out. While I was putting my feet in the pan, Jody had opened her robe up. Underneath was a nightgown that I instantly knew she had not had on in the morning. I was embarrassed, and quickly looked back at my feet in the pan. I watched the bottom of her robe to see if it was closed. Thank heavens, it was. I raised my eyes up her robe slowly, making sure not to raise my head. When I got to her waistline, I could see she was tying a bow in the robe belt.

I was afraid to look at her eyes. I wondered if she had noticed that I had seen her with her robe open.

"Are you sick?" I asked, looking back down at my feet.

"Why?" she replied.

"Oh, I thought maybe you were since you had your robe on now, and you were dressed this morning."

I looked up at her to hear her answer.

"Oh, oh," she stammered, brushing a long strand of reddish brown hair from her forehead. "Oh, no, Ralph. I'm not sick. I just felt more comfortable this way. Sometimes I sit around all day in my nightgown and robe."

"Oh," I answered, not knowing what to believe. I had a strange feeling again, like I had had on the train, that something was not right. My sisters never did anything like that. Mother wouldn't allow it. Oh, well, maybe she was different.

"Hello, there."

I turned, startled by the voice behind me. A man was standing in the kitchen doorway behind me. A white, broad-rimmed hat sat on his head. The man had a brown leather coat with a white fur collar hanging over his left shoulder.

"Remember me?"

I looked at the man for a moment. He looked familiar, but I couldn't remember who he was or where I had seen him.

"You remember, don't you, Ralph?" Jody said.

"No, no, I can't remember," I replied, still eying the man.

"It's Chris Jennings. Now do you remember?" Jody returned.

"Oh, yeah, I remember. I saw you at the wedding."

"That's right," Mr. Jennings said, winking at me. "You sure have grown up, Ralph."

"Yeah, maybe a little," I agreed.

"I rode over here to see you and Jamie. Where is he anyway?"

"He's down at the river with Mr. Northfield getting firewood," I replied.

"How come you're not with them?"

"Ralph fell in the river and had to come back before he froze to death," Jody cut in, laughing. Mr. Jennings leaned his head back and laughed heartily.

"Too bad I wasn't here to see you come in," he said, still laughing. He lifted his hat from his head and strolled over to the kitchen table. He set his hat on the table and pulled out a chair, turned it around and, straddling it, sat down.

"Yeah, too bad," I agreed, looking at his boots. "You should have been here ten minutes earlier. You would have seen how wet and cold I was."

I looked at the floor by the kitchen doorway. I couldn't see any water or snow that would have been left by his boots. I looked at the kitchen doorway that led outside. Little puddles of water were sitting on the floor from the snow I had tracked in. And I hadn't been here for more than ten minutes myself. He had to have been here when I got back, I thought to myself. Something was wrong. I knew it, but I couldn't figure out exactly what.

I sneezed twice into the blue blanket. My rose was starting to run. I knew I was coming down with a cold. I was starting to get chills again. Jody must have sensed the same thing. She told me to get up and said that I was going to go upstairs to bed. I didn't really want to go. I wanted to stay around to see what happened. But being a guest, I knew I had to mind my manners, so I got up and headed for the bedroom upstairs. Jody followed behind me. When we got upstairs, Jody got me out a fresh undershirt and underwear.

"Here, put these on and get in bed," she ordered.

"Please turn around," I said, embarrassed once again. She did so, and I quickly pulled off my underwear and put the dry ones on. I pulled the undershirt on and slid into bed before I told her she could turn around.

"I'll bring you up some hot soup in a little bit," she said, picking up my underwear. "Just stay in bed under the covers."

She turned and left the room, closing the door behind her. I pulled the heavy quilt up over my shoulders. My chills were getting worse it seemed to me. I stared at the ceiling. The only thing I could hear was the clock ticking on the wall. Suddenly I heard a loud crash of something breaking in the kitchen below me. I could hear Jody say something but couldn't understand what she had said. I heard Mr. Jennings say something back, but once again I couldn't make out what it was. I could tell they were arguing about something. I decided to find out what was wrong.

I got out of bed and went to the door. I opened it slowly and peeked outside. I didn't see anyone, so I opened the door and stepped out onto the balcony overlooking the living room. I could hear the voices clearer now. I lay down on the balcony and leaned over the edge, looking upside down through the kitchen doorway below me.

"For Christ's sake, Jody, what's the matter with you?" Mr. Jennings yelled.

"Nothing," Jody replied.

I leaned over farther, trying to see either of them, but I couldn't. They were over by the stove where I couldn't see.

"What do you mean 'nothing'? Mr. Jennings exclaimed. For two years I've watched you live with that man. For two years! And all that time you have wanted children and couldn't have them. Now, after all that time, you think you are pregnant. You know damn good and well it isn't his. It's mine, and you know it! So leave with me, damn it. I'll sell my ranch, and we will leave. You have said you loved me, so leave with me."

"Damn it, Chris, you know how I feel. I love you, but I'm not sure which of you is the father if I am pregnant. It could be John's."

"Jesus Christ, Jody. Don't be ridiculous. If it was his, you would have been pregnant long before now! You know it. Leave with me—you know you want to."

"I do, Chris, I do. But there is no way I can leave John. It would just kill him to think that I would leave with the best friend he has ever had all his life. You two are like brothers."

"I don't give a damn."

"You do too, and you know it. Let's wait and see whose baby it is. If it's yours, then we will leave. There is no other way."

"Yes, there is."

"What do you mean?"

"Never mind what I mean. You love me, don't you?"

"Yes, Chris, you know I do—with all my heart."

"Well ... well, what if John had an accident?

"Chris!"

"Well, what if he did?"

"I ... I don't know. Yes, yes, I do know. Chris, if you really love me you will do what I want. Do you love me?"

"Yes, I've loved you ever since I first saw you."

"Then forget this talk. You wait. You wait, just like me, to find out. If it is your baby, I'll know, and I'll leave with you."

"And if it is not?"

"Then ... then I don't know. But I know this: if you do anything before that baby comes, you'll never see me again, Chris. You swear to God to me that you won't do a thing. Understand? Swear to me."

"Alright, Jody. I swear to God I won't do anything. I'm just so in love with you I forgot myself. I promise I'll wait. I'll never do anything that will keep you from loving me. Do you believe me?"

"Yes, yes, I believe you, Chris. I believe you."

"Then come here, Jody, and let me hold you in my arms. I can wait, I suppose, but let me hold you now while I can."

"Alright, Chris, but just for a moment. I've got to get that soup up to Ralph."

I laid on the balcony in silence. I couldn't believe what I had just heard. Jamie's sister was in love with someone else. So that's what it was.

I could hardly believe it, but I had heard it for myself. I promised myself that I would never tell Jamie or anyone else. I was sorry that

I had heard it myself. I lay there going over in my mind what I had just heard. My daydreaming almost got me caught. Jody and Chris's footsteps beneath me under the balcony returned me to my senses. I quietly got up and slipped back into the bedroom. I quickly got into bed and pulled the covers over me.

I don't believe it, I repeated over and over to myself. *I wish I were home.*

No one—no one—could ever know what I had heard. I knew I mustn't tell anyone, ever.

Chapter

10

"Well, Ralph, are you ready to go?" asked Mr. Northfield.

"Yes, I'm ready," I replied, putting on my coat and stocking cap.

"You don't seem very excited," he replied.

"Well, I'm still a little stiff and achy," I said, standing up. After staying in bed for two and a half days with a cold, I was stiff. I still had a bit of a head cold, but I did want to go hunting. It was Wednesday morning. Christmas was Friday, and I figured that everyone would be preparing for Christmas tomorrow, so I didn't want to miss out.

Jody entered the kitchen carrying three guns in cases. I spotted my new gun case and Jamie's under her right arm. In her left arm, she cradled Mr. Northfield's gun. She walked past me over to the kitchen door leading outside. She set the guns down by the door and pulled the curtain hanging over the door window to one side.

"Here comes, Chris!" she said, not turning her head. "I thought I heard someone outside."

She stepped back from the door just as it opened, Chris Jennings stepped inside and stomped the snow from his boots on the old brown and yellow rug that lay by the door.

"Hello, everyone," he announced. "Ready to go hunting?"

"Sure," Jamie chirped, more excited that I was.

"How about you, Ralph?" he said, looking into my eyes.

Somehow, I found it difficult to return the look into his light-blue eyes. I couldn't forget the conversation I had heard two days before.

I almost thought that he knew I had overheard something. His eyes seemed almost hard and cold to me.

"Sure," I replied softly.

"Well, you don't seem very excited," he said, repeating what Mr. Northfield had said moments before.

"I'm a little stiff and achy," I repeated.

"Well, let's go if we're going," Mr. Northfield said. "We haven't got all day."

He walked over to the door near Mr. Jennings and picked his gun up and tucked it under his right arm. He opened the door in front of him and stepped outside. Chris Jennings followed him. Jamie and I both headed for the door at the same time. Jamie got there first and picked up his gun and went outside. I picked mine up and followed him. Mr. Northfield and Chris Jennings had already mounted their horses. Tied to the rail by the back door, was Tinker.

"Hand me your guns," Chris said, extending one arm out to Jamie. "I'll hold them until you get mounted. Have you boys got your shells?"

"I've got them," Mr. Northfield cut in.

Jamie handed his gun up to Chris. I walked over and did the same. I followed Jamie back over to Tinker.

"You want to ride in front, or do you want me to?" Jamie said, turning to me.

"I don't care."

"Come on, Ralphie, decide."

"Oh, you ride in front."

"Then help me get up," Jamie smiled with satisfaction. I helped lift his foot up high enough to reach the stirrup. Jamie grabbed each side of the saddle with his gloved hands and started to pull himself up. I could see he was struggling a bit so I put both my hands on his rear and pushed him up. Once he was in the saddle, I untied Tinker and handed Jamie the reins. I slowly lifted my aching leg to the stirrup. Finally, my foot found it, and I grabbed the saddle and pulled myself up. Jamie tried to help me by grabbing the back of my coat and pulling with his left hand. I swung my right leg over Tinker's back and settled behind Jamie.

"We'll head south toward the river and hunt some of the draws that look good," Mr. Northfield said, pointing the direction we would head. He turned Midnight south and headed out in a walk. Jamie and I followed, with Chris Jennings bringing up the rear.

It was a beautiful day. The sun was rising in the east. There was not a cloud in the sky. The snow was glistening white as it stretched out on the land before us. There was no wind, and it was not cold. That was one reason why I was able to go hunting. The sun felt good for a change. I wasn't cold, and I started feeling a little better. I started to get a little excited about hunting.

We headed straight south, just as we had done when we went to the river for wood. The horses walked along quietly and effortlessly through the eight inches of fluffy snow on the ground. Up and down three ridges we went, just as we had done before. When we reached the fourth ridge, I looked off to my right, and I could see the cattle shed down in the valley off in the distance. I had remembered it from the trip before. We turned left and headed down to the long valley that lay before us.

"How about that draw over there?" Chris Jennings said, pointing to a small patch of trees to our right several hundred yards from us. "There might be a few rabbits in there."

"Alright with me," Mr. Northfield called back, turning his horse that direction. "At least there aren't any creeks for anyone to fall in."

I failed to find what he said funny, even though the other three laughed. Within a few moments, we were at the bottom of the draw. It wasn't a long draw, maybe about eighty to one hundred yards long. It was V-shaped and narrowed to a point. It was maybe thirty-five yards wide at the bottom where we stopped our horses. There were quite a few trees and bushes though and lots of high grass sticking up through the snow.

"There goes one," Jamie yelled in front of me. "See it?"

He pointed off almost straight in front of him. Sure enough, I could see it. It was a jack rabbit, for sure. I could tell by his long ears, and he was almost completely white in his winter coat.

"Well, that's a good sign," Mr. Northfield said, dismounting. "Come on."

I reached for the left stirrup with my foot to dismount. Before I could find it, Jamie had his left foot in it and was swinging his right leg over Tinker's back. It hit me in my right side, causing me to lose my balance. Since I had nothing to hang on to, I started to fall off the left side of Tinker. I grabbed for Jamie to keep from falling. Instead, I caused Jamie to lose his balance and both of us fell in a pile in the snow.

"What are you doing?" Jamie yelled, getting up and brushing off the snow.

"Me! What about you? You darn near kicked me right off the horse."

"You! What about me? You didn't have to pull me off."

"Hey, boys," Mr. Northfield interrupted. "Do you want to hunt, or do you want to fight?"

"Hunt," we both replied, forgetting our accident and remembering the rabbit that was getting away. Chris Jennings had dismounted and uncased our guns while Jamie and I were arguing. He walked over to me and handed me my brand new gun.

"Go over and get some shells from John," Mr. Jennings said.

I walked over to Mr. Northfield, and he handed me six shotgun shells. He told me to put them in my pocket. I did as he said and waited for instructions. When Jamie had gotten his shells, Mr. Northfield told us that he and Jennings would go up the middle of the draw and that I should walk on one outer edge and Jamie walk the other.

When we had spread out as we had been told to do, Mr. Northfield told us to load our guns and to be sure the safety was on. I lifted the bolt and pulled it back. Reaching into my coat pocket, I fumbled for a shell. I grabbed one with my gloved right hand and pulled it from my pocket. Quickly, shoved it into the barrel, closed the bolt, and checked the safety. I was ready.

"Now, stay in line with Chris and myself," ordered Mr. Northfield. "If anything jumps up, don't get excited. Take your time and be careful."

He motioned for us to start up the draw. Everything was quiet except for the crunching of the snow under my feet. I kept searching through the trees for the sight of a rabbit running over the snow. I saw nothing. I glanced to my right every few moments to make sure that I was staying in line with the others. Mr. Northfield I could see easily, and every so often I could see Chris Jennings moving through the trees. I was not able to see Jamie at all. I checked my safety again to see if it was on. It was. My eyes strained through the trees looking for game. Still I saw nothing.

Bang!

The noise exploded over the quiet countryside. I wondered who had shot, but I didn't have to wait long to find out.

"I got him, I got him!" I could hear Jamie yelling from the other side of the draw. I was excited from his yelling. I wanted to see what he had gotten. I could hear Chris Jennings and Jamie saying something to each other, but I couldn't make out what it was. I started into the trees over to Jamie. My curiosity was killing me. I trotted fifteen or twenty feet into the draw when Mr. Northfield yelled at me.

"Ralph, get back where you were. You can see what he got at the end of the draw. A good hunter stays put unless he is called on, remember that."

I turned, half mad and dying of curiosity, and went back to the edge of the draw. I had walked a few feet when a sudden movement caught the corner of my eye. I turned my head to see a rabbit running up the draw to my right. I turned excitedly, releasing the safety from my gun. I lifted the gun to my shoulder, aimed, and fired. *Bang!* The noise seemed deafening in the trees. The gun kicked hard against my shoulder, bending me backward. The front of the barrel raised upward. I quickly lowered my gun to see if I had gotten the rabbit I wanted so badly. I searched the snow for the rabbit. I couldn't see anything. I headed to where I had fired at the rabbit. When I got there I saw nothing but the snow torn up from the pellets from the shotgun shell. I surveyed the ground beyond only to find rabbit tracks leading on up the draw.

Darn it, I said to myself.

Bang! Bang! A gun cracked to my right. I turned and saw Mr. Northfield lowering his gun.

"There's your rabbit, Ralph" he called to me. "It doubled on back down the draw after you fired. He came right back to me."

I didn't say anything. I watched Mr. Northfield head up the draw twenty feet or so. He bent over and picked up a large rabbit. I was sick. My rabbit had gotten away from me, and someone else had gotten it. I put my right hand on the bolt of my new gun and ejected the shell. I reached in my pocket for another and loaded it in my gun.

I gotta get something, I thought to myself. *I just have to.*

We started up the remainder of the draw. I searched every inch of ground for another rabbit, hoping I'd get another chance. It never came.

Within a few moments, we came to the end of the draw. I looked toward Jamie to see him proudly carrying a nice large rabbit. I envied him.

"How about that, Ralphie?" he said excitedly. "Where is your rabbit?"

"Mine? I missed him," I said, burning up inside. I could have killed Jamie, I was so mad.

"Maybe I better walk along with you and shoot one for you," Jamie returned.

"Cut it out, Jamie," Mr. Northfield cut in. He probably sensed how mad I was, and I was glad if he did. "Everyone will get one, I'm sure of it. Ralph just had a hard shot that's all. I was watching him."

In my mind, I agreed with him. But in my heart, I knew I should have had that rabbit.

We turned and headed back down through the draw to return to the horses. I had hoped, along with the others, that we would maybe run into another rabbit. We never did. We all reached the end of draw at the same time and headed back to the horses. Mr. Northfield pulled a leather strap from his saddle bags and tied each end around one of the hind legs of each rabbit. Then he hung the rabbits over the back of Midnight in front of the saddle horn. One rabbit hung on each side.

Chris Jennings took mine and Jamie's shotguns, which we had already unloaded. We mounted our horses. This time I got in the saddle first with Jamie behind me. I didn't want him knocking me off Tinkers' back like he had done before. Jamie squawked a little about this, but I guess he was too happy to really care. We turned our horses and headed on down the valley.

"Let's hunt that long draw over there," Jennings said, pointing to a heavy patch of timber up ahead of us on the opposite side of the valley from where we had just hunted. "That one is really thick, John, but is not very wide. Think we could drive some game down to the boys?"

"What do you mean, down to the boys?" Mr. Northfield asked.

"Well, we'll let the boys stay down at the bottom, and we'll start at the top and walk down to them."

"Don't you think that is a little risky?" returned Mr. Northfield.

"Nah, they're big boys, they're not going to shoot anybody, are you?"

"No, sir," I replied, shaking my head. Jamie didn't answer. I guess he was still thinking about his rabbit.

"Why don't I take one of the boys and you one of the boys," asked Mr. Northfield. "That way we can keep an eye on them."

"What are you gonna do, pamper them?" answered Jennings, seeming rather irritated. "If they want to hunt like men, they have to be treated like men."

"Well—"

"Ah, come on, John. Let's try it one time and see how they do," Jennings cut in. He kicked his horse in the haunches and took off in a trot for the draw. The white snow flew from his horse's hooves. I watched him break into a gallop; I was afraid that Jennings was going to drop our guns. He quickly covered the distance to the draw. I watched Jennings get off his horse and lean our guns against a large tree. He tied the reins of his horse to the branch of a nearby tree.

It took us several minutes to reach the lower end of the draw where Jennings was waiting for us. Mr. Northfield dismounted and tied Midnight up to the same tree as Jennings's horse, Paint. I brought Tinker to a halt and waited for Jamie to dismount. I guess Jamie thought he would be cute, because to get off, he slid off the rear end of Tinker. He lost his balance and fell on his seat in the snow. We couldn't help but laugh as he got up brushing off the snow. I thought it had served him right for what he had done to me. I dismounted and picked my gun up, brushing the snow off the butt. Jamie did the same.

"Okay, boys," said Jennings. "You walk in about twenty yards and post yourselves so you each can see the edge of the draw. Make sure you can see each other so you don't shoot each other. Understand?"

We shook our heads, indicating that we did.

"Now, John and I will circle around to the top of the draw and head down to you. Be alert and keep your eyes open for us. We don't want anyone to get shot now. Come on, John. Let's go."

"I don't know, Chris," Mr. Northfield said slowly. "This may not be too good an idea."

"They know what to do, John. They're not stupid, you know."

Jennings slapped gently at Mr. Northfield's left shoulder with the back of his right hand. He turned and headed up the hill leaving Mr. Northfield behind.

"You boys sure you'll be alright?" Mr. Northfield said, with a concerned look on his face.

"Sure, we'll be just fine," smiled Jamie. Strange as it seemed, it was about the friendliest I had seen Jamie treat his brother-in-law. I didn't care how happy Jamie was about shooting that rabbit, Jamie's friendliness to Mr. Northfield took me by surprise.

Mr. Northfield turned with Jamie's answer and headed up the hill after Jennings. He turned part way up the hill and called back to us.

"It will take about thirty minutes for us to work our way back to you because it is relatively thick in there. So be patient. If you hear us shoot don't worry about it, just stay where you are. Okay, boys?"

We waved to him to indicate that we had heard what he said. I turned to Jamie and asked which side of the draw he wanted. He wanted the west side. I nodded and pulled a shell from my pocket. I loaded my shotgun once again and headed to the east side of the draw. When I got to within twenty feet of the edge I turned to Jamie. He was standing inside the west edge maybe thirty yards from me. I waved my left arm, signaling for him to enter at the same time I did. We both walked into the draw about twenty yards and stopped, making sure that we could see each other clearly. We had done exactly what Mr. Northfield had instructed us to do.

We stood there in the cold silence looking uphill into the thick brush, trees, and grass. My feet began to get cold from the lack of movement. Five minutes or so went by. Neither Jamie or I saw anything. Time seemed to pass slowly. I didn't have a pocket watch, so I didn't know for sure how much time had passed. I stood quietly, leaning against a tree, watching the draw in front of me. I was hoping for another chance at a rabbit. I would not miss this time, I was sure.

Bang! The sound of a shotgun shattered the stillness about one hundred yards up the draw. I got my gun ready in case something came my way. I looked at Jamie quickly to see if he was ready. He was. He looked at me to see if I was ready. We both turned our heads back to the draw in front of us. Suddenly a blood curdling scream filled the air. A wild scream from a man that brought goose bumps to my arms. I looked at Jamie to find him standing there with his eyes and mouth wide open. Something had gone wrong, and I was scared!

Chapter

11

"*Help, help,*" we heard a voice calling from up the draw. "*Help.*"

"Come on, Jamie. Let's go!" I yelled over to him, starting up the draw.

"Wait, wait, Ralphie. Let's go together," Jamie yelled as I started up the draw. I stopped and waited for Jamie. I watched him plow through the snow as quickly as possible to reach me. Within a few moments, he was beside me, panting heavily.

"What do you think is wrong, Ralphie?"

"I don't know. Let's just get up there," I returned.

We started up the draw together. We moved as quickly as we could through the trees, bushes, and grass. Branches slapped at our bodies as we trotted as fast as possible up the thick, dense draw. It seemed as though it would take us forever to get to the person yelling up ahead of us. Once I heard a thump on the ground behind me. I turned, to find Jamie sprawled in the snow. Somehow it wasn't too funny this time. We could still hear the voice calling *"Help"* in front of us.

The voice was very near to us now. There was a small rise in front of us, and the voice was just over the other side, I was sure. I reached the small crest before Jamie, to see Chris Jennings standing with his back to me. He was twenty yards or so in front of me.

"What's the matter?" I yelled to him, panting heavily. The sound of my voice startled him. He turned around quickly.

"Stay there!" he yelled fiercely at me.

"What's the matter?" I said, stopping in my tracks.

"Just stay there, it's too late," he yelled, raising both hands as if to push me back. My eyes widened at the sight of his hands held before me. They were covered with blood. Blood so fresh that I saw it drip from his hands onto the white snow.

"What's happened?" yelled Jamie, who was now standing beside me. "Are you hurt?"

"He's ... he's dead," Jennings said softly. He lowered his head and dropped his arms to his sides. Muffled noises came from beneath his hat that hid his face from us.

"He's dead?" screamed Jamie. "Who's dead?"

Jamie and I waited for an answer. Jennings said nothing for a long moment.

"Who's dead?" Jamie screamed again.

"John—your brother-in-law, John!" screamed Jennings, not raising his head.

"Oh, Jesus," I yelled, forgetting that my father would switch me for saying that word. "Where ... where is he?"

I started running up to Jennings who did not move as I approached. I ran past him to see for myself. My eyes searched the ground before me. I guess I just didn't believe him, or maybe I just had to see for myself. It just couldn't be true.

"Don't look, Ralph. It's not very pretty." I heard Jennings say behind me. I turned around to see him facing me. His eyes were red with tears. He took several deep breaths that made him calm down somewhat.

"Where is he?" I repeated. "Are you sure?"

"Over behind that fallen tree," Jennings said, pointing to the right of me. "He was climbing over the tree when his gun went off. It struck him in the chest. He never had a chance. He's gone."

I turned and walked slowly to the downed tree. I felt two hands grab my arm that made me jump. It was Jamie. He must have run up behind me to see for himself. I nervously inched closer to the downed tree.

"Oh, Jesus, Jamie. I ... I see his feet. I ... I can see blood in the snow. Do you see it?"

"Yes, yes, I see it, Ralphie," Jamie's voice started to crack. I leaned over the tree slightly to get a better look. What I saw made me sick.

"Oh, my God," I yelled, dropping my gun in the snow. "I don't believe it."

I covered my mouth with my hands at the sight before me. My stomach felt queasy. Mr. Northfield was laying on the ground on his back. The shotgun blast had ripped a large hole through his leather coat. I saw pieces of flesh dotting the jacket and the ground around his chest. His eyes were wide open and rolled back, showing only the whites of his eyes. Blood ran from his mouth onto the white snow.

"Jesus, Jamie, don't look," I said, turning away from the bloody body before me. It was too late. Jamie had already seen him. He turned away from the tree, gagging and coughing. Wild grunting noises came from his mouth as he vomited on the white snow. It was too much for me. I ran away from him back to Mr. Jennings, trying not to get sick.

"What … what should we do?" I said, gasping for breath to clear my nose and mind.

"Go … go get the horses, Ralph, and take Jamie with you. Hurry."

"Come on, Jamie," I yelled, not bothering to look back at him. I took off down the draw to get the horses. I could feel branches slapping my face and body as I went. Somehow they didn't hurt like before. All I could think of was what I had just seen. Every time I closed my eyes I could see Mr. Northfield lying in the snow, dead.

I could hear Jamie behind me, coming down the draw. He was crying out loud. His crying bothered me, and I wished he would stop. It only seemed to make things worse. I reached the end of the draw and found the three horses where we had tied them. I quickly untied the horses and, holding on to the three sets of reins, mounted Tinker. I waited for Jamie to catch up. When he reached me, I held my left hand out to him to help him mount. I pulled with all my strength to get him up behind me.

"Shut up, Jamie," I said, when he was sitting behind me. "You're making things worse by crying."

"But, geez, Ralphie—"

"'But, geez' nothing, Jamie. Shut up, will ya?" I cut in angrily. "Here, hold the reins of the other two horses."

He grabbed the reins from my hand. I headed Tinker out as fast as I could up the east edge of the draw. Up ahead of me I could see Chris Jennings standing at the edge of the draw waving both arms back and forth over his head. Within moments, Jamie and I reached Jennings. I noticed that the blood on his hands was gone and that he had his gloves on.

"You boys stay here" he said calmly, as he untied a blue wool blanket from behind his saddle. Pulling the blanket free, he turned and entered the draw. Jamie and I sat quietly on Tinker, waiting for what we both knew would happen. Shortly, I could see the figure of Chris Jennings moving through the trees back to us. And, as I knew it would be, he was carrying the blanket-covered body of Mr. Northfield over his right shoulder. Jamie and I watched silently as Jennings walked slowly back to us. As he emerged from the draw, I could see Mr. Northfield's hands swinging freely back and forth beneath the blue blanket. Fresh blood was still dripping from his hands leaving little red spots in the glistening white snow.

Jennings walked directly to Midnight. The beautiful black horse bolted slightly as if sensing that his master was dead. Jennings calmed the horse by patting him on the shoulder with his left hand. Carefully he lifted the lifeless body from his right shoulder and laid it over the saddle. He loosened a rope tied near the saddle horn and wrapped one end around the black boots hanging beneath the blue blanket and tied it. He tossed the other end under Midnight's belly. Slowly Jennings walked around the rear end of the horse and picked up the other end of the rope. He wrapped the rope around Mr. Northfield's bloody hands and tied them together. He pushed gently on Mr. Northfield's body to see if it was securely tied. Satisfied that it was, he silently walked to his horse and mounted it.

"What about our guns?" I asked, suddenly remembering we had left them in the draw.

"Oh, yeah, I … I almost forgot," he said, calmly dismounting his horse. "I'll go get them.

Quickly, Chris Jennings retraced his footsteps back into the draw. A few minutes passed before he reappeared with four guns cradled in his arms. He placed his gun in the sheath attached to his horse. He went over to Midnight and carefully placed Mr. Northfield's gun in its sheath.

"Can you carry your own guns, boys?" he said softly.

I reached out for my gun without saying anything. He handed it to me. Jamie did the same.

"I unloaded them already," Jennings continued. He mounted his horse once again and slowly raised his right arm and swung it forward, indicating for us to move out. Slowly and quietly, our horses continued up the east side of the draw. Jennings stopped his horse at the top of the draw and stopped Midnight when he came up beside him. He leaned over and grabbed the string that tied the two rabbits together that we had shot. He lifted them up and studied them silently. Suddenly he threw the rabbits over his head back into the tip of the draw. We all watched the rabbits bounce once in the snow and disappear beneath it. Neither Jamie nor I seemed to care. Jennings started his horse off in a trot over the top of the hill. Midnight trotted behind him. Jamie and I followed on Tinker. The only thing I looked at was the bouncing dead body on the horse in front of me. We turned northwest heading back to the ranch. Jamie had calmed down now, which helped me settle down also. I tried to get my mind off of what had happened by looking at the countryside. I kept telling myself how beautiful it was, but it didn't do any good. I wished with all my heart that I was home with my family. I remembered how I thought something was wrong on our way out on the train. This had to be a dream I thought, it just had to be. This just couldn't be happening.

"Ralphie."

I heard Jamie whisper in my ear.

"What?" I said softly.

"What's gonna happen when we get back to the ranch. What's my sister gonna say?"

"I don't know, Jamie. Don't even talk about it."

"I can't help it, Ralphie," Jamie said, starting to cry again. "Geez, he's dead, Ralphie. He's dead. Don't you know that?"

"Of course, I know that, Jamie," I said, trying not to show my feelings.

"Have you ever seen a dead person like that before?" Jamie continued.

"No."

"Neither have I, Ralphie, and it makes me sick. I didn't really like him that much and now I'm sorry—so sorry he's dead. I wish he wasn't dead, Ralphie."

"So do I, Jamie. So do I. I never want to see anything like it again as long as I live. It just happened. It was an accident. There's nothing we can do, Jamie."

"I know, Ralphie, but—"

"Just be quiet, Jamie. I don't want to talk about it. Okay?"

"Okay."

Off in the distance, beyond Mr. Northfields' body that I suddenly had found myself staring at, I could see the ranch. Silently, we rode on. I was glad no one said anything, especially Jamie. My stomach was still in knots, and I wished more than anything that this whole thing was over. It seemed that, for the first time in my life, I was trying to be as grown up as possible. And here I was, thirteen years old.

As we neared the house, Jennings raised his gun, signaling us to stop.

"You boys stay here. I'll have to go and tell Jody."

I stopped Tinker. Slowly Jennings headed out toward the ranch house a hundred yards away. Midnight walked slowly behind them, still carrying his dead master. It was one of the worst things I had ever seen. Jennings walked his horse and Midnight up to the side kitchen door. We watched him dismount, tie up the horses, and go inside.

"Ralphie, take me up to the outhouse. I have to go," Jamie said.

"No, Jamie, Mr. Jennings said to stay here."

"I can't help it, Ralphie. Take me, or I'll get off," Jamie said firmly.

"Okay," I said reluctantly, heading Tinker to the outhouse. When we got there, Jamie jumped off, still holding on to his gun. He leaned his gun up against the side of the outhouse and went inside. I stared ahead at the house in front of me. The only thing I looked at was the body of Mr. Northfield lying sideways over the saddle of Midnight.

As I sat on the back of Tinker, I suddenly picked up the sound of voices. At first I was not able to tell where they were coming from. My ears strained, trying to pick up the faint sounds again. There they were. I could hear them. They were coming from the house. They were getting louder, but I still couldn't hear what was being said. I heard a crash inside the house. I wondered if something had happened. Did Jody pass out, I wondered. Did they need help? I didn't know what to do, but I decided to find out. I kicked Tinker in the side, and she trotted off toward the house. As I reached the back door I dismounted and tied Tinker up next to Midnight and Point.

"You killed him! You killed him!"

"No, no, I didn't, Jody. I didn't."

"Yes, you did!" I could hear Jody yell hysterically. I crept up to the back door to listen. Carefully I peeked through the kitchen door window. I could see Jody and Chris Jennings facing each other with the kitchen table between them. I could see Jody's face, but Jennings' back was to me so I couldn't see his.

"Whose gun were you using?" Jody yelled at Chris.

"My own, Jody," he returned quickly.

"Are you sure, Chris? Are you sure? You know damn good and well that I know that you and John hunted with each other's guns. Always having your little contests with each other about this thing or that. How can I believe you, Chris? How can I believe you?"

"You just have to—"

"But after what we talked about, and after what you said the other day, how can I?" Jody cut in, calming down. "What will people say, what will they think? What can I think? Damn it, Chris, don't lie to me."

Jody sat down at the kitchen table and crossed her arms on top of it. She dropped her head into her arms. I was sure she was crying, but her face was hidden. Jennings walked around the table behind Jody. He placed both his hands on top of her shoulders and massaged them gently. He was speaking softly to her. I strained trying to hear what he was saying. I just couldn't make it out. I wished that he would speak up so I could hear.

The conversation I had just heard flashed over and over in my mind. I turned and looked at the blanket covered body of Mr. Northfield tied on the back of Midnight. I remembered the conversation between Jody and Jennings I had heard the day I fell in the creek. I remembered promising myself that I wouldn't tell anyone what I had heard and knew.

But now, I wondered. Did Jennings really shoot Mr. Northfield as he mentioned wanting to do? Who was using whose gun? Was it really an accident? Those questions and more went through my mind. But the biggest question was trying to decide if I should tell someone. Should I, or shouldn't I? The problem flashed over and over.

I didn't know what to do, and it scared me. I wished I was back home.

Chapter

12

"What's going on, Ralphie?"

"Jesus, Jamie. Don't scare me like that!" I exclaimed, startled at the sudden sound of Jamie's voice.

"Ralphie, you said 'Jesus' again."

"Yeah, I know," I answered angrily, glad that my father wasn't here to hear me say it. "Knock on the door, and ask if we can come in."

I wanted Jamie to take the blame in case someone got mad, since we didn't stay where we were told to. I didn't want Chris Jennings or Jody to know that I had heard their conversation. I figured if we knocked at the door together they would think nothing much about it. Jamie knocked on the door. I watched Jody lift her head from her arms. Her cheeks were damp from crying.

"Come in," she called, with little emotion.

Jamie opened the door and stepped inside. I followed and closed the door behind me. Jody said nothing. She just turned in her chair and extended her arms outward to Jamie. Jennings released his grip on Jody's shoulders and stepped back. He said nothing. Jamie quickly went around the table to his sister's arms. They hugged each other tightly for a long moment. Jody closed her eyes as she held Jamie. A single tear slowly ran down her left cheek to her chin. I watched her wipe it away with the back of her left hand as she held Jamie. She released Jamie and held him back at arm's length with both her hands on his shoulders.

"You … you and Ralph go upstairs and pack your things," Jody said calmly. "We are going to town, and then we will be going back to Selby. Understand, Jamie?"

"Yes" Jamie said, sniffling his nose.

"Chris," Jody continued, turning to him, "you go out and hitch up the team. Then I want you to take John to town. You know what I mean. I want you to send a wire to my father and have someone take it out to him. Tell him what has happened, and have him come out here on this afternoon's train if at all possible. It is still early enough that he can get the late afternoon train. Then go to the hotel, and get me two rooms. Please go right now. I'll talk to you in town."

"You sure you'll be all right?" he asked, walking past me to the kitchen door.

"Please hurry, Chris, and do these things for me," Jody returned. Chris placed his hat back on his golden hair, opened the door, and went outside. I watched him trot off to the barn west of the house to fetch the team as Jody had asked.

"Boys, you go upstairs and get your things."

Jamie and I did as she asked. We left the kitchen and went up to the bedroom that we had slept in. We pulled our suitcases from under the bed. We laid them on top of the bed and opened them. We packed our suitcases in silence. I was glad Jamie didn't ask me if I had heard anything at the kitchen door. As I put some socks in my suitcase, I watched through the west window and saw Chris Jennings appear from the barn. He was walking the team over to the house.

I put another pair of socks in my suitcase and then walked over to the window. I could see Jennings standing outside the kitchen door below me. I watched his hands move in front of him and his head bob occasionally. I figured he was talking to Jody, although I couldn't see her.

"What are you looking at," Jamie asked from behind me.

"Oh, I was just watching Mr. Jennings, that's all," I replied.

"Why, what's he doing?" Jamie questioned, walking up beside me.

"Nothing, I just watched him walk the team over to the house, that's all."

"Oh."

We both watched as Jennings turned and got on his horse. He grabbed Midnight's reins and turned his horse. Jamie and I watched silently as he led his horse out the lane followed by Midnight with the body of Mr. Northfield. It was a sad, terrifying sight, I thought to myself. We watched Jennings until he reached the end of the lane.

I returned to my suitcase on the bed and finished my packing. Neither Jamie or I spoke. In the silence, I began recalling all of the events of the past few days. I wanted to say something, or do something, but I just didn't know what to do. I tried to push everything out of my mind.

"Come on, Jamie. Let's go," I said, slamming my suitcase shut and fastening it. I picked up my suitcase and headed to the kitchen. Setting down my suitcase, I again went upstairs. I quickly rechecked the bedroom to see if I had left anything behind. Satisfied that I had everything, I left the bedroom and returned to the kitchen. Jamie followed close behind me.

We sat down at the kitchen table and waited for Jody. We could hear her opening and closing dresser drawers in the bedroom next to us. I glanced at the clock on the west wall. It wasn't quite eleven thirty. I was surprised at the time. Somehow I thought it just had to be later, after everything that had happened. I watched the pendulum slowly swing back and forth, making the tick-tock sound I was used to from our grandfather clock back home.

"Are you ready, boys?" Jody said, appearing in the kitchen doorway. She was dressed in a long, black dress. In each hand she carried a suitcase. She quietly crossed the room to the outside kitchen door and set the suitcases down. She mumbled, "Oh, I almost forgot."

She retraced her steps and went back to the bedroom. Within a few seconds she reappeared. This time, a gold locket hung from her neck. I recognized it as the locket she was wearing the day she was married. I remembered that it had been her mother's and grandmother's. Even though I had only seen it a few times, I had remembered it from the wedding.

"Is that the locket you wore when you got married?" I asked, wanting to make sure my memory was right.

"Yes ... yes, it is, Ralph," Jody said, starting to cry. I realized that I had said something wrong. I was sorry for that.

"Gee, I'm sorry, Jody, I didn't mean—"

"That's ... that's alright, Ralph. I understand," Jody said, brushing the tears from her eyes. "Just get your things; we have to go to town."

Jamie and I got up at the same time. We picked up our things and headed for the outside kitchen door. I put my suitcase down and opened the door. After opening it, I grabbed my suitcase and shotgun and went outside. Jamie followed behind me. I went to the wagon and carefully laid my gun down under the wagon seat. I lifted my suitcase into the back of the wagon. Jamie stood there beside me, silently watching. When I had finished, I stepped back and watched Jamie lay his gun beside mine. Then he put his suitcase down beside mine. Just as he finished, Jody walked out the kitchen door toward the wagon. She was wearing a dark blue overcoat with a matching bonnet. She carried her suitcases in each hand. A little black purse with a gold chain hung from her right arm. She placed both suitcases next to Jamie's and mine. Without saying a word, she returned to the kitchen. Seconds later, she returned carrying two boxes. Just as before, she placed the boxes next to our suitcases.

"Get in the wagon, boys," Jody said.

We watched Jody climb in the left side of the wagon and grab the reins. She looked very calm. After she sat down, Jamie and I climbed into the wagon. Jamie sat in the middle. Jody pulled back on the reins, making the wagon move backward. After moving the team away from the rail, Jody pulled hard on the left rein, making the team turn toward the lane. Silently, the horses headed out the lane to the road. The sun was high overhead, and it seemed almost warm. The snow was a glistening white. It was such a beautiful day, I thought. It was hard to believe that we were headed home. Christmas was two days away.

As we left the lane onto the road to town, I looked over my left shoulder back at the ranch. It looked beautiful. The brown logs of the house stood out brilliantly against the white snow. The snow on the roof made the house look more beautiful. The two barns looked just as pretty. It was quiet and peaceful. Silently, we rode toward town. We went west down the road. Shortly, we reached the road that headed to town. We turned right, heading north to Red Elm.

Everything was so quiet; I wanted to yell just to hear some noise. The South Dakota countryside was beautiful in the bright sunlight. Time passed slowly as we headed north toward town. In my mind, I was glad that I was going home. We all rode along in silence. I was afraid to say anything. I didn't want Jody to cry again.

"We're almost there, boys," Jody said, breaking the silence. I looked up the road and could see Red Elm in the distance. The buildings looked like little dark matchboxes against the white snow. I sat in silence and watched the buildings grow larger as we get closer to town.

"Is that someone coming?" said Jamie, raising his right arm and pointing down the road.

"Yes, it is," answered Jody.

I wondered who it was. Within a few minutes I would know, I thought to myself. I could see two people on horseback headed up the road toward us. When they came up beside us, Jody stopped the wagon. The man on the lead horse was dressed in a brown leather coat with a white fur collar. He had on a big, white broad-brimmed cowboy hat. Pinned on the left side of his leather coat was a sheriff's badge.

"Jody, I'm real sorry to hear what happened," the sheriff said through a thick black mustache.

"I know you are, Mr. Allard," Jody replied softly. "Thank you."

"We were on our way out to your place to make sure you got to town alright."

"Thank you, sheriff."

"I'm afraid that when you get to town I will have to ask you to stop at my office. You know what I mean?"

"Yes, I know."

"Are these the boys that were there when it happened?"

"Yes, this is my brother, Jamie, and that's his friend, Ralph," Jody said, pointing to me. "They came out from Selby to spend Christmas with us."

"I'm afraid I'm going to have to ask them some questions too. I have already gotten a statement from Chris, but I will have to hear the boys' side of the story too. Chris has sent a wire off to Selby to your father and mother. Undertaker Barlow is taking care of the body right now. Is that alright?

"Yes, but I want his body shipped back to Iowa. Understand?" Jody snapped, suddenly becoming angry. "I want him buried back where he was born. He would want it that way. Understand?"

"Sure, sure, Jody. We'll see he's buried wherever you think is right."

"Okay," she replied, lowering her voice and calming down. "Please wire the undertaker in Storm Lake, Iowa, that he will be coming and that someone will be accompanying his body."

"Okay, Jody," the sheriff said. "What day should they expect—"

"Either Christmas day or the day after," Jody cut in. "If my father gets here tonight, we will be leaving on tomorrow's morning train. Otherwise, we will leave on the evening train. It depends upon when Father gets here."

Jody's voice seemed cold and stern as I listened to her speak. She seemed almost mean to the sheriff, I thought. It was very businesslike the way she gave instructions. It reminded me of mother when she ordered me to do the chores. Maybe this was Jody's way of hiding her sorrow. I didn't know.

"Would you like to get something to eat before or after you come to my office?" the sheriff said as politely as possible.

"Well, I think we would all rather get it over with," Jody said, in a soft voice. "Wouldn't you, boys?"

I almost wondered why she bothered to ask, the way she had been throwing out the orders. I was starting to get hungry now, but I nodded my head yes. Jamie did the same.

"Okay let's get to my office now," the sheriff said, turning his big chestnut mare back toward town. "I'm sure it won't take long to get each of your statements."

We all started back to town together, except for the man who went on ahead to send the wire. As we rode along, I wondered what kind of questions the sheriff would ask. What could I tell him? I didn't see it happen. I wonder if he would ask me if I saw the body. I closed my eyes at the thought of having to describe what I had seen. I remembered once again the conversation I had heard between Jody and Chris Jennings when I was sick. The words I heard between Jody and Mr. Jennings at the ranch not an hour ago flashed through my mind. Would the sheriff ask me if I had heard anything?

If he does, what should I say? Should I tell him what I heard, even if he doesn't ask me?

Those questions raced through my mind. I didn't know what to do, and the thought of answering any questions suddenly scared me.

What should I do? I thought. *What should I do?*

Chapter
13

T he sheriff's office was a big square room. Opposite the door we entered were four small jail cells. I couldn't ever recall seeing jail cells before. I quickly checked each cell with my eyes to see if any of them were occupied. I was disappointed to see that they were all empty. In the center of the room, near the middle jail cell, was a black potbellied stove with a chimney pipe going straight up through the roof. There was a desk that faced the cells on each side of the door we entered. On each wall beside the desks were gun racks that held shotguns and rifles. There was a billboard on the wall beside the door we entered that held several "wanted" posters.

I took my hat and coat off and placed them over the back of my chair. As I sat down in a chair facing the front door, I tried to study the posters that were pinned to the board. I could see the pictures of the men that were wanted. The print wasn't big enough for me to see what each was wanted for. I studied each picture carefully to see if I recognized any of them. I didn't.

Jody, Jamie, and I were all seated together facing Sheriff Allard, who was now seated behind his desk. Two other men sat down in two chairs over by the other desk. Just as the sheriff began to speak, Chris Jennings walked through the door.

"Sit down in my deputy's chair, Chris," the sheriff said, pointing to the chair behind the other desk. "Now, Jody, I need some information regarding John, Okay?"

Jody nodded silently. The sheriff asked her questions about his age, height, birth date—things like that. I listened quietly as the sheriff would ask a question and then write down Jody's answer.

Then sheriff asked Jody if she was there when her husband was shot. I thought it was a stupid question to ask and wondered why the sheriff asked it. Jody said that she wasn't. The sheriff said he had one final question. I listened silently as the sheriff asked Jody if she had any reason to believe that Mr. Northfield's death had been anything other than an accident.

"No," Jody said softly. As the sheriff began to write, I watched Jody turn her head toward Chris Jennings. She looked at him for a brief moment and then looked back at the sheriff. Neither Judy nor Chris Jennings had any expression on their faces when they looked at each other.

"Now, boys, which one of you wants to tell me what happened, in your own words? I want one to tell his story only, and then the other will have a chance to add anything he wants. I may have a few questions after, okay?"

Jamie and I both nodded.

"Which one wants to talk?"

I looked at Jamie, and he looked at me.

"You do it, Ralphie" he said.

"No, you talk, Jamie."

"No, I don't want to. Please, Ralphie."

"No," I said sternly, wiggling in my chair.

"Okay, boys, I'll decide," the sheriff declared. "Which one of you is older?"

"I am," I said, not very happily.

"Then you tell me what happened first," the sheriff said, pointing at me.

"Alright," I said, and I proceeded to tell the sheriff and the others exactly what had happened. I told how Jamie and I had been waiting at the bottom of the draw when we heard a shot go off. How we both had heard a wild scream and then the calls for help. The room was very quiet while I spoke. I watched the sheriff take down a few notes on a notepad in front of him. I told him how Jamie and I ran up the draw and that

I had reached Chris Jennings first. I mentioned how I had startled Mr. Jennings, and then he had told me that Mr. Northfield was dead.

"How did he know he was dead?" the sheriff interrupted me.

"I don't know," I said. "All he said was that he knew he was dead."

"Was he by the body when you got there?"

"No, he was twenty feet or so from the body, I guess."

"Then what did you do?"

"Well, I didn't know for sure or not if everything was true or not, so I went over to see for myself."

"What did you see?"

I told the sheriff how I had seen Mr. Northfield laying on the ground with a hole in his chest. That there was blood and flesh all over his chest, and there was blood running out of his open mouth down into the snow.

"Did you check to see if he was alive?" the sheriff asked.

"No, sir."

"Why not?"

"Because the sight of him almost made me sick to my stomach. Jamie looked at him right after me, and he threw up from the sight of it. I never want to see anything ever again like that."

"Then what happened?"

"Mr. Jennings asked us to go get the horses and bring them back up to him. When we got back with the horses, Mr. Jennings took off a blanket and went back in to get Mr. Northfield."

"What do you mean, 'back in'?" the sheriff asked me.

"Back into the draw."

"In other words, you were not there to see him cover the body and bring it to the horse?"

"That's right. We waited out at the edge of the draw. We couldn't see through the trees to watch him. I didn't want to watch anyway."

"How long was he in there?"

"Oh, I don't know; maybe five, ten minutes maybe."

"And then when he got back, he tied Mr. Northfield's body to his horse, and you and Jamie then headed to the ranch," the sheriff said. "Right?"

"Well, he had to go back in to get the guns," I said. "We didn't want to leave them behind."

"Oh, I see," the sheriff said, raising his eyebrows as he wrote on the pad. "One question, Ralph, and then I think we can finish. Do you remember seeing any tracks near the body when you arrived?"

"No, no, I don't remember seeing any," I said, trying hard to remember.

"How about you, Jamie" the sheriff asked.

"No, I don't remember," Jamie answered.

"Do you know if each man was using his own gun?" the sheriff said, looking at me.

"As far as I know they were," I answered.

"How about you, Jamie," the sheriff asked again.

"I don't know—I suppose so," Jamie answered.

"Do you believe it was an accident?" the sheriff said, looking at me again.

"I ... I don't know for sure, sir, but I think it was."

The sheriff asked Jamie the same question. Jamie answered the same as I did. As he spoke, the conversation I overheard in the kitchen raced through my mind. I wondered if I should say anything.

"Ralph!"

"What?" I said crossly, wondering who had called my name.

"Answer the question, Ralphie," Jamie pleaded.

"What question?" I said, not knowing one had been asked.

"Can you think of anything else that we should know? Anything that was said or something that maybe we should know?"

"No, no, I can't," I answered, amazed at the question. For a moment, I wondered if somehow the sheriff could have read my mind. I looked about the room only to find Chris Jennings sitting back in the deputy's chair staring at me. His light blue eyes had a cold look about them. I turned my head away from him. I wondered what he was thinking about. Had he read my mind too? Did he know I had overheard the conversation in the kitchen? I didn't know, and it scared me a little. Should I tell or not? I looked back at Jennings quickly only to find him still staring at me. Maybe I had better tell.

"Sheriff," I said, looking away from Jennings, back at him. "Sheriff."

"Yes, what is it, Ralph?"

"I ... I ...I was wondering if we were done now," I said, backing down. "I'm getting hungry. I hope you're done."

"Yes, I think that about covers it," the sheriff said, standing up.

I stood up and grabbed my coat and hat off the back of my chair. I quickly put them on and started walking to the front door. I wanted to say something, or thought maybe I should have said something, but I was afraid to. I knew what I had heard, but I wasn't sure what to do. After all, I had heard Jennings promise Jody he wouldn't do anything. It just had to have been an accident, I thought.

Chris Jennings met me at the door. He placed his right hand on my right shoulder. I felt his hand tighten on the muscle near the bottom of my neck. He squeezed hard enough that he pinched my muscle causing it to hurt a little.

"You did just fine, Ralph," he said, looking down at me. He and I walked out onto the front porch.

I looked out into the western sky beyond the buildings across the street from me. Dark gray clouds were off in the distance. I studied them silently, wondering if they were headed this way.

"Chris, I want you to take us out to where it happened," I heard the sheriff say behind me. "Let's get going, because it looks as though we are going to get some snow."

Quickly, the sheriff and his men passed me on the porch, followed by Chris Jennings. As he passed, he patted me on the head and said, "Fine job, Ralph, fine job. You and Jamie look after Jody." I watched him mount his horse with the others. The four men quickly turned their horses south and started out of town in a gallop. I watched them head down the street past the train station. My eyes were focused on Jennings. I wondered why he had pinched me so hard. What did it mean? As much as I had liked him before, I found myself not liking him now. I didn't like it when he pinched me. It made me mad. Somehow, he was acting differently. Why, I wondered. Why was he different now than he was before? Jamie, Jody, and I went over to the town hotel. The sheriff had gotten us rooms, and we took our suitcases inside.

There was a knock at the door that startled Jamie and me as we sat on the bed looking out the hotel window.

"Come in," Jamie called.

The door swung open. Jody was standing in the doorway. The gold locket still hung from her neck. She stepped inside and closed the door behind her. She sat down in a high-backed chair in the corner near the door.

"I just got a telegram from Dad. He will be on the train this afternoon. I have already been to the station, and I have bought tickets for the eight o'clock train tonight. I want to leave as soon as possible. So you may as well get some rest since we will be home late tonight. Understand?"

Jamie and I nodded in agreement. Jody seemed very calm. She showed little emotion as she spoke. I wondered if my sisters would be as calm as Jody after everything that had happened.

"We'll go down and have dinner in a little while. Until then, stay in your room and look at the books you have or take a nap or something."

Jody got up and went to the door. Quickly, she opened it and stepped into the hall. She closed the door behind her. I was glad to hear what she had said, but I didn't say so to Jamie. More than anything, I wanted to get home. Since we had left, it seemed that everything had gone wrong. I looked out the window. It was still snowing. It had been for about an hour. I wondered where the sheriff and his men were. I wondered what they were doing out at the draw. What were they looking for? What did they find—if anything?

I turned around on the bed, laying my head on the pillow. I closed my eyes, trying to take a nap before dinner. Every time I closed my eyes, I could see Mr. Northfield lying in the snow. I opened my eyes every time the sight of him lying in the snow appeared in my mind. I was beginning to tire of the thoughts that were going through my mind. I turned my head to the side and watched Jamie at the other end of the bed with his back to me looking at a book. I turned back, staring up at the white ceiling. It reminded me of all the snow we had. I tried to think of something happy.

Christmas—Christmas was a happy time. I'd be home for Christmas. I felt comforted and calm as I thought of being with my brothers, sisters, mother, and father. I pictured each of them and called each by name in my mind. I was unable to get through them all before I fell asleep.

"Wake up, boys, it's time to eat."

Someone was tugging at my pant leg, I thought, or was it in the dream I was having? Again I felt a tug on my pant leg. I actually moved in bed from the force of it. I opened my eyes and sat up quickly. Quickly, my eyes focused on a figure at the foot of the bed.

"Mr. Bucklin," I said, surprised to see him. "What are you doing here?"

"I came to take you home," he remarked.

"Oh, yeah, I remember," I returned as my mind cleared. "What time is it?"

"It's six thirty, and we have got to go down and eat. We're leaving on the eight o'clock train back to Selby tonight."

"Dad, Dad," exclaimed Jamie, just waking up next to me.

"What, son?"

"Boy, Dad, I'm glad you're here. I feel better already," Jamie exclaimed, hugging his father around the neck while standing on the bed.

"Jamie, you have to be strong for your sister about this. Do you understand?"

"Yes, sir."

"You too, Ralph. You know that, don't you?"

"Yes, sir."

"Well, let's all agree that we'll try to be as happy and cheerful as possible. Try not to say anything to remind her about what happened, okay?"

"Yes, sir," Jamie and I said together.

"Well, let's go eat. Jody is downstairs waiting for us now."

Jamie and I both got off the bed. As I walked over to the door, I checked myself in the mirror on the wall by the door to see if my hair looked alright. I straightened my hair with my fingers until I thought it looked neat. Satisfied with how I looked, I walked into the hall where Mr. Bucklin was waiting for us. I turned and watched Jamie looking in the mirror, just like I had done.

I used to get mad when he would copy everything I did, especially two or three years ago when he first started doing it. My brothers and sisters would tease me about it. They would say Jamie was my little slow shadow. Even though I was used to it by now, it still made me mad at times. This was one of them.

Downstairs, we found Jody sitting at a round table for four people over in one corner of the hotel dining room. There were maybe ten tables in all in the room. The walls were covered with his pictures with scenes of Indians chasing buffaloes on horseback or fighting battles with cavalrymen. They were pretty and interesting to me. I sat down in the chair opposite Jody. Jamie sat on my left, Mr. Bucklin on my right.

Jody wondered if Jamie and I had taken a cap. We both told her we had. We listened as she told Mr. Bucklin that the arrangements had been made at the funeral parlor to have Mr. Northfield's body at the train station by seven thirty. She talked softly and slowly. She seemed very tired and pale. Her face seemed whiter than usual against the black dress she had on. Her fingers fumbled with the little gold locket that hung from her neck as she spoke. She would rub it gently between her thumb and forefinger of her right hand. I became fascinated with her rubbing the little locket and paid little attention to what was being said.

A large platter of chicken being placed in the middle of the table brought me out of my trance. I watched as a short, dark-skinned woman with long black hair set a large bowl of mashed potatoes on the table beside the chicken. Mr. Bucklin picked up the platter of chicken and handed it to me, telling me to take some and pass it on. I took a leg and a thigh and passed the plate to Jamie. When the plate got to Jody, she removed a single chicken wing from the platter. Mr. Bucklin protested, telling her that she had to eat and to take more. Jody refused, saying she wasn't very hungry. I could see that Mr. Bucklin was not happy by the look on his face, but he said nothing. Instead, he picked up the potatoes and scooped up a big spoonful of potatoes and flopped them on Jody's plate. Then Mr. Bucklin filled his plate with potatoes and handed me the bowl.

We ate in silence. Remembering to do what was right, I ate everything on my plate. So did Mr. Bucklin. Jody, however, never even touched her chicken. She sat there, instead, with her fork and played with the mashed potatoes. Every once in a while she would take a small bite. I could see Mr. Bucklin was not happy with her, but he said nothing. I guess he didn't want to upset her. Jamie only ate half of his food. Mostly, he sat on the chair and fidgeted as though there were bugs on his seat.

After a while, Mr. Bucklin asked Jody to eat some food so that she would feel better. She answered that she just wasn't hungry. Then the woman returned who had served us our food. Mr. Bucklin asked if it would be alright to take some of the chicken with us since we had a long train ride ahead of us. The woman said it would be okay. She picked the platter of chicken up and went to the kitchen. She returned moments later carrying a brown paper bag. She placed it on the table between Mr. Bucklin and me.

"How much is the bill," Mr. Bucklin asked the lady.

"Six dollars," she replied. Mr. Bucklin pulled some money out of his pocket and paid her.

"You boys run upstairs and get your things ready. We'll have to be at the station soon. Come down to the lobby and wait for Jody and me."

Jamie and I got up from the table and went back to our room. I opened the door to our room and walked in, followed by Jamie. All of our things were ready. We had never bothered to unpack anything since we would not be staying the night. Never having spent a night in a hotel before, I was disappointed. I walked over to our window and looked out. It had stopped snowing, and it was dark now. I couldn't see any stars. I looked down to the street below me. There was not much light showing from the buildings across the way. Even though it was dark, and there were not many lights, I could still see people and horses on the street because of the white snow. I figured it was really cold by the way people hurried about, bundled in their heavy clothes.

I started to turn away from the window when I saw a wagon pull up between two buildings across the way from me. In the shadows I couldn't see who or how many people there were. I watched silently as a door opened on the side of the left building. Light shone through the door into the little alley on the wagon. I watched three men go into the building. They left the door standing open. How stupid of them, I thought. Shortly, two of the men backed out through the door into the alley. I could see that they were struggling with a box that must be heavy. As they packed out farther it was easy to see that the box was long and bulky. Two other men came through the door carrying the other end.

A coffin!

That's Mr. Northfield's coffin, I thought to myself. *Somebody's stealing his body!*

Chapter

14

"**M**r. Bucklin, Mr. Bucklin," I called, leaving the window and running to our door.

"What's the matter, Ralphie," Jamie said to me. I ignored Jamie's question and hollered down the hall for Mr. Bucklin. Within seconds, Mr. Bucklin appeared at the end of the hall and trotted up to me.

"What's the matter, Ralph?" he said, placing his right hand on my left shoulder.

"Some … someone is stealing Mr. Northfield's body," I said.

"Where," Mr. Bucklin returned, wrinkling his eyebrows down over his eyes.

"Out there," I said, pointing to the window.

Mr. Bucklin pushed me aside and hurried over to the window. I followed him.

"Where," he repeated, not seeing the wagon.

"Right there," I said, pointing my finger against the window in the direction of the wagon.

"Oh, Ralph," Mr. Bucklin sighed, holding his right hand to his forehead. "They are not stealing his body; they're only taking it to the station."

"Oh," I said sheepishly. "I really thought—"

"I know, Ralph, I know," Mr. Bucklin said, patting me on my shoulder. "It's alright. Come on, we best be going.'"

Mr. Bucklin watched as Jamie and I put on our coats, hats, and gloves. He picked up our shotguns and started out the door, leaving the suitcases for us. Jamie and I each grabbed our own stuff and followed him. Down in the lobby, Jody was standing by the front door, staring through the glass. I wondered if she had seen the men in the wagon too. She already had her winter hat and coat on and was ready to go.

Mr. Bucklin asked if everyone had their things. Everything seemed to be together so he opened the door, and we headed for the station with Jody in the lead. The night air was very cold. It was bitter cold, in fact. As we walked to the station, our footsteps creaked loudly in the white snow. It was several hundred yards south to the station. I could see it plainly lit up in the darkness. There, in the lights from the station, was the train. I could see it. I hoped it would wait for us. As we neared, I could see the number on the engine, number 51. It was the same train we had ridden out on.

By the time we reached the station platform, the tips of my ears were cold. I set my suitcase down and pulled my stocking cap down over my ears.

"Have you got the tickets, Father?" Jody asked, breaking the silence.

"Yes," Mr. Bucklin said, displaying four tickets that he pulled from his pocket.

"And what about John?"

"I'll check, Jody," Mr. Bucklin said softly. "Conductor, would you come here?"

A man in a dark uniform came walking over to us. He was not the same conductor we had had on the way out.

"Has everything been taken care of?" Mr. Bucklin asked.

"You mean with the—"

"Yes," Jody said, cutting him off.

"Yes, ma'am, we're all set to go when you are."

"Where is he?" Jody said sharply.

"He's in that car right there—the baggage car."

"I want to ride with him," Jody said, looking the conductor straight in the eye.

"Well, I'm afraid, ma'am, that it's against the regulations of the—"

"I don't care about the damn regulations. My husband is dead; don't you understand?" Jody shouted, starting to cry. "Wouldn't you want to be with your wife, if you have a wife, if it were you?"

"Yes, yes, I would," the conductor answered. "It's against the rules, but I suppose, in this case, it will be okay."

"Thank you, conductor," Jody said, holding a little pink handkerchief to her nose.

"You people get on board," the conductor said to us. "After I get the ticket, I'll take you up to the baggage car, ma'am. I'll have to tell the baggage man its okay, or he won't let you in. Just get on that car right there behind the baggage car. It's a passenger car."

We picked up our belongings and went to the car the conductor pointed out to us.

"Wait a minute," the conductor called to us when we reached the steps. He trotted up to us in the snow. "Let me have the guns, please. No guns allowed on the passenger car."

Mr. Bucklin gave the conductor our shotguns. He headed off toward the baggage car with them. We all watched as the conductor put them on the baggage car. We saw the door slide back and two arms reached out and pulled the guns in. Satisfied that they were on the train, the four of us climbed the steps to the passenger car. Jody opened the door and walked in. The rest of us followed her. She walked down the aisle to the other end of the car and sat down in the last seat close to the back door that led to the baggage car. She motioned to me to sit down on the seat across the aisle from her. I slid in and sat down next to the window after putting my suitcase down on the seat in front of me. Jamie set his suitcase beside mine and sat down beside me. Mr. Bucklin sat down next to Jody.

The passenger car was similar to the car we had ridden out on. Two kerosene lamps were attached to each side of the wall at each end of the car. Also at each end was a small stove that wood or coal was burned in to heat the car. The smoke stack went right through the ceiling. The car was not as long as the one we rode out on, only having ten seats on each side of the aisle. I looked right away to see if there was a toilet on the car. There wasn't. I wondered what I would do if I had to go to the bathroom.

Unlike the trip out, most of the seats on the car were occupied. I could see suitcases and wrapped packages on the racks overhanging the seats. The people must be going somewhere for Christmas, I thought to myself. I wondered what was in the packages. Up ahead of me was a little girl with red hair bouncing up and down on her seat by the window. I could hear her asking when the train was going to start again.

I looked over at Jody. Her head was down, looking into her lap. Her hands were clasped together, and she was rolling her thumbs over one another. She never looked up or smiled; she just watched her thumbs go round and round. At the sound of the engine whistle, she looked up. Slowly, the train started to pull out of town. I watched the lights of Red Elm disappear through the window across the aisle from me. I wondered what had happened to the sheriff, Chris Jennings, and the other men. Did they find anything? What were they looking for? I wondered if I would ever visit Red Elm again.

Within moments, the lights of Red Elm were gone. All I could see was the light from the passenger car dancing on the white snow outside as we traveled through the dark Dakota countryside. The only sound now was the sound of the wheels clacking over the tracks. *Click clack, click clack.* The steady sound was rather comforting to me. The sudden bang of a door slamming open brought me out of my trance-like condition. It was the conductor. I watched him as he made his way down the aisle, checking people's tickets and asking if anybody needed anything.

"Do you have your tickets, boys?" he asked as he reached our seat.

"I've got theirs, conductor," I could hear Mr. Bucklin say from across the aisle. The conductor turned his back to Jamie and me and put his left hand on the back of the seat in front of them to steady himself against the slight rocking motion of the car. I watched him put the tickets into his right pocket with his free hand. He bent over and said something to Jody. I couldn't make out what he said. The conductor stepped back, and Jody got up and stepped into the aisle. She walked to the passenger car door behind us, followed by the conductor. I could hear the door open. The clanging of the metal wheels against the rails grew louder and then got softer as the door closed.

I turned my head back toward the window. I looked out into the darkness. I couldn't see very much, so I tried to imagine what was out there. As I tried to picture the countryside in my mind, I heard the passenger car door open behind us. It was the conductor. He stopped and sat down in the vacant seat beside Mr. Bucklin. I watched the two of them with their heads together talking in low tones. Every so often, Mr. Bucklin or the conductor would shake his head in agreement.

I strained to hear what they said, but I heard nothing. Shortly, the conductor stood up to leave.

"Mr. Conductor," I said, wanting his attention.

"Yes, son," the conductor said, turning around to me.

"Could I please have a blanket?"

"How about you, do you want one?" the conductor said, bending over Jamie.

"No, I think Ralphie and I can share one, can't we, Ralphie?" Jamie said, looking at me.

"Sure, it's okay with me," I answered.

"Fine, I'll get you one," the conductor replied. He turned and headed up the aisle in front of us to the other end of the car. We watched as he opened a little door in the wall up near the little stove and pulled out a red blanket. He draped it over his left arm and headed down the aisle back to us. When he reached our seat, he unfolded the blanket and laid it across our laps.

"How is that, boys? Just unfold it all the way if you want to cover all the way up."

"Thank you, sir," I replied, "but can you also tell me, do you have a toilet?"

The conductor grinned, revealing large, yellow teeth under his brown mustache. One tooth in the very front was completely gone. Strange, I hadn't noticed it before. The conductor looked funny without it.

"There's a toilet on the next car back. But if you go back there, be careful. Sometimes the landing between the cars is slippery and icy. I don't want anyone falling off the train."

"I'll watch them if they have to go back there," Mr. Bucklin said from across the aisle.

"Fine. Now, if everything is alright, I'll tend to my business," the conductor said. With that, he turned and headed down the aisle back to the next car where the toilets were. He opened the door and went through to the next car.

I took my coat and hat off and laid them on top of my suitcase in the seat in front of me. Jamie did the same. I settled back in my seat and unfolded the blanket. I pulled one end up around my shoulders after covering my legs with the other end. I looked back out the window at the white snow shining beneath me in the light from the passenger car. The gentle rocking of the train car soon had me drowsy. Within minutes, I was fast asleep.

"Wake up, boys. Do you want to stretch your legs?"

I turned to see Mr. Bucklin standing in the aisle over us.

"Where are we?" I asked.

"Mobridge. We have a ten-minute stopover."

"What time is it, Dad?" Jamie asked, rubbing his eyes.

"About ten o'clock. We had to slow down a little, I guess. It started to snow again. Do you want to get some fresh air?"

"I think I'll go to the toilet," I said, beginning to wiggle a little in my seat.

"Me too, Dad," Jamie seconded.

Jamie and I stood up together. I pulled the blanket from him and rolled it into a ball and set it on our seat. We stepped into the aisle and headed down to the toilet on the next car. Mr. Bucklin followed us. The cool air of the car gave me goose bumps after being covered up in the blanket. I didn't bother to take my coat since I wasn't going to get off the train. I reached the back door and opened it. Big white flakes of snow drifted down between our car and the next. I stepped outside onto the landing in the cold night air.

I quickly opened the door to the next car and stepped inside. Just inside the door was a door on the right that said MEN. I grabbed the handle on the door and turned it. It wouldn't open! *Jammed*, I thought, and now I had to go bad. I tried the handle again and shoved on the door. I couldn't get it open.

"Just a minute," came an angry voice from inside.

"Oh … Oh, I'm sorry," I said, surprised by the voice from inside the door. I stepped back and leaned as patiently as possible against the wall opposite the door. I put my hands together and held them down in front of me. *Hurry up*, I thought to myself. Jamie leaned against the wall next to me.

It seemed that it took forever for the door to swing open. A man with a full red beard stepped into the aisle. He had a broad-rimmed black hat pulled low over his eyes. I knew he was looking at me.

"Now you can go in, boy," the man growled at me. He turned and walked down the aisle back to his seat. I quickly went into the toilet and closed the door behind me, leaving Jamie outside. The first thing I noticed was the foul odor in the air. I looked into the toilet to see the bowl half filled with urine and more. I wanted to flush it since I was sure it was responsible for the foul odor, but I remembered the conductor said it could not be flushed while the train was in a town or passing through one. There was a sign over the toilet to remind people of this also.

Quickly, I went about my business. I was glad that I didn't have to poop since it didn't look clean at all. The air in the toilet seemed to worsen as I relieved myself. I almost thought I was going to vomit, I was gagging so bad. I held my breath. Soon I was finished, and was I glad. I fastened my pants and opened the door. The odorless air from the passenger car was refreshing. I stepped out and told Jamie to hold his breath and to hurry when he went in because of the odor. He looked at me with his nose all crinkled up and mouth twisted in a look of disgust. He sucked air in and out deeply three times. On the fourth time, he held his breath and in he went. I went back to my seat.

Shortly, the train was moving again. Jamie had returned to his seat and told me I was right about how bad the toilet was. Strange how excited I had been about wanting to try the toilet out on the trip to Red Elm and that I was disappointed about not using it. But now, after actually doing it and seeing what it was like, I had lost all interest in ever wanting to use one again.

The train rolled on toward Selby. I knew we would be home shortly, and I was happy to be getting home. It had been a long, long day, one I knew I would never forget as long as I lived. I looked out the window. It was not hard to see the snow coming down, even though it was dark outside. Big flakes would bounce off the window next to me. It seemed like no time at all before I noticed the train slowing down.

"Selby, South Dakota; next stop in about five minutes," I heard a man yell from the back of the railroad car. I figured it had to be the conductor even though I didn't turn my head to look. Suddenly the door in front of me swung open. Jody burst through the doorway and quickly sat down on the edge of the seat beside her father with her back to Jamie and me. I watched her whisper something to him that I couldn't hear.

"What?" Mr. Bucklin exclaimed loudly, turning his back to the window so that he could face Jody better.

"I'm not going!" Jody said, loud enough for most of the people in the car to hear.

"What do you mean, you're not going?" Mr. Bucklin replied.

"I'm not going on to Iowa for the funeral. I can't stand this anymore. I'm getting off at Selby. You'll have to take him there for me."

Mr. Bucklin's mouth dropped open in surprise. His eyebrows dropped down low over his eyes at the same time. "I don't believe you, Jody. In fact I am surprised at you. Your own husband and you can't see that he is buried properly."

"I know you can do it, Father. You will have to. The man in the baggage car told me how long it would take to get there, and I just can't take it. It would seem like forever, and I can't take that. If you don't want to go either, then you get off at Selby too. The people on the train can take care of it. They know how."

"Jody Bucklin, I'm surprised at you," Mr. Bucklin scoffed, forgetting to call her last name Northfield. "I thought I raised a girl with more feelings and scruples than you're displaying."

"What are scruples?" Jamie whispered to me.

"Sh," I said, not knowing the answer and wanting to hear what was being said.

"Daddy, I just can't take any more. You just have to understand. I just can't take it. I'm just not up to having to make a trip all the way out there to Iowa and then having to come back. You just have to understand. It's not that I don't care of anything like that. I do care, but it's too much to take, all this. I will go to Iowa later on, after things settle down, to visit his grave."

At the sound of her own words, Jody began to cry. She placed the little pink hanky to her nose as she cried openly. Mr. Bucklin quickly put his right arm around Jody and tried to console her. He kept reassuring her that everything would be all right and that he would go on to Iowa to see that John was buried. Shortly, Jody calmed down. Tears still ran from her eyes, but the almost uncontrollable sobbing had stopped. Almost everyone in the car was watching her.

Through all of the excitement, no one had even noticed that the train had stopped. The conductor had come down the aisle from the back of the car. He told us that this was our stop. Mr. Bucklin told the conductor that Jody would not be going on to Iowa but that he would be going.

I pushed the blanket from myself and got up and put my hat and coat on. Jamie did the same. I grabbed my suitcase and started toward the back of the car. I was followed by Jamie, Jody, and Mr. Bucklin, in that order. When I stepped out the door of the car onto the little landing I could see my father, my mother, Artie, and Mrs. Bucklin standing on the Selby train-station platform. I bounded down the three steps, dragging my suitcase, and ran as fast as I could through the snow to them. Mother gave me a big hug, and my father and Artie just patted me on the back. Mom wanted to know how I was. I told her, "Fine."

I noticed Mrs. Bucklin was crying. I looked over my mother's shoulder and saw Jody and Mrs. Bucklin coming together, both crying and hugging each other. Mr. Bucklin came up to them and tried to console them. Mother released me and turned to the two ladies standing in the falling snow. She went over to them and hugged both of them, and she, too, started crying. It was just too much. Jamie and I both started crying. Everyone was crying except for Dad and Artie. Even Mr. Bucklin was crying. After a few minutes, everyone seemed to quit crying all at once. Everyone was brushing away tears and wiping their noses trying to get hold of themselves once again.

It was then that Mr. Bucklin told Mrs. Bucklin that he was going on to Iowa to see that there would be a proper burial for Mr. Northfield. Mrs. Bucklin did not seem to mind that at all that Jody would not be going on.

Down at the baggage car, I could see Artie and Dad. I could see the man in the baggage car hand two guns to Artie. My dad was handed a suitcase. I guessed that it was Jody's since I knew that Jamie and I both had ours. I turned and looked at Mr. and Mrs. Bucklin, Jody, and mother. All of them had their eyes focused on the baggage car.

"All board," the conductor yelled from behind us. "The train is leaving in one minute."

"I guess I better get on the train," Mr. Bucklin said softly. He looked at Jody, who turned to him as he spoke.

"Thank you, Daddy. I love you," she said. She turned and headed down to the baggage car. The man in the car started to roll the door shut. "Wait, wait a minute, please!"

133

Slowly, the door on the baggage car reopened. Artie and Dad were still standing by the door. Jody quickly went the short distance to the open door. She placed both hands on the floor of the car in the open doorway and leaned her head inside. A few feet behind her stood Artie and Dad. She turned her head slightly to the right. I knew she was looking at the coffin containing her dead husband's body. All of us knew it. She stood there looking for what seemed a long time. Then she looked up at the baggage man and said something. I could not hear what it was. Then she put her hands down and clasped them together. She turned and, with her head down, she walked back to us.

"You can get on now, Daddy," she said, when she reached us. She never raised her head. But standing close to her, I watched her eyes follow her father's feet as he turned to board the train. Somehow, I knew it would be a long, cold ride home, with the snow and all.

"All aboard."

Chapter

15

Over the next several months I never saw Jody. At least not close enough to speak to her. I would go up to see Jamie, and sometimes I would see Jody, but it was always at a distance. She would never speak to me or even wave to me, and I wondered why. Jamie would tell me that she would spend a lot of time by herself in her room. Sometimes, he told me, Jody would walk out to the old well where she had gotten married. She would even do this in the freezing cold weather Jamie said. I wondered why.

The old well had dried up the previous summer, and Mr. Bucklin had boarded it over. I remembered him saying that he didn't want Jamie and me falling into the well and getting hurt. Even the big old cottonwood tree that stood guard by the well was down. It had been struck by lightning during a thunderstorm last August or September and had been knocked to the ground. The trunk of the big tree missed hitting the well by fifteen feet or so. Even when the big tree went down, Jamie and I still had fun climbing on it.

My folks were really happy to see spring come. Dad said it had been the worst year for snow since '92. I really didn't know though, because I was only five years old then. But I figured it must have been bad because we took very good care of our livestock. We had to make sure they had plenty of feed. With the drifting snow that we had, we tried to keep everything as close to the house as possible. The snow was so bad at times that my sisters, brothers, and I never bothered to try to get to school, those of us that had to go. That was the one part about the snow that I liked—no school.

May had rolled around, and the weather had started to warm. The grass in the fields for the cattle had turned green. Our garden had been planted two weeks earlier, along with the flower seeds Mother had received as one of her Christmas presents. The whole month of April, my father and Artie had been busy planting oats, wheat, corn, and barley. April was always one of the busiest months of the year. All the neighbors helped one another with the planting of their crops. When it was time for our crops to be planted, the house would be alive with activity. Everyone was up before dawn doing their chores, from making coffee to slopping down the hogs. The odors from the food being prepared in the kitchen seemed to always make you hungry. At noontime, Mother would call in the men by clanging the large iron triangle that hung on the back porch. It was the same at all the neighbors' homes. The amounts of meat, potatoes, bread, and coffee that the men ate really kept Mom and my sisters hopping. Mom was lucky she had a lot of helpers, although the wives would help one another if there weren't children in the family to help out.

It was really one of the fun times of the year when each neighbor's turn came for planting. Even though there was a lot of hard work, it was a time when everyone got to see everyone else all at the same time, which was especially welcomed after the long, cold winter. And even though the kids were still in school and saw each other almost every day, we still had fun when we got together on the weekends at planting time.

How much of what was being planted always determined how many would be over at planting time. This year we were planting forty acres of oats, twenty acres each of corn and barley, and seven hundred acres of wheat.

Each year, everyone varied the amount of each grain they planted. Later, after the harvesting was done, the crops would be exchanged between everyone. This year, our neighbors would be helping us plant our wheat. Dad and my brothers could easily plant the corn, barley, and oats.

The second Saturday in May was a beautiful day. The sun was shining brightly, and there were no clouds in the sky. The air was crisp and fresh. Everyone got up early and did his or her assigned chores as usual. On days like this, it was almost even fun doing the chores. Especially if it was Saturday and there was no school. All of us seemed to hurry a little faster so we could get done and have the rest of the day to do what we wanted. Eddie and I had decided we were going fishing right after lunch. There was a stream a couple of miles or so west of our place that we would fish. The stream eventually flowed into the Missouri River. There were some good catfish in that stream, and we planned on catching some of them.

We had a lot of fun digging for the worms. Dad showed us the easiest way to find them whether it was spring, summer, or fall. It didn't even make any difference if it was a very dry summer or not, we would always find them around a manure pile. The ground would always be damp underneath, and we would be able to dig up some nice fat wiggly worms in a matter of minutes.

"Wow, look at this one, Eddie," I exclaimed, holding up a big fat night crawler.

"Yeah, that's a good one, Ralph. That's the biggest one yet."

"Hurry up and dig up another shovelful of dirt. I'll bet there are some bigger ones." Eddie quickly pushed the shovel into the ground with his right foot. He pulled back hard on the handle loosening a big shovelful of earth. He turned it over and smashed the big clod with his shovel, breaking it up. Four worms wriggled wildly in the damp soil, having been disturbed in their homes. I bent over and grabbed them as fast as I could and put them in a rusty old can we had.

"Look at that big one in the hole," Eddie said excitedly, pointing down into the hole he had just made. My eyes lit up at the sight of the big worm's head sticking out of its tunnel. I grabbed for it, but it was too fast. It ducked back inside before I could catch it.

"Hurry up, Eddie. Dig behind it so we can get it." Eddie shoved the shovel into the ground, trying to cut off the worm's retreat. He turned over the pile of dirt on the shovel and smacked it as he had done the others. "There it is, Ralph. See it?"

I saw it at the same time Eddie spoke. I reached into the wet soil for the worm. I grabbed its head and proudly held it up for Eddie to see. "Doggone it, Eddie. Look."

"What?"

"Look at the worm. You cut it in two with the shovel. Doggone it. I'll bet he would have caught the biggest fish in the stream."

"Well, half a big worm is better than no worm."

"No, it's just not the same and you know it. A whole worm is better than half a worm."

"Look, Ralph," Eddie said, pointing behind me. "It's Jamie and Jody."

I turned and looked back toward the house. Sure enough, pulling into our lane were Jamie and Jody in their buckboard.

"Let's ask Jamie if he wants to go with us," Eddie said.

He dropped the shovel and took off in a run back to the house. In his excitement, he kicked over our can of worms scattering the wiggling worms about the ground.

"Hey," I yelled angrily at him. "Look what you did."

Eddie never even looked back. I bent over and picked up the can. I looked at the half of the big worm I still held in my hand. I held the worm over the can and dropped him in. He landed with a thud in the bottom of the empty can. I got down on my hands and knees with the can and started picking up all the worms that were now wiggling and crawling all over the ground trying to get away. Satisfied that I had recaptured the majority of them, I put the can on the ground and put the blade of the shovel over the can to keep the sun off of the worms. I got up and brushed the dirt from the knees of my pants. All that remained were two wet spots from the moisture in the soil. I clapped my hands together to remove as much of the soil from them as I could. I took off for the house in a run.

When I reached the house, my brothers and sisters were gathered around Jamie and Jody on the front porch. Everyone was scurrying around for a place to sit. Artie pulled up a chair for Jody to sit on. I just sat down on the porch steps next to Jamie.

"Jody's gonna have a baby, Ralphie. What do you think of that?" Jamie whispered leaning over to me.

"What?"

"Jody's gonna have a baby," he repeated louder.

"Who's going to have a baby?" my oldest sister Lydia said, overhearing Jamie.

"I am," snapped Jody, looking angrily at Jamie. "Can't you ever keep your mouth shut for a minute, Jamie?"

"I'm sorry, Sis, but—"

"That's alright," Lydia cut in. "I think it's wonderful, Jody. We all do, don't we?" She nodded her head in a way that the rest of us understood. We all eagerly agreed. "That must make you very happy, Jody," she continued. "Especially because—"

"Of what happened?" Jody cut in.

"Why … why, yes, Jody. You … you know what I mean, don't you?"

"Yes, I know what you mean," Jody returned, giving Lydia a cold stare. "You think it's wonderful that since John is dead, by having a baby, his memory will live on. Well, I wish I weren't having the baby. All it will be is a reminder of the past. Something that should be dead and buried."

"No, it's not like that."

"Oh, yes it is, and, with a baby around to raise, who will want me? I don't want to be a widow the rest of my life. Do you understand?"

"We understand," Lydia said, looking around to the rest of us. "You are just upset still about everything that's happened. I'm sure you will feel differently later on."

Jody didn't say anything. She sat staring at the house wall in front of her. I don't believe she even heard what Lydia said. We all sat silently, waiting for someone to say or do something.

"She's been like that a lot lately," Jamie whispered in my ear.

"What do you mean?" I asked, not understanding.

"Ever since she found out she was going to have a baby, she has acted real strange. She spends a lot of time in her room by herself. Sometimes she won't even eat. Sometimes she will be in a happy mood and then in a minute's time she will be yelling, screaming, or crying for no reason at all. Other times, she will just sit there and stare, just like now. Sometimes, even in the cold of winter, she would walk out to the old well and sit there. Mom and Dad are really worried about this. They think she is getting worse all the time. They are just hoping that all of this is due to the baby and that once she has it she will be fine."

"Gee, is that why nobody has seen her much, and why she wouldn't speak to me?" I asked.

"Probably."

It was almost as if Jody had overheard part of Jamie's and my talking. Suddenly she broke into tears. She covered her eyes quickly with her hands and sobbed loudly. We were all surprised at the sudden change that had come over her. All of us sat silently watching her, wondering what she was going to do next.

Within a few moments, her crying slowed. Lydia had handed Jody a handkerchief to wipe her eyes with. When she finally took her hands away from her face, Jody's eyes were red and her nose was running slightly. Everyone always said how pretty a girl Jody was. At that moment, she didn't look so good, I thought to myself.

"I ... I'm sorry, everybody," Jody said softly, sniffling her nose. "When, when this is all over and the b ... baby is here, and when I find out who—I ... I mean *what* it is, either a boy or a girl, I'll be better. I'm sure of it. Right now, it seems as if there is so much pressure."

Who? I wondered.

What she said flashed in my mind. I looked at the faces of the others on the porch to see if I could find a reaction from them. No one seemed shocked or upset. Everyone silently listened to Jody as she spoke. I guess no one thought anything about "who." I wondered. My mind flashed back to the conversation I had heard between Jody and Chris Jennings. I recalled his asking her to leave with him, and Jody's unhappiness at not having any children.

Whose is it? I wondered; maybe this was why she wouldn't speak to me. Maybe it was why she acted so strangely at home and had her parents wondering. Maybe I knew why and no one else did.

"Come on, Jamie. We had better be going," Jody said, catching my attention. Jamie dutifully got up and started to the buckboard. My sisters tried to persuade Jody to stay a while longer and have some cake and milk, but Jody said that she was tired and felt that she should be headed for home. Jamie had already reached the buckboard and had climbed in. The rest of us followed Jody. Lydia had taken Jody's arm as they walked and when we reached the buckboard, Lydia helped her in. Jody thanked my sister for the use of her handkerchief and handed it back to her.

"Everything will be fine" Lydia said cheerfully. "Just fine. We all know it. Now you take good care of yourself and you come down and see us often, okay?"

"Sure, sure," Jody said softly, with a faint smile crossing her lips. "I'll come back again."

Her words seemed to drift away softly. She turned her head slowly looking straight forward out over the horse. Her eyes seemed almost glassy as she stared straight ahead. "Let's ... go ... Jamie."

Jamie raised the reins and snapped them across the rump of the horse. The crack made Jody blink her eyes, but she stared straight ahead as Jamie turned the buckboard around and headed down our lane to the road. Jamie waved back to us, not bothering to look over his shoulder. Jody never waved or looked back.

Chapter

16

The summer passed quickly, I thought as I stood leaning against my hoe in our garden. It was the first of August. The grass fields had started to turn brown from the hot summer sun and the lack of rain. The crops were dry and needed water badly. We hadn't had rain for over three weeks. To make things worse, the temperature had been in the nineties every day over that period.

It was hot as I stood there looking off into the South Dakota countryside. It was just mid-morning, and already I was sure it was at least ninety degrees. In the distance, I could see the black smoke of the threshing machines drifting lazily into the sky. There wasn't any breeze to comfort me. Dad and Artie were over there, I thought to myself, looking at the smoke. I didn't want to hoe the garden. I wondered if it would be better to be in school instead of doing this. School started next week.

"Come on Ralph; start hoeing so we can get this done," Eddie exclaimed.

"Yeah, yeah, I know," I returned, irritated by his jabbing. I slanted my hoe into the dry, crusty soil. Dirt clouds and dust flew out from under the head of the hoe. I studied the ground. It was dry and cracking. Some cracks were pretty big, I thought.

I wondered what Jamie was doing. I hoped that he would be down to see me. I knew I could put him to work if he showed up. It had been a long time since I had seen him. I hadn't seen him since Jody had had her baby. That was nearly ten days ago. He came down to our house to tell us all that Jody had a little girl. Oh yes, and I remembered what she was named. Christine Lee Northfield. I wondered how she arrived at the name. None of us had been invited to see what she looked like, and we all wondered why. Even I was curious to see her. I wondered what color hair she had, if any. I wondered if there was something wrong with the baby. I knew there was something wrong with the mother. Jody acted really strange the last two months according to what Jamie told me and from what I was able to see when I went to the Bucklins. She stayed by herself almost all the time. She insisted on eating alone in her room. She would go out on long walks by herself, and if Jamie's parents objected or wanted to go along with her, she would go into a rage.

Sometimes, Jamie said, she would be gone for hours at a time. On many occasions, she wouldn't return until after dark. All of these things worried her parents terribly. She wouldn't go anywhere with anybody for anything.

"Damn it, Ralph. Get to work!" Eddie yelled at me.

"Oh, shut up," I yelled back at him.

"What are you doing then?" he returned.

"I'm thinking."

"You think too much. All you do is daydream. You do it all the time."

"I do not."

"Then how come you were just standing there staring off into space?"

"I was not."

"Were to."

"Was not."

"Were to."

"I was not," I yelled, picking up a dirt clod. I threw it at Eddie, but he ducked and it went over his left shoulder.

"You little stinker," he yelled, throwing his hoe down. I'll fix you." He took off after me. I threw my hoe down and started running to the house. I ran like the devil to keep Eddie from catching me. I knew I'd have to make it to the house to be safe. I could hear Eddie's footsteps right behind me. At any second I expected to feel a hand on my shirt collar trying to pull me down. I dodged and swerved whenever I thought he was right on me to try to keep him off balance. Once I felt his hand hit my right arm. I dodged just in time, and Eddie lost his balance and tumbled to the ground. I laughed out loud at the sound of Eddie hitting the ground. I was not stupid enough to make the mistake of stopping to look at him. I continued running to the house and the safety of Mother inside. She would protect me from Eddie, at least until he calmed down.

I reached the back porch and quickly stepped through the door into the kitchen. I closed the door and looked out the window for Eddie. There he was forty yards away limping slightly coming toward the house. I could see dirt on his pants and shirt. I figured he must have rolled when he hit the ground. He looked funny, I thought, but when I saw the look on his face, I knew he didn't feel the same way. I went looking through the house for Mother. I was going to need her.

We had just finished supper when we heard someone knock on the back door. "I'll see who it is," Artie said, getting up from his chair. He walked to the door and opened it.

"Hi, Jamie, come on in," Artie said.

"Thanks."

"Anyone else with you?" Artie asked, searching out the back door.

"No, I'm by myself."

"Did you come to see Ralph?" Mother asked.

"No, I have to get back. From the looks of it outside it will have to be soon too. It's getting real cloudy outside. The wind is picking up a lot. I'm sure we're gonna get some rain."

"We can use it though, Jamie. We can use it," my father said, nodding his head and still holding his pipe in his mouth with his right hand. "Well, if you didn't come to play with Ralph, what brought you?"

"My dad was wondering if you might have an extra razor around that no one is using. Seems he lost his a few days ago, and he can't find it. His whiskers are driving him crazy, he says, and he hasn't had time to get to town to get another one."

"I was wondering why he hadn't shaved the last few days when we've been working in the fields. It's not like your father not to shave," Father replied. "Artie, go get your razor. You can use mine for a couple of days until Mr. Bucklin can get to town."

As Artie started for his room the sound of thunder rolled across the sky. I got up from my chair and walked to the door to look out.

"Ouch," I said sharply. "Damn it, Eddie."

"Ralph, watch your mouth," Mother scolded.

"Doggone it, Mom. He kicked me."

"Cut it out, Ed," Father cut in.

"I will. I was just getting even for this morning, that's all," Eddie replied.

"What about this morning," Father asked.

"Never mind, honey," Mother said. "It's really nothing."

I looked out the window of the door just in time to see a large flash of lightning off to the northwest. The sky was really dark in the west and northwest. As I looked out the window, I could hear the sound of the thunder rolling through the sky overhead. It sounded just like potatoes rolling on the floor, I thought. The rumble was faint at first, then it would grow louder and louder, and it would roll right overhead and then get fainter and fainter until the next bolt of lightning came along and let the potatoes loose again.

"Wow, we're really going to get a storm," I said, looking at the sky. "It is really dark out there."

"Just like I said, Ralph. We can use the rain," Father repeated.

"Here you are, Jamie," Artie announced as he reentered the kitchen carrying his straight razor in his right hand. "Better tell your dad to sharpen it up a bit though before he uses it."

"Thanks, Artie" Jamie replied. "Dad can really use it. Well, I suppose I better get back before it starts to rain. Boy, I hate lightning; it really scares me."

"How did you get down here," Mother asked.

"I got one of the horses."

The words were no sooner out of Jamie's mouth when a brilliant bolt of lightning flashed out in the distance west of the house.

"Maybe you ought to wait to see if it blows over, Jamie," Father said.

"No, I think I can make it if I hurry," Jamie said, and quickly stepped to the kitchen door. I pulled it open for him.

"See ya," he said.

"Bye, Jamie," we all replied together.

Jamie passed through the door onto the back porch. Quickly, he untied the horse from the porch corner post and mounted. He took off at a gallop down our lane to the road. All of us immediately went to the east windows of the house to watch him. The wind was really blowing.

Clouds of dust would spring up with each gust of wind. We watched as Jamie reached the road and headed east up to his house. Each bolt of lightning that flashed lighted the way for Jamie. Between flashes Jamie and the horse were only a dark shadow silhouetted against the countryside.

Raindrops sounded on our rooftop, big raindrops. They cracked like gunshots on the wooden roof. At first there were only a few. Then they came in buckets. It came down so hard and fast that at first we all thought it was hail. Another bold of lightning flashed, this time nearby. The force was so great that it shook our house. In the light, we could see that it was rain and not hail. By this time, it was raining so hard that we couldn't even see the road at the end of our lane.

"I sure hope Jamie made it back in time," I said softly.

"I do too, Ralph," my mother replied, placing her arm around my shoulders. "I do too."

Chapter
17

The next morning, Eddie and I were back working in the garden. It had rained most of the evening and had quit sometime in the night. The rain had softened the ground, and it was easy to work. The ground was still so wet that the soil stuck to our shoes. The bottoms would cake up, and every so often we would have to kick our legs to throw the dirt from our shoes.

The sun was out brightly. The rain had cooled the air, and I knew it was going to be a pleasant day even though there was no breeze. I looked off to the south, and I could see the black columns of smoke rising straight into the sky from the threshing machines. I leaned against my hoe and watched the columns slowly grow in the sky. From this distance, they took on the shape of small tornado funnel clouds. There were three of them. As I watched, the sound of someone yelling way off caught my attention.

"Hey, Eddie, hear that?"

"Hear what."

"Listen."

We stood silently, our ears straining to pick up the call. "Ralphie, Ralphie," we could hear a little better now.

"See, I told—"

"Look, Ralph, it's Jamie. He's running this way."

Sure enough, it was Jamie. He was running as fast as he could in our direction. He was waving his arms wildly over his head as he ran toward us.

"I wonder what's wrong," I asked.

"I don't know, but let's go see," Eddie said, throwing his hoe on the ground. I did the same, and we both took off running to meet Jamie. Quickly, we closed the distance.

"She's gone, she's gone," Jamie yelled, when we were fifty yards apart. Eddie and I stopped and waited for Jamie to cover the remaining distance.

"What did he say?" I said, looking at Eddie.

"I … I don't know."

Breathlessly, Jamie reached us, almost staggering the last few feet. "She's gone, Ralphie! She's gone!" Jamie shouted, gasping for breath.

"What do you mean?" Eddie said, trying to calm Jamie down.

"When … when we got up this morning, Jody was gone. We … we can't find her anywhere."

"Try to calm down, and tell us exactly what happened," Eddie said, placing his hands on Jamie's shoulders.

"Okay … okay," Jamie said, beginning to catch his breath. "When we got up this morning, Dad and I went about our chores. After we finished, we went in for breakfast. It was about eight thirty. Mom, Dad, and I ate. We called for Jody several times to come and join us, but there was no answer. When she didn't come, we didn't think much about it since she has done that so much lately anyway. Well, about nine fifteen or so, Dad decided maybe he better go wake her up 'cause the baby started crying. He went to her room, and she was gone. The window was open and that's it. We checked the whole house, the other buildings, everything, and nothing. All of her clothes were there—everything. She left, from what Dad figures, in her nightgown. She didn't even take any shoes. Dad also figures she left sometime during the storm, since the curtains were wet and there was some water on the floor. That's when Dad told me to come down here and try to get Artie and your dad for a search party. We've got to find her, Ralphie. We've got to."

With those words, Jamie started to cry. Eddie spoke softly to Jamie, trying to tell him everything would be all right. Eddie put his arm around Jamie and started walking him to our house. Jamie had covered his eyes with his hands while he continued crying.

"Ralph, you run ahead and tell Mom and the others what has happened. Maybe you will have to ride over and get Dad and Artie and the others."

"Okay, Eddie. Everything will be okay," I tried to assure Jamie, squeezing his right arm with both hands. I took off and ran to the house to tell the others. I ran into the kitchen, and I found my mother and my sister Lydia doing some baking. Quickly, I told them what had happened as best I could. Both of them looked at me in shock. They looked at me with their eyes and mouths open in disbelief. I told them that Eddie was coming with Jamie now.

"Go get one of the horses and get your father and Artie," Mother said excitedly. "This better not be a joke, Ralph."

"It's not, it's not," I assured her. I turned and ran from the kitchen to the barn. I passed Eddie and Jamie on the way. Jamie was still crying. "I'm going to get Dad and Artie."

I entered the barn and saw Artie's horse in his stall. Quickly, I grabbed the bridle from a peg on the wall next to the stall door. I opened the stall door and went in. I pulled on the horse's neck to lower its head so I could put the bridle on. Once that was done, I moved him over next to the stall gate so I could climb up it to get on him. I'd have to ride him bareback since I didn't want to take the time to saddle him. I wasn't any good at saddling horses anyway.

Once mounted, I headed out of the barn. I had to duck so I wouldn't hit my head going out the door. I headed down the lane to the road in a gallop. I hated riding bareback because I had a hard time staying on, but I would just have to this time. Once I reached the road, I looked for the columns of smoke in the sky. There they were, off to the south, reaching high in the sky. I headed west down the road. I knew that I would shortly reach a gate that would allow me to go cross country to reach my father and Artie. As I rode along, I searched the countryside for signs of Jody. For some reason, I had the strange feeling that I would see her. I wondered where she might be or why she had disappeared in the night. Where could she have gone? Was she all right? I wondered these things as I rode to get my dad and my brother.

"Okay, men, we will split up into groups of three and start searching in different directions. If you find Jody or any clue of her, fire three shots in the air, ten seconds apart."

Mr. Bucklin was standing on the porch giving out the instructions for the search party. It seemed as though every neighbor in the area was there. All of the men were saddled and ready to go. Jamie, Eddie, and I sat on the porch steps watching and listening.

"You think we can help?" I asked Eddie softly.

"I don't know, Ralph. I suppose we better ask Dad if we can go along."

"Hurry up and find out, 'cause I wanna go."

Eddie got up and walked over to where Dad was sitting on his horse. I watched as Dad leaned over and spoke to Eddie. I crossed my fingers, hoping we could help. After a minute or so, Eddie returned and sat down beside me.

"What did Dad say?" I asked.

"He said as long as we don't get in the way and can keep up, he didn't care, but we have to go with him."

"Good, let's ride double so we can keep up. You're better guiding the horse than I am."

Mr. Bucklin had just finished giving his instructions. The fifteen men began breaking up into groups of threes. Off they headed into various directions. Mr. Bucklin and Dad were going together along with Eddie and me. Jamie had been instructed by his father to stay with Mrs. Bucklin. He complained but to no avail. Mother had also come up to stay with and comfort Mrs. Bucklin. Mrs. Bucklin was taking the whole thing very hard, Jamie had told me.

Mr. Bucklin stepped from the porch, went over to his horse and mounted. Eddie and I went over to our horse. Eddie put his left foot in the stirrup and swung himself up into the saddle. He extended his left hand down to me. I grabbed it with both hands and lifted my left foot up to the same stirrup. When I had done so, Eddie pulled me up behind him.

"Ready boys?" Father asked.

"I guess so," Eddie returned.

"Which way you want to head?" Father asked Mr. Bucklin.

"Well, I thought maybe we ought to head toward town. Maybe, for some reason, she went to town."

"Sounds like a good idea—"

"Oh, Dad," I said, hesitantly raising my hand for permission to speak.

"What, Ralph?"

"Don't you think we maybe should go out toward the old well north of the house?"

"Ralph," Father said sternly, "if Mr. Bucklin wants to check town first we'll check town. I said you could go along, but you have to do as you're told or you can't go."

"Wait, Frank," Mr. Bucklin said. "That's a good idea. She's been spending a lot of time out there. Besides, we could head cross-country toward town going that way. I checked the well out from the top of the hill this morning, but I didn't go on out there. It certainly can't hurt."

"Alright," Father agreed, "if you want to head that way, it's fine with me. Let's go."

With that, Father swung his horse around and headed north. Eddie and Mr. Bucklin quickly did the same thing. All of our horses were side by side as we headed out behind the Bucklin house between the barn and sheds to the dirt lane that headed back to the old well. I wanted to go faster, but everyone else was apparently satisfied to just walk their horses. I could hardly stand the suspense as we slowly walked our horses up the hill to the well. I just knew we would find her. I could just feel it in my bones.

I strained forward to see over Eddie's shoulder when we reached the crest of the hill. I saw the big old cottonwood tree lying on its side behind the well. All of our eyes searched for Jody. She wasn't there. In my mind, I was really disappointed. I thought for sure she would be sitting right there by the well. As we got closer to the well, we were positive she wasn't hiding from us. She just wasn't there.

"Nope, she's not here," Mr. Bucklin said, with a little disappointment in his voice. "Let's swing off toward town."

"Oh, Mr. Bucklin," Eddie said softly, noting Mr. Bucklin's sadness. "Look at the—"

"Eddie, I told you boys you are gonna have to mind or stay home. Now, what's it gonna be?" Father really flew into Eddie. I don't know why he seemed so grouchy. Maybe he thought—oh, I didn't know what he thought. I figured I was gonna keep my mouth shut though because I wanted to go.

"Wait, Frank," Mr. Bucklin said, without raising his voice. "Don't be hard on him. The boys are only trying to help. You're just upset about this whole thing as I am, but you can at least let him say what's on his mind."

"You're right," Father said, looking at Eddie. "Sorry, Eddie, what did you want to say?"

Eddie sat there in front of me quietly. I knew he was a little afraid to speak after Father chewed him out. I would have been afraid too. "Come on Eddie, what was it?"

"Well," Eddie said, with a raspy voice. He had to stop to clear his throat. "I was just looking at the old well," he raised his arm and pointed to it. "See … see how some of the boards that covered it are off. I just thought that—"

"Jesus Christ, Ed! Are you nuts?" Father yelled at Eddie, "You and Jamie get—"

"Wait," Mr. Bucklin yelled over my Father's voice. He grabbed Father's arm at the same time. Father stopped speaking but continued looking angrily at Eddie. "I know what you're thinking, Ed, and you're right. I don't want to check, but we're gonna have to. I … I just hope we don't find her there. Come on, let's check out the well."

Mr. Bucklin snapped the reins on his horse's rear end and took off in a gallop to the well. Father followed him as a close behind as he could. Eddie and I brought up the rear. When we reached the well, the four of us dismounted. Mr. Bucklin and Father walked to the well and leaned over and looked down into the opening.

"See anything?" Eddie said excitedly. He quickly covered his hand over his mouth. I knew he was afraid he had spoken out of turn, and he didn't want to be chewed out again.

"No, it's too dark down there," Father said, not raising up. "We can't see anything."

"Look," I yelled, spotting something. Mr. Bucklin and Father raised up and turned to me at the same time. I pointed to one of the boards lying on the ground behind them. "What's that under that board?"

"Where?" they said together.

"Right here," I returned, running over to the board. I bent over and turned the board over. It was a white piece of material. I pulled it off the board.

"Let me see that," Mr. Bucklin said, grabbing it out of my hand. Quickly, he inspected it. "It's hers alright."

"What do you mean?" Father asked.

"It's part of her nightgown. The one she had on last night. I'm sure of it. She's been here alright."

"Do, do you think she's down there?" Father said reluctantly. "There aren't any footprints."

"The rain probably washed them out. Eddie, go back to the house and get a lantern. We're going to have to go down there to find out for sure. Don't tell anyone what you want it for. If someone asks, just tell them we might be out all night, and we figured we better have one with us. Hurry up now."

Eddie ran over to our horse and mounted. He snapped the reins and gave him a kick in his flanks. Off he took in a gallop back up the hill. We all watched him until he reached the crest and disappeared over it. Mr. Bucklin went back to the well and sat down on the wall. He quietly studied the piece of white material. Father joined him by the well, but instead of sitting down, he looked down into the well. He shaded his eyes with his hands and looked down. Slowly, he moved around the well, looking intently into it. I sat down on the ground and watched him. The sun by this time had dried the ground.

It seemed like an hour before Eddie returned. I watched the hill constantly until he reappeared. When I saw him, I announced it. They both stood up and watched as Eddie came galloping back to us. When he arrived, he handed the lantern to Father before dismounting.

"Ralph, get the rope from my horse," Father ordered. I went and got the rope and returned to him. He grabbed it from my hand and began tying the one end in a loop. Father had already handed the lantern to Mr. Bucklin, who was snapping a match on the side of it to light it.

"Slip this end of the rope around your waist or lower back. You are going down the hole."

"Me?" I looked at Father in surprise. I didn't really know what to think.

"You're small and light. You said you wanted to go along and help, so here's your chance." I was a little excited and scared. I wanted, I thought anyway, to go down the hole, but I didn't want to find anything down there. My stomach began to feel a little funny.

Father lifted me up under my arms and swung me out over the well. Slowly, he lowered me until I was down inside the well. He let go. The rope strained at my weight and dug into my back. I saw an arm swing out above me holding the lantern. It was Eddie's arm. I watched as Father's arm reached out and took it. He lowered it to me, and I grabbed it with my right hand. With my left hand grabbing the rope that was tied around me, I was slowly lowered into the well. I looked up and saw the hole above me grow smaller. There were three heads watching me from above. The farther down I went, the colder it got. Goose bumps grew on my arms. I wasn't sure if it was from the cold of the well or from the thought of what I might find at the bottom.

For the first time, I looked down. I could see something! But I couldn't quite tell what it was. My heart started to pound wildly. I strained as hard as possible to make it out. I could only tell for sure that it was getting larger as I was slowly lowered. Then I made it out. I knew what it was. It was the reflection of the lantern in the well water below me. Strange though, I thought the well had dried up.

"Hey, up there, stop," I yelled. My voice echoed against the well walls up to them.

"What's the matter? Did you find something?" echoed Mr. Bucklin's voice back down to me.

"No, not yet, but there is water below me. I didn't want to get wet. I don't know how deep it is though. Drop a dead branch down, but not on my head. Within moments, I could see a branch or stick above me. It appeared to be about two feet long from where I was. I watched as the fingers spread open against the sky to let go. It came hurtling down the well to me. It whistled by me and hit the water with a splash. I could feel some of the drops hit my pant legs even though I couldn't see them.

"Lower me a little," I yelled up. "That's good." I tried to lean forward as much as possible to see. I also tried to hold the lantern down as much as possible to see. The rays of the lantern bounced off the sides of the well better now. I could also see the stick. It was standing almost straight up at me out of the water.

"Hey, this must be the bottom of the well," I yelled, not looking up. "The stick is pointing up at me."

"Well, grab it and feel around in the bottom to make sure," someone yelled back.

"Okay," I yelled, grabbing at the stick. I couldn't reach it so I yelled back up to them to move me on around the well a little. Slowly they moved me around the well. I bounced back and forth off the wall as I was moved along. I was also getting very cold. "Hold it."

I reached for the stick and dropped the lantern. Unbelievably, it hit the water with a splash but didn't sink. It was standing there with the light still burning. "Hey, let me all the way down. There's just rain water here. I won't get wet."

"Well, if there's nothing down there, why not come back up," Father yelled down at me.

"Because I dropped the lantern, that's why, and this rope is just killing me. I've got to adjust it."

I was immediately lowered to the bottom of the well. My feet hit the water with a light splash. I stood up quickly and readjusted the rope to another position on my back. I figured the water wasn't too deep since I couldn't feel any on my toes. As I reached for the lantern, I could suddenly feel the water running around my toes. Boy, it was cold. I grabbed the lantern handle just as a little flash of light caught my attention, not too far from the base of the lantern. I sloshed in the water, trying to find the flash of light, but I didn't see it. Maybe it was nothing, I thought to myself. I shrugged my shoulder and began to raise up. It flashed again. I was sure this time. Slowly, I moved the lantern over the surface of the water.

"Ready to go," my father's voice crackled and then rumbled like thunder as it echoed down to me.

"Quiet, Dad," I yelled, not looking up. I moved on until I saw it. I reached down to pick up the thing giving off the light. I picked it up and held it in front of the lantern. It was a ring, a gold ring. "Wow," I whispered to myself. Quickly, I put the ring in my left pants pocket. "Okay, bring me up."

I was jerked off my feet at the first tug. I banged against the side of the well wall almost causing me to drop the lantern. I rolled back and forth against the wall. The side pulled at my shirt and head as I was dragged. Dirt would hit me and fall into the water. I looked up to see how much farther but dirt landed in my eyes so I didn't have a chance to see. I could tell it was getting warmer though, so I was nearing the top. With my eyes still closed, I felt a hand grab my upper left arm. I lifted the lantern up with my right arm for someone to take it. Someone did, but I couldn't see who. Four hands grabbed at me at once, and I could feel myself being swung into the air. I was set on the ground, and I started rubbing my eyes to clear them. Someone was tugging at the rope around me at the same time.

"Didn't find anything, huh, Ralph?" Mr. Bucklin said. "That's a relief. I was afraid—"

"This is the only thing I found," I said, reaching into my left pocket and pulling out the ring. I held it out with my left hand for everyone to see. I continued to rub my right eye to clear it up.

"Let's see that," Mr. Bucklin said, grabbing it out of my hand. He inspected it carefully. "It's Jody's. It's her wedding ring."

"Are you sure?" Father said, pressing forward to look at it.

"I'm positive. Amy would know for sure, but I'm nearly certain it is. Strange though, I'm sure I saw Jody with her wedding ring on just recently."

"If that's true, it probably means she was out here sometime during the night. At least it's a clue. We know what direction she is or was headed. Do you want to check first to make certain on the ring, or start looking?"

"Let's spread out and start looking. There is no point in getting my Amy upset. I'm sure it's Jody's ring. Let's spread out a little and head northeast to town and see what happens."

Mr. Bucklin put the ring in his right pants pocket and headed for his horse. I, with Eddie's help, brushed myself off quickly. My feet were wet, but other than that I wasn't too dirty. Eddie and I headed for our horse. Once we were all mounted, we headed out in a northeasterly direction toward Selby. We rode along in silence about fifty yards apart or so. We searched the grassy ground around us for clues. The warm sun felt good to me after being in the cold well.

After checking with the people in town, we started to search the countryside to the west. No one in town had seen Jody. Some of the men offered their help and organized a search party of their own. They said that if they found any sign of her, they would to go Mr. Bucklin's house and wait. Mr. Bucklin thanked them for their concern.

All afternoon we searched the countryside and found no sign of Jody. We were all getting tired of riding. I was saddle sore and hungry, but I didn't complain. I figured we all were. We told the people we ran into what had happened and asked that they be alert for any sign of Jody when going about their business. We would stop at each house along our way and do the same thing.

"Wonder what time it is?" I said to Eddie. "Oh, it must be about six o'clock, judging from the sun."

"Boy, I'm hungry. When are we gonna quit?"

"I don't know. It shouldn't be too long, I hope."

It was almost as if our words had been heard by Mr. Bucklin.

"Let's stop for now, and go back to the house," Mr. Bucklin said, reining his horse to a stop. "We haven't heard any shots or seen anything. I suppose we ought to check to see if anyone else did."

"Sure you want to go back?" Father asked.

"Yes, let's go."

Mr. Bucklin kicked his horse in the flanks and headed in a southerly direction at a gallop. Eddie and I followed on our horse. I couldn't believe how much my bottom hurt when our horse took off in a gallop. I put my hands under my butt to try to ease the pain a little. How Mr. Bucklin and Father knew exactly where to go amazed me. Much of the countryside I had seen in the afternoon I had never seen before. I really had no idea exactly where we were. All I knew for sure was that we were somewhere west of Selby. Every so often we would come to a fence line, which we would have to follow one way or the other until we came to a gate where we could get through. I liked seeing the fences appear, because I knew we would have to stop our horses and it made my bottom feel better.

I really didn't have any idea how long we rode before I started to recognize some of the countryside. Off in the distance, I could see our house and barns to my right. We were coming in from the northwest. We finally cleared a small rise, and I could see the old well and the fallen cottonwood tree where we had been six hours or so earlier. I couldn't wait to get off that darn horse. But at least I knew it wouldn't be much longer.

We galloped past the well and headed up the lane leading to Mr. Bucklin's. When we cleared the hill, we could see the buildings that blocked the view of the house. We still couldn't tell for sure if anyone was there or not. As we rounded Mr. Bucklin's biggest barn that had blocked our view, we could see a number of horses tied up along the east side of the house. We all headed in that direction. We went around the horses and pulled up at the front porch. At the sight and sound of us approaching, a dozen men or so got up and came to meet us.

"Did you find her?" Mr. Bucklin asked loudly, dismounting his horse.

"No," came the reply from one of the men.

"Damnation!" Mr. Bucklin exclaimed loudly in disgust. Mrs. Bucklin, followed by my mother, came out the front door onto the porch.

"You didn't find her?" Mrs. Bucklin asked, looking at Mr. Bucklin. She held both hands clinched together in front of her mouth. Her eyes were red from crying.

"No," Mr. Bucklin replied. Mrs. Bucklin started to cry. "All we found was this." Mr. Bucklin pulled the small gold ring from his pants pocket and the piece of her nightgown and held them up to her. She grabbed the ring from his fingers and inspected it.

"It's her wedding ring," Mrs. Bucklin exclaimed. "Where did you find it?"

"Ralph found it down in the bottom of the well out back."

"What … what can it mean?" she asked, shaking her head slowly back and forth.

"I don't know, I just don't know."

"We think we may have picked up her trail," one of the men said, stepping over to him. It was Wendell Smith, who lived over by the Missouri River.

"What?" Mr. Bucklin said excitedly. "Where?"

"About a mile and a half or so southwest of here. We found some tracks that we think might be hers. We weren't too sure. We tried to stay off of them so we wouldn't mess them up if they were hers. We thought if they were her tracks we could maybe go get those tracking hounds from that man over in Mobridge and see if they could find her."

"Good thinking," Mr. Bucklin agreed, nodding his head.

"We tried to follow them for a ways," Mr. Smith continued, "but we lost them in the high grass. If they are hers, it looks as though she's headed toward my place for some reason or other."

"I know this is a lot to ask, but would a couple of you men go to Mobridge and see if you can get the dogs?" Mr. Bucklin asked.

"Sure," replied a small man wearing gold wire-rim glasses. I knew him to be George Powell. He had the ranch the other side of Mr. Smith's. Mr. Powell's ranch bordered the Missouri River.

"Thanks, George," Mr. Bucklin replied, resting his right hand on Mr. Powell's left shoulder. "Wendell, would you take me out to where you found the tracks? I'd like to look at them."

"Sure," replied Mr. Smith. "Let's go."

The two men mounted their horses. Father asked if we could go too, and Mr. Bucklin said it was all right. We all headed out the lane to the road and turned west heading down the road toward our place. When we passed our house and continued down the road about three quarters of a mile, we came to a gate on the south side of the road. Mr. Smith dismounted and opened the gate. He pulled it back, allowing us to pass through. Once in, Mr. Smith swung the gate back and fastened the latch. He mounted and pointed his right arm in a southwesterly direction. He kicked his big, black and white horse in the flanks and took off in a gallop toward some trees a mile or so away. We all followed.

It took several minutes to cover the distance to the small grove of trees. As we neared them Mr. Smith stopped and got off his horse. The rest of us did the same. Mr. Smith started walking toward the small grove of trees.

"Leave your horses here," he said, tying the reins to a small sapling. We followed his instructions. Mr. Smith walked carefully through the trees down to the bottom of a small draw. We all followed him in single file. Mr. Bucklin was right behind Mr. Smith. Dad, Eddie, and I followed in that order.

"See right there?"

Mr. Smith stopped and pointed down near the bottom of the draw.

"They're awfully faint, aren't they" Mr. Bucklin said, kneeling down to get a better look.

"Yes, they are," Mr. Smith said. "See over there, on the other slope? There are some more. I figure the rain or mud runoff washed out any tracks that would be in the bottom of the wash. What do you think?"

"Sounds logical," Father said, squatting down beside Mr. Bucklin to get a better look. "If those are her footprints, she didn't have any shoes on."

"She didn't," injected Mr. Bucklin. "That's what I said earlier, remember? We couldn't find any sign of her taking anything other than the white gown she had on."

"We tried to search on the other side but couldn't find anything," Mr. Smith said. "Like I said, we didn't get too close, because we didn't want to disturb anything."

"You did the right thing, Wendell," Father assured him.

"I sure hope it doesn't rain tonight," Mr. Bucklin said, standing up and checking the sky overhead. There wasn't a cloud in sight.

"I know what you mean," Father said, placing his left arm over Mr. Bucklin's shoulder. "I know what you mean."

"What does he mean?" I whispered to Eddie.

"So the rain doesn't wash out any of the tracks, dummy," Eddie whispered to me gruffly.

"Oh," I said, nodding my head up and down.

"Let's get back and get some food and rest," Mr. Bucklin said, turning. "We'll get a fresh start at daybreak. I hope we can get the dogs."

"I'm sure we will," Father said, trying to give Mr. Bucklin encouragement.

We all turned and walked back through the trees to our horses. Mr. Smith said he would just go on home, but that he would see us in the morning. The rest of us headed back across the field to the gate. Eddie and I listened as Mr. Bucklin and Father discussed the day's happenings. They both wondered where she could be, if she was alright or not. Mr. Bucklin told us how she had been acting strange over the past several months, just like Jamie had said. Mr. and Mrs. Bucklin had been very concerned he said, but he thought everything would get better after the baby was born. However, according to Mr. Bucklin, after she had the baby she was just as bad as before. Eventually, we reached the lane leading to our house. We all stopped our horses in the road.

"Frank, do you think that after you eat you could come up to my place?" Mr. Bucklin asked.

"Sure, John. Why?" Father replied.

Well, I thought maybe I would light some torches and put them out tonight. Maybe she will see them and find her way back to the house."

"Sounds like a good idea, Bob. I'll be up in forty-five minutes."

"Thanks, John; I appreciate it."

Mr. Bucklin kicked at the flanks of his horse and galloped off to his house. Father and Eddie headed our horses down the lane to our house. We were greeted by the other members of our family who had seen us approaching. Artie asked if we had found anything. Father related the things we had found and done during the day, but that other than the ring and piece of gown that we had found and the tracks that Mr. Powell and his group had found, there had been nothing else. Artie said that his group had searched south and southeast of Mr. Bucklin's place, and that they had found nothing.

Mother, according to Artie, was still up at the Bucklin's helping take care of the baby since Mrs. Bucklin was so upset at what happened. My sisters had prepared dinner for us and had it waiting inside. I was glad to hear that, because I was starving. My stomach had been growling for the last two hours. Before we could eat though, Eddie and I were informed by Father that we had to take our horse to the barn, put him away, and feed him. Eddie and I hurriedly went to do that. As we headed to the barn, I looked over my shoulder and watched Father dismount, tie his horse to the porch rail, and go inside.

Around the dinner table we continued to discuss Jody. Where could she be? Why didn't she take any clothes? Why was the ring in the well? Those questions and more were some that were asked. Father ate quickly and headed back to Mr. Bucklin's. Artie offered to go along too, but Father made him stay to see that the basic chores were completed that hadn't been done during the day. By the time Eddie, Artie, and I had completed them, the sun was down. When we returned to the house, my sisters had already washed the dishes and cleaned up the kitchen. I looked at the kitchen clock. It was a quarter to nine. My sisters already had their nightgowns on and were preparing to go to bed.

"Come on, fellas. Time for bed," Artie said, checking the clock. "If you want to be up first thing in the morning, you better get going."

I don't know about Eddie, but I was bushed. It had been a long, exciting day. I headed for our bedroom upstairs. Eddie followed me. Artie stayed in the kitchen to leave one of the kerosene lamps lit for

Dad. Upstairs, I groped in the darkness for a match to light one of the lamps with. I found one on the table near Eddie's bed. I struck the end of it on the match box beside it. The end of the match burst into flame. I lifted the chimney and lit the wick. I turned the knob of the lamp to raise the wick to enlarge the flame. The light grew, filling the room. I replaced the chimney and went over to my bed. I sat down on the edge of my bed and pulled off my shoes and socks. After removing my shirt and pants, I laid down on my stomach on my bed. I was really bushed.

"Open the windows, Ralph; it's stuffy in here," Eddie said, while pulling off one of his boots over by his bed.

You do it," I returned. "I'm too tired."

"You do it," Eddie replied, his voice raising. "I'm tired too, you know."

I didn't move or say anything else. I closed my eyes, pretending to be asleep. Quietly, I laid there until a sudden blow to my bottom jolted me. I rolled over and sat up quickly. Eddie was sitting there, laughing at me. His boot was lying at the end of my bed. Angrily, I picked the boot up and raised my arm to throw it.

"Don't do it, Ralph," Artie said, entering the room. "You are sure to break something if you do."

"He hit me with it, Artie. That's not fair."

"I don't care—now put it down," Artie said sternly. "And open the windows; it's stuffy in here."

"See," Eddie said sarcastically.

I tossed the boot to Eddie, which he easily caught. I got up slowly and walked to the window near my bed. I pulled at the little handle in the center of the window frame. The window went up easily. The fresh night air felt good. I stuck my head out and inhaled a deep breath. The stars shone brightly in the sky. The moon was just appearing on the east horizon. It was half full.

"Hey, you guys, look! Look there," I shouted excitedly. "I've spotted something."

"What?" Eddie and Artie said together.

"I don't know. It's some kind of light or something."

"Where?" my brothers said simultaneously, rushing up to the window to join me.

"Out there, see?" I said, pointing out into the black night with my right hand.

"I see it," Eddie said excitedly. "Look, it seems to be moving. Think it's Jody?"

"I don't know," Artie said softly.

The three of us leaned out the window, watching the light move slowly through the darkness. Eddie had crammed his way into the window beside me. Artie was leaning over both of us to see out the window.

"Artie, look out the other window," I said angrily, pushing him back. "You are leaning on me, and you are heavy."

"Oh, alright," he replied, moving away quickly to the window to our right.

"It can't be Jody," Eddie surmised. "Remember, she didn't have a light or anything with her. It must be Dad or Mr. Bucklin."

"Look, there's another one," I said, pointing off to the left of the first light.

"Yeah, it's Dad and Mr. Bucklin all right," Artie called from the window to our right.

We watched the two lights silently from our windows. The light at the left stopped moving. Within seconds, another light separated from it and moved off down the field after the first light. Soon it stopped. The same thing happened with the first light. It stopped and then another light separated from it and moved farther down the field. Within minutes, a row of six lights stretched across the countryside. A chill ran down my back from the eerie feeling it gave me.

"Think she'll see them, Artie?" Eddie asked.

"I don't know," he called back.

"Wonder why they put the torches there?" I asked.

"Because that's the way they think she went, dummy," Eddie answered.

"Oh, yeah, that's right. I forgot."

"Come on, let's go to bed. It could be a long day tomorrow," Artie said, moving away from the window over to his bed. Eddie left the window and went to his bed.

"Coming, Ralph?" Eddie called from his bed.

"I want to watch a minute."

The room went black. I heard Eddie blow out the lantern on the table next to his bed. I stared at the six torches burning out in the field way off in the distance. I guessed that they were several hundred yards apart, but I wasn't sure. It was hard to tell in the darkness. Since I could see all six lights, I knew that the last light wasn't close to where we had seen the tracks during the day. The lights were in a line south and slightly west. I wondered why they weren't run in a line more west, over to where we had seen the tracks. I couldn't come up with an answer.

I looked up at the stars in the sky. It was a beautiful night. The moon had completely appeared above the east horizon. It was above and slightly behind the Bucklin house. I could see the silhouette of the house easily. There was light coming from the first floor windows at the front of the house. I hadn't noticed it before, but maybe I just hadn't paid any attention. Silently, I stared out the window looking at the lights. Behind me, I could hear Artie begin to snore as he always did. He would start slowly with a low rumbling noise and get louder as he fell deep into sleep.

I sat down on the floor in front of the window and laid my forearms across the sill. I rested my chin on the top of my knuckles of my joined hands. I stared out, not really looking for anything. My mind wandered, and my eyelids became heavy. I shook my head to fight off my drowsiness. For a moment, I thought I saw something. No, it was my imagination. I rubbed my eyes with both hands. It took them a second or two to focus when I stopped. I got up on knees again and looked out the window.

There was someone down in our lane. I could see a figure walking down the lane to our house! My eyes bugged out at the sight of the figure. It wasn't Dad; I knew that because he left on horseback. A lump formed in my throat, making it difficult to swallow. It was Jody. I was sure now; it was Jody. It was definitely a woman coming up the lane to our house.

"Eddie, Artie," I turned and called softly to them after clearing my throat. "Eddie, Artie, wake up." There was only the sound of Artie's snoring. "Wake up, you guys, wake up," I said, raising my voice a little.

Still no one moved. Only the sound of Artie snoring indicated anyone else was in the room with me. I looked back out the window at the figure. It was almost underneath me now. I got up and moved quickly over to Artie's bed. In the darkness, my toes struck something hard near the foot of Artie's bed. I yelled out in pain and fell forward, landing on Artie in his bed.

"Jesus Christ, what's going on?" Artie called out, sitting right up in his bed, knocking me to the floor.

"Sh, Sh," I hissed loudly at him, grabbing the toes of my right foot with both hands to comfort them.

"What the hell are you doing?" Artie said, loud enough to wake Eddie.

"Quiet," came Eddie's voice from the darkness of the other side of the room.

"She's here, Artie. She's here," I said softly, still holding my foot.

"Who's here?" Artie said, rather loudly.

"Quiet, Artie, we don't want to scare her off," I said. "It's Jody. I just saw her come up our lane to our house.'"

"You are seeing things, Ralph. Go back to bed," Artie said, laying back down.

"I am not; I saw her with—"

I stopped speaking at the sound of knocking coming from downstairs.

"Hear that?" I said, shaking Artie with both my hands.

"Hear what?" he replied, not too enthusiastically.

"The knocking on the door. She's knocking on the kitchen door. Listen."

In the darkness of our room, Artie and I waited to hear some sound that told Artie I was not seeing things. I figured Eddie was asleep again since he hadn't said anything more. It seemed as though minutes went by. There was no sound.

"You are crazy, Ralph. Now go to sleep," Artie said sternly.

"But Artie—"

"Get to bed, Ralph. Enough is enough," he ordered. Quietly, I got up. I stood silently in the dark room. Slowly I started to inch my way back to my bed. I didn't want to stub my toes again. I found the edge of my bed and sat down.

Bang! bang! bang! came a sound from another part of the house.

"What in the hell are you doing now, Ralph," Artie called from the other side of the room.

"Nothing," I said, in a low excited voice. I knew now that Artie had also heard the banging. It came from downstairs.

Three more knocks sounded down below. This time they were louder.

"You are right, Ralph. There is someone down there," Artie said, rustling around on his bed. "Let's go see who it is."

I stood up and as quickly as possible moved through the darkness back over to Artie's bed. I bumped into Artie, knocking him down on his bed.

"Watch out, Ralph. What do you think you are doing anyway?" Artie scolded me.

"Sorry, Artie," I whispered. "I didn't see you."

"Come on, let's go," he said, getting back up. Artie reached out and found my left arm. He grabbed me by the wrist and started pulling me to the bedroom door.

"Shouldn't we get Eddie up?" I whispered.

"No, let him sleep" Artie answered.

"He'll be mad, I bet."

"He'll probably be madder if we wake him," Artie returned. We reached the door, and I could hear Artie grab the door handle and turn the knob. He pulled the door back slowly. It started to creak when he did so. He opened the door just far enough to let both of us pass through. Artie quickly stepped through the doorway into the hall, pulling me along with him. We could see faint light at the bottom of the stairs that was coming from the kerosene lamp that Artie left on in the kitchen. Slowly we descended the stairs trying not to make the boards beneath our feet creak. When we reached the bottom step, Artie poked his head around the corner leading to the kitchen.

Bang! Bang! Bang! came three more knocks from the back door. They were much louder than the others we had heard. The noise at the door excited me. My heart began to beat faster. Artie pulled me from the last step, and slowly, together, we headed into the kitchen. The lamp on the kitchen table cast eerie shadows on the kitchen walls. As Artie and I crossed the kitchen to the back door, our shadows came up behind us and passed us on the left kitchen wall. It startled me. I thought for a moment that there were two people following us. Artie grabbed the door handle with his right hand and twisted the door latch with his left.

The lock clicked loudly. Slowly he pulled open the porch door. I stood behind Artie peeking out around him, not knowing what to expect.

The door was open now and the light from the lamp rushed through the doorway into the darkness. In the shadows of the porch, we could see a lone figure standing there. The light touched the bottom part of the figure revealing a dark blue skirt. Silently, Artie and I waited for the figure to step to the doorway.

"Jody?" Artie spoke out boldly.

"Jody? It's me, your mother," came a voice from the porch.

"Mother!" Artie and I exclaimed together. The figure stepped forward into the light of the doorway. It was Mother.

"We thought ... we thought it was Jody," Artie said, stuttering slightly.

"No, it's only me, boys," she said, stepping into the kitchen. "Amy was feeling better and said that I should go on home, so here I am."

"Jody didn't come home then?" Artie asked.

"No, she's not home yet. You better get to bed now if you're going to get up early in the morning to search for her."

Disappointed, I turned and started walking back to my bedroom.

"And you thought it was Jody," Artie called after me. "Can't you see?"

"That's enough, Art," mother said. "He didn't know. I probably would have thought the same thing! But I wish you would have left the door unlocked."

"I forgot," I could hear Artie say as I started to climb the stairs to my bedroom. My legs felt heavy. I was worn out. It had been a long day, and there had been too much excitement.

I reached the bedroom doorway and stepped in. The light from the moon came through the window next to my bed. I walked to the window and looked out. The moon was way up in the sky now. A light was still on at the Bucklin's. I looked to the south and stared at the torches burning out in the field. All six were still going.

"See anything else?" Artie said, chuckling as he entered the room.

"Aw, shut up," I said, turning back to him.

"It's alright, Ralph. You didn't know. I probably would have thought the same thing," Artie said, sounding sympathetic.

"You mean it?"

"Sure I mean it, Ralph. Now let's get some sleep, okay?"

"Okay," I said feeling better. I got up and went to my bed and lay down on top of the covers. I lay there listening to the crickets out in the field. I knew they were rubbing their legs together. Everything seemed peaceful. As I lay there listening, I wondered about Jody—about all the things that had happened. Everything flashed quickly back into mind. Everything about her seemed strange. I wondered if we would find her.

Oh well, I thought to myself, *we'll all find out in the morning.*

I said my prayers and went to sleep.

Chapter

18

"I wonder where in the hell they are." Mr. Bucklin said, pacing back and forth on the front porch. "It's eight thirty, and they still aren't here. What's keeping them?"

"I don't know, John," Father replied from his seated position on the porch steps. "Maybe they couldn't find the man with the dogs."

We were waiting at the Bucklin house for the men to return from Mobridge with the search dogs. We had all been up since sunrise. My brothers and I had done our chores so that we could go on the search for Jody. Fortunately, it had not rained during the night, which would have washed out any possible chance of having the dogs find Jody's trail. Mrs. Bucklin and Jamie served us all hot coffee while we waited for the dogs. The members of the search party—which numbered twenty including Father, Artie, Eddie, and me—milled around, discussing the situation.

"Here they come," one of the search party said, pointing down the road toward our place. In the distance, we could see two men on horseback followed by one man driving a wagon pulled by two horses coming up the road toward us.

"It's about time," Mr. Bucklin said impatiently, pulling out his pocket watch by its chain. He flipped the lid up to check the time. "Quarter to nine already."

We all watched as the little party reached the lane leading to the Bucklin house. The two men on horseback turned into the lane first, followed by the man in the wagon. I couldn't see or hear any dogs, and I wondered if there were even any dogs with them. I had never seen the man in the wagon before. The men on horseback were the ones Mr.

Bucklin had sent to Mobridge. As the group pulled their horses and the wagon to a stop by the porch, the men who had been waiting for them gathered around them.

"Where in the hell have you been?" Mr. Bucklin said, looking up at one of the men on horseback. "Do you know what time it is, man?"

"Well, there wasn't a—" the man started to answer.

"Let me explain," came the booming words from the man in the wagon. "I am Pierre Beauchard. I tell them no point in leaving till morning. No point in riding most of the night to get here, only to be tired in morning. The tracks still keep if it not rain. My dogs find your girl. They best dogs in South Dakota."

The man stood up in the wagon and bent over, extending a very big right hand to Mr. Bucklin to shake. He was huge, standing up in the wagon. A buckskin coat covered his broad shoulders. I wondered why he wore the thing since it would probably be warm again today. He had a brown broad flat-rimmed hat pulled down on his head enough to touch his bushy brown eyebrows. He had a full-grown gray-brown beard and mustache that were neatly trimmed.

After shaking hands, Pierre jumped down from the wagon and stretched his arms above his head and yawned loudly. He made me yawn watching him. Standing beside Mr. Bucklin, I could see that Pierre was a good three inches taller. I remembered that Mr. Bucklin was about six feet four or so, Father had said. This man looked almost like a giant compared to the other men who were shaking his hand. Pierre had to have weighed around two hundred fifty pounds or more, I was sure. I tried to determine how old he was, but it was hard to do. The gray-brown beard made him look old in one way, but the twinkling blue eyes and the straight white teeth made him look younger in another. His face and hands were dark brown from the sun, but they didn't look leathery and wrinkled like an older man's.

"Why's he talk so funny" I whispered to Eddie, who was standing beside me.

"He's French, dummy, that's why," Eddie whispered back. "Don't you know anything?"

"Well, if I didn't know, how did you know? I've never seen a Frenchman before. So how do you know?"

"I just know," Eddie said back, perturbed. "Be quiet will you?"

I was mad. I wanted to know how come Eddie knew he was French and I didn't. I had never seen a Frenchman before that I knew of, so how did Eddie know. He wasn't that much older than me.

"I charge you fifty dollars for my dogs," the big Frenchman said, looking at Mr. Bucklin.

"Fifty dollars!" Mr. Bucklin exclaimed loudly. "That's absurd."

"That's only if my dogs find your girl," Pierre said, holding up one finger. "If we no find girl, you owe me nothing. My dogs best in South Dakota. That fair?"

"Fair enough," Mr. Bucklin said, calming down. "Let's get started."

The big Frenchman gently pushed through the gathered men to the back of the wagon. We all followed him. We formed a half circle at the back end of the wagon as we watched Pierre unfasten the latches of the wagon tailgate. Once unfastened, he pulled the gate back, and it swung down on its bottom hinges until it hung straight down. Two large wooden crates sat side by side in the back end. A square hole was cut in each door near the top. Printed on one door in white paint was the word "Louie." On the other cage door the word "Henri" was printed. Quickly, Pierre pulled a little wooden peg from the latch of Louie's cage and swung the door back. A big red dog stood up in the wooden crate.

"Gentlemen, this is Louie," announced Pierre proudly, standing back from the dog with his hands on his hips. "Come, Louie."

The big red dog jumped from the back of the wagon and went to his master and sat down beside him.

"What kind of dog is that?" I said to Eddie standing beside me. "I've never seen one like that."

"It's an English bloodhound," Pierre said, overhearing my words. "He came all the way from England. Best tracking dog there is, boy. Stay, Louie."

Pierre went to the other cage and pulled the peg from its door latch. He pulled the door back to reveal another dog that looked just like Louie. Pierre went back to Louie and called the other dog.

"Henri, come, boy."

The big red dog jumped from the back of the wagon and went over to Pierre and sat down beside Louie.

"They good dogs," Pierre announced proudly. "Well trained. Best tracking dogs in South Dakota. They find girl."

"Do, do you think they can pick up her trail?" Mr. Bucklin asked, moving closer to look at the dogs.

"Sure," Pierre answered. "Scent should be strong enough to pick up. Since it not rain, it should still be there for my dogs."

"Well, let's get started then," Mr. Bucklin said, moving to his horse.

"Wait," Pierre boomed out in his deep voice. "You got horse for me?"

"Take that horse," Mr. Bucklin said, pointing to a brown horse tied up beside the horse Eddie and I were riding.

Pierre moved over to the brown horse and quickly mounted it. Louie and Henri never moved a muscle the whole time. "Now, I need piece of her clothing for the dogs to get scent from."

"Jamie, go in and get something for Mr. Beauchard," Mr. Bucklin ordered. Jamie, who had been standing on the front porch, turned and quickly went into the house.

"I wonder how come Jamie isn't going," I said to Eddie as we walked to our horse.

"His dad won't let him go."

"How come?"

"I heard him say so to Dad," Eddie said, swinging himself into the saddle. Eddie reached out with his left hand to help pull me up behind him. "Mr. Bucklin wanted him to stay with his mom since Mother won't get up here for a while, but more so, because Mr. Bucklin is afraid of what we might find—if we find anything. That's probably why he didn't say anything to us this morning."

"Probably feels bad he can't go, huh?" I asked.

"Probably, so don't say anything about it, Ralph, okay?"

"Sure, Eddie. I won't."

Jamie came back out onto the porch carrying a white blouse in his right hand. He walked to the edge of the porch and handed it to his father. Mr. Bucklin grabbed it and then turned his horse in our direction. He walked his horse over to Pierre mounted on the brown horse beside us.

"Here," Mr. Bucklin said, handing him the blouse.

"Has it been worn since it last washed?" Pierre asked, examining the blouse.

"I believe she had it on the day before last, didn't she, Jamie?" Mr. Bucklin asked, looking over his left shoulder at Jamie standing on the porch.

"She wore it the day she disappeared," Jamie answered.

"Good, good," Pierre's voice boomed. "Now, you have idea which way she go first?"

"Well, we have two clues, we believe," Mr. Bucklin said. "The first is out behind our place to the north. There's an old well back there where we found her wedding ring yesterday. So we think she was there, but we don't know when for sure. Then there's a small draw southwest of here where some of the men found some foot prints that we think are hers."

"Good, good," Pierre boomed again. "Which is closer, we check that first."

"The well," Mr. Bucklin answered.

"Let's go then. Which way to get there?" Pierre said. "Come dogs, you stay with me."

Both dogs stood up at once and came over to Pierre. They looked like twins. They were both the same size. They had droopy ears and wrinkles on the tops of their foreheads over their saggy eyes. Their baggy lips flopped up and down as they trotted together over to Pierre.

Mr. Bucklin moved his horse past Pierre and headed toward the lane that would take us back to the well. Pierre followed him on his horse with the dogs patiently walking beside him. The rest of the search party including Eddie and me followed.

"This is exciting, isn't it, Eddie?" I said, seated behind him.

"Yeah, it's exciting alright. Who knows what we'll find."

"Yeah, who knows."

"Well, don't get too excited, Ralph."

"Why?"

"Because ... because we may find her dead, you know."

"Oh ... oh, I hadn't thought of that." Eddie's words didn't make me feel too good; all of a sudden I felt queasy in my stomach. "Really, Eddie, you are kidding, aren't you?"

"Who knows, Ralph. Who knows."

"Well, well, I hope not."

"I do too, Ralph."

When we approached within forty yards of the old well, Mr. Bucklin raised his left hand above his head signaling us to stop.

"This is it, huh?" Pierre said, staring at the old well.

"This is where we found her ring yesterday," Mr. Bucklin said.

"Well, let's see what we find," Pierre said, dismounting.

"Here, boys. Smell. Smell." Pierre bent over the two dogs and shoved the white blouse into their noses. The dogs eagerly sniffed the garment, and their long, red tails began to wag. I got the feeling that the dogs knew they were about to play a game that they had played before and enjoyed. I wondered if it was really just a game to them or if, in their own minds, they could sense the seriousness of the situation.

"Go, find, boys," Pierre continued, waving the dogs off in the direction of the old well. "Find her, boys, find her. Good dogs."

The two bloodhounds started searching the ground with their big, black noses. For the most part, the dogs always stayed pretty close together. One didn't go one way and one the other as I had expected them to do. The dogs sniffed the ground all around the well and the old downed dogwood tree at a brisk pace. To me, the dogs just seemed to run about in a reckless manner. I wondered how they could find anything. They ran back and forth re-covering ground they had already been over. These couldn't be the best search dogs in South Dakota unless they were the only search dogs in South Dakota, I thought to myself.

Suddenly, Louie came to a halt about five feet from the well. He stuck his nose against the ground, sniffing heavily. Little clouds of dirt rose as he exhaled hard into the ground. Henri, seeing Louie stop, came over and searched the ground with him. Slowly they moved toward the well, sniffing the ground.

"Did they find something?" Mr. Bucklin said excitedly.

"Not yet," Pierre said calmly. "We know for sure if they start to howl. When they howl, they have the scent."

We all waited quietly as the dogs sniffed around the well. Everyone's eyes were glued to the dogs in fascination. Louie and Henri slowly disappeared behind the well. Within seconds they reappeared on the west side of the well. As suddenly as Louie had stopped, he took off in a trot continuing to search the ground with his nose near the ground.

"No, no scent here," Pierre announced. "We move on to the other place."

"Are you sure?" Mr. Bucklin said, disappointment written on his face. "We found her ring here though."

"I sure" Pierre said. "There is no scent here. Ring maybe here two, three days. Maybe rain wash away scent night she leaves. But there is no fresh scent. Let's move on."

"Okay, if you are sure."

"I sure, let's not waste time. Scent not going to last forever," Pierre said, irritated.

He turned and remounted the brown horse. Everyone mounted and sat silently waiting for Mr. Bucklin. He turned slowly to his horse and mounted. I don't believe he was convinced that the dogs had not found something. He continued to watch the dogs, who were still searching the area around the well.

"Louie, Henri, come, boys. Come by me. Here, boys." Pierre whistled loudly, and the dogs' heads snapped up at the sound. They looked at Pierre, waiting. Pierre whistled again and pointed with his left hand down at the ground beside him. The dogs immediately trotted back to Pierre and stood beside him waiting for his next command.

"They sure are well trained, aren't they?" I whispered into Eddie's ear.

"Yeah, they are," he whispered, turning his head back to answer. "I'd like to have a dog like that."

"Me too."

Mr. Bucklin raised his left arm and waved it forward signaling us to head out. He turned his horse and headed it back up the lane leading back to his place. Pierre and the two dogs followed close behind him. The rest of us all turned our horses and followed them. When we passed by Mr. Bucklin's house in the lane leading out to the road, Mrs. Bucklin and Jamie came out on the front porch. I saw Mr. Bucklin look over at them and slowly shake his head from side to side. I wondered to myself what he meant by that. Was it "no" that we didn't find any clues, or was it "no" that he didn't think the dogs would find anything?

Our search party turned west upon reaching the road that headed down toward our place. Slowly, we walked the horses down the road. Even at a walk, the hooves of the horses kicked up clouds of dust in the dry, hard road. I was glad Eddie and I were near the front so the dust didn't get in my nose. My sisters and mother came out on our front porch as we passed. Eddie and I looked silently over at them. None of them waved and neither did we. I wondered what they were thinking.

Within a few minutes we reached the gate that opened into the field leading to the small draw where we had seen the footprints the day before. Way off in the distance, I could see the tops of the trees where I knew we were headed. Mr. Bucklin dismounted and went over to the gate and pulled it open for the rest of us. We all passed through into the field and waited as Mr. Bucklin closed the gate behind us. Quickly, he mounted his horse and headed south toward the trees. Pierre, his dogs, and the rest of us followed close behind. As we neared the draw, Mr. Bucklin raised his left hand signaling us to stop.

"The tracks we found are down in the draw," Mr. Bucklin said, pointing to the trees some forty yards away. "What do you want to do?"

"Keep the men and horses away. Too many scents make it hard to find one scent that is fading anyway. I take the dogs to the draw and let them work. You all wait here."

Pierre dismounted and walked to the draw. He took long strides and covered the distance to the trees quickly. With his brown buckskin coat on and his big brown flat-rimmed hat, he lumbered up to the trees like a big, brown bear. We all watched as Pierre knelt down on his right knee near the edge of the draw and pulled the white blouse from his belt. He grabbed one dog by the loose skin on its neck and pushed the blouse into its nose. I couldn't tell which dog it was because both dogs looked identical from a distance. Pierre grabbed the other dog by the neck and shoved the blouse to its nose too. I could see that he was talking to the dogs, but his words could not be heard due to the distance.

"I don't know," Mr. Bucklin said, scratching the side of his head with his left hand.

"You don't know what, John?" Father asked.

"I'm not so sure about this man. I don't think his dogs can find her."

"Well, let's not be too hasty. After all, the man did say no fee unless his dogs find her. I'd say he would have to be pretty sure of his dogs to say that."

"I ... I suppose that's right," Mr. Bucklin said, watching Pierre with his two dogs. "But there just can't be too much scent left. I don't think his dogs can find her scent. It's been too long, I think."

"Well, we will all know shortly, I suppose. If those are her tracks in there, and there is any scent left, those dogs should find it."

Pierre stood up and pointed with his right arm into the draw. Louie and Henri abruptly went the direction their master pointed. They quickly disappeared into the trees and bushes of the draw. They were followed by Pierre. We all stared intently at the draw waiting for the sight or sound of one of the dogs or Pierre. Every so often we would hear the crack of a branch or twig snapping or breaking.

A howl suddenly filled the air. One of the dogs was howling loudly down in the draw. Within seconds, the first howling dog was joined by the second and that were both howling together. We could tell from the howling that the dogs were heading down the draw to the southwest.

"They have found something," Mr. Bucklin said excitedly. "Come, let's go."

"Wait, John. Pierre said to stay here, remember? Let's wait until he returns."

"Come men, bring my horse," said Pierre's booming voice from somewhere in the draw. He suddenly stepped out of the dense draw about thirty-five yards west of where he went in. He waved his arms calling us to him. The search party went in a trot to him.

"Did they find the track?" Mr. Bucklin said excitedly, handing Pierre the reins to his horse.

"They find alright. Hear them," Pierre said proudly, cupping his left hand over his left ear to gather in the sound of his howling dogs. "Henri find scent first. Louie come over quickly and second that it her track alright. Now all we do is follow the sounds of my dogs, and we find her. They howl whole time until she found. They good dogs—best there is."

Pierre mounted his horse and told everyone to follow him now. He would take over, and everyone should do what he told them to do. He kicked the brown horse in the ribs and trotted off along the edge of the draw in the direction of his baying bloodhounds. We followed him in a trot. When we reached the southwest end of the draw, we crossed it and headed up the south side after Louie and Henri. We could hear them howling over the pounding hooves of the search-party horses. The dogs were heading in a southwestern direction, through a grass field so high that we couldn't see the dogs up ahead of us. The legs of our horses were hidden by the high grass. We trotted on through the grass field after the dogs.

"What a place to hide in, huh, Ralph?" Eddie said over his right shoulder to me as we trotted along.

"Yeah, you could hide real easy in this high grass," I agreed as I hugged Eddie's stomach to keep from falling off. My bottom was beginning to hurt from the pounding it was taking from bouncing on the back end of our horse.

"Looks like she's headed toward your place, Wendell," one of the men called out from behind us as we trotted along.

"Looks that way, don't it?" came another voice from behind us.

Up ahead of us we could still hear Louie and Henri howling. The sound of their cries were louder than before, so I figured we were beginning to catch up to the two dogs. Just as quickly the howling of the dogs suddenly grew fainter. As we neared the top of a small hill, Pierre raised his right hand high in the air signaling us to stop. We all stopped at the top of the hill. To the south and west of us, the countryside turned into rolling hills. I knew that it meant we were heading into the rough Missouri River bottom country. Way off in the distance I could see some of the buildings of Smith ranch. I knew that there was only one other ranch between his place and the Missouri River.

"They've turned," Pierre said loudly, his left hand cupped around his left ear as he listened for his dogs. "I hear them. They headed to the big draw down there."

Pierre pointed down the hill to a long, heavily timbered draw south of us. The draw ran east and west. He headed his horse to the center of the draw. It didn't take much time for our horses to go down the hill to the draw. As we approached the north side, we could once again plainly hear Louie and Henri howling. They were somewhere in the thick-timbered draw. It was impossible to see them. It sounded to me like they were moving back and forth through the trees, but I wasn't sure.

"Look," Eddie said, pointing to the west end of the draw. I turned my head in time to see a magnificent buck deer bolt from the trees. It had a huge rack on it. The spooked buck took long bounds as it quickly climbed a small ridge and disappeared over the top.

"What a beauty," I said, staring at the spot where the deer disappeared.

"You better believe it," Eddie agreed.

"I think she know what she doing," Pierre said to Mr. Bucklin.

"What are you talking about?" Mr. Bucklin inquired.

"I think your girl know what she doing. She's trying to hide."

"What do you mean?"

"Louie and Henri confused. That means trail crisscross or backtrack in there. Girl, who not right in head, not think to do that."

"What do you mean, not right in head?" Mr. Bucklin said, fire in his eyes.

"Calm down, John," Father put in.

"Men tell me how strangely she act lately. If that case, don't think she would think to backtrack or crisscross trail. So far, she seek cover of high grass or draws to stay out of sight. If she sick, she probably just go straight. Somebody probably would see her. Maybe I wrong, but I not think so. I think she knew what she doing."

"It's a good point, John," Father said, agreeing with what Pierre said.

"But what about her not taking any clothes or shoes?" Mr. Bucklin said.

"Hmm, can't answer that," Pierre said, rubbing his chin with his left hand. "Maybe we find answer to that when we find her. Listen, Louie and Henri have picked up her trail again."

From the west end of the long draw we could hear the dogs howling. Pierre led the way after the sound of his dogs.

"There they are," Mr. Bucklin called out, pointing to a spot near where the deer had run. We could see Louie and Henri near the top of the steep hill. "Maybe they are chasing the buck?"

"No, they no chase deer. Never have and never will," Pierre answered as we rode along.

Our horses strained and struggled to climb the steep hill after the two dogs. They puffed heavily, their hooves digging deep into the steep hill as they climbed. Pierre reached the top of the hill first and stopped his horse. He looked back over his shoulder and watched as the rest of us climbed the hill.

"Come on, boy, just a little farther," Eddie said, urging our horse on. When we reached the top, Eddie pulled our horse to a halt. We waited for the rest of the men, our horse breathing heavily beneath us. My bottom hurt from the bouncing. I adjusted myself on the back of our horse to try to ease the pain. I looked off into the distance. The rolling hills looked like gold with the sun beating down high above us. Every so often there were green patches of trees that dotted the hillsides. It was really pretty. To the southwest of us, down at the foot of a big valley, was Wendell Smith's ranch. The road that led to his place cut across the golden hills down in front of us. Louie and Henri were somewhere down near the road. I could hear them.

When the last man reached the top, Pierre kicked his horse in the flanks and started after his dogs. Our horses had an easy time going down the long hill to the road. As we rode down the hill, Louie and Henri stopped howling.

"Did they find her?" Mr. Bucklin said excitedly as we rode through the high-grass field to the road. "I don't hear or see them."

"I don't know," Pierre answered. "They find something, I sure. We find out soon."

Chapter
19

"Look on the fence, near Louie and Henri," Pierre called out as we neared the road. "There is something hanging there. See it?"

I looked over Eddie's shoulder in the direction Pierre had pointed. I could see his dogs standing by the fence with their noses pointed upward, but I didn't see anything else.

As we neared the dogs, Mr. Bucklin dismounted before even bringing his horse to a stop. He ran the remaining few yards to the fence and stopped. He held his head downward as if looking at the two dogs below him. I could see that he was moving his arms, but with his back to all of us we couldn't tell what he was doing.

"Look, it's her handkerchief," Mr. Bucklin said, turning back to us raising his right hand. "And it's covered with blood. My razor, the one I couldn't find, was tied inside it."

Mr. Bucklin raised his left hand displaying a black-handled straight razor. I could see dark spots on the blade that looked like dried blood. The handkerchief he held in his right hand was all white other than a rather large red spot in the middle.

"Is it dry?" Pierre said, pulling the handkerchief from Mr. Bucklin's hand. He examined the piece of material carefully. We all watched as he wet his right index finger with his tongue back and forth several times. He rubbed the red spot with his finger. "It not real fresh blood. Probably done late last night or early this morning."

"What was done early this morning?" Mr. Bucklin said, his face suddenly turning pale.

"Don't know for sure. Blood come from something though, that for sure, and it come from something this morning."

"Do you think she cut herself?" Father asked, inspecting the razor Pierre handed him.

"Possible. If she cut herself real bad we find blood trail. It explain reason for leaving razor on hanky. It warning to us what happen. But if there no blood trail, then why she leave hanky when she can use it to cover or stop bleeding?"

"What does it all mean though," Mr. Bucklin asked, obviously upset with what we had found.

"I don't know," Pierre said, shrugging his shoulders. "We have to keep searching. Someone have wire cutters with them?"

"I do," came a voice from behind me. It was one of the ranch hands of Wendell Smith.

"Cut the fence here then. We keep searching from this point. One group of men go up road and one group down road and search for blood and footprints. If she cut herself bad, she may be able to cover up blood trail for several hundred yards."

The man came forward with the wire cutters and quickly cut each of the three barb wires. Each wire snapped back with a "twang" when cut. Pierre then ordered the ranch hand to cut the fence on the other side of the road in case Jody had crossed the road at this point. Eddie and I watched as the men behind us divided into two groups. One group headed south, down the grass ditch beside the road; the other group headed north, up the ditch. The men had dismounted at Pierre's orders and were searching the ground on foot, followed by their horses. Pierre told the men not to search in the road itself. The dirt and dust in the road would reveal her track if she crossed. Father, Pierre, Mr. Bucklin, Eddie, and I watched as the men searched. Louie and Henri sat quietly by Pierre's feet, catching their breath.

"No unusual tracks here," Pierre said, studying the ground.

"What do you mean?" Mr. Bucklin said, watching Pierre.

"Well, just wagon tracks and horse tracks in dirt road," Pierre said, pointing down at the road before him. "Not see any footprints, shoe or no shoe. Dust thick enough should leave mark easy. See?"

Pierre lifted his right foot covered by a big brown leather boot and stepped into the road. Light puffs of dust rose with the slightest bit of contact with the boot and the road.

"Don't think kangaroo could jump over road; think your girl can? We should find track soon."

The two search parties had moved a hundred yards or so in opposite directions of us. No one found a clue. I waited excitedly for someone to find something. I tried to study the handkerchief that Mr. Bucklin was once again holding. It had fancy little lace down around the edges of it. I could see some of the red stain on it, but most of it was concealed by Mr. Bucklin's big hand.

"Find anything?" Pierre called out in his deep loud voice.

"No," came back calls from both directions.

"Hmm," Pierre mused to himself. "Should find clue in few moments."

We tried patiently to wait for a signal. The two groups moved farther and farther away from us. Still there was no signal from either party. The sun was warm on our backs, and it was getting hot.

"Let's move Louie and Henri across the road and see if they pick up the scent," Father said, breaking the silence.

"What do you think, Pierre?" Mr. Bucklin asked impatiently.

"Can't hurt," Pierre agreed. He walked to the other side of the road raising little clouds of dust as he went. When he reached the other side, he turned and called to his dogs to come. Louie and Henri went to him. Once again, Pierre pulled the white blouse from his belt and held it down to the dogs' noses to smell. "Find her, boys, find her."

He waved his right arm in an outward direction, and the dogs started out once again in search of Jody's trail. The dogs ranged back and forth sniffing the ground their tails wagging sluggishly behind them. Louie, or was it Henri, had barely reached the fence line when he let up a large howl and headed off in the field directly west of where Pierre was standing. The other bloodhound, hearing the bay of his companion, took off after him. Soon he was howling too. Pierre, seeing his dogs running out into the field west of him turned and ran back toward us.

"Mount up," he said, grabbing the reins of his horse. "They find the trail."

"Are you sure?" Mr. Bucklin said, putting a saddle on his horse.

"Of course I sure. I know my dogs."

"Well, how come no tracks them?" Mr. Bucklin said, with a puzzled look on his face.

"Don't know, can't explain it. But she somehow cross right there," Pierre said, pointing to the spot where he had just been standing. "But dogs have track. Let's go."

Pierre kicked the flanks of his horse and headed for the opening in the cut fence on the other side. As Eddie pulled me up into the saddle behind him, the other members of the search party were galloping back to us from both directions. They had heard the howl of the dogs too. Mr. Bucklin and Dad had already crossed the road and were past the cut-down fence line, chasing after Pierre.

"Come on, Eddie. We're getting behind," I yelled excitedly into his ear.

"Hang on, Ralph," Eddie raised his feet and brought them back sharply into the sides of the horse beneath. He bolted forward when he felt the heels of Eddie's boots strike his side. I would have tumbled off had it not been for grabbing Eddie's shirt with both hands. We galloped across the road and through the fence after the others. The two search parties reached the downed fence line only moments after Eddie and I passed through. Forty yards in front of us were Mr. Bucklin and Father in hot pursuit of Pierre who was another twenty yards in front of them. Off in the distance, I could hear the howl of the dogs, but I couldn't see them.

Pierre suddenly turned his horse south and disappeared down the hill. Eddie, seeing this, changed directions and headed to the point where Pierre disappeared. We would gain some ground on the three men in front of us. We were only forty yards or so behind Pierre when Eddie and I started down the hill. Way down below me, I could see the Smith ranch. I could see the dogs headed toward a creek bottom that lay several hundred yards this side of the Smith ranch. Pierre was gaining on his dogs, followed closely now by Mr. Bucklin and Father.

Eddie and I were halfway down the hill when the dogs disappeared into the trees that lined the creek. Once again their howling stopped. Within moments after the dogs disappeared, Pierre reached the trees and quickly dismounted. He, too, disappeared into the trees.

"Think the dogs found something?" I asked Eddie as we neared the spot where Pierre left his horse. Eddie didn't answer. Mr. Bucklin and Father were off their horses, trotting the few remaining yards on foot to the spot where the dogs and Pierre disappeared. As Eddie reined our horse to a halt, they too disappeared into the trees.

"Get off, Ralph. Let's see what they found," Eddie said quickly. I hurriedly swung my right leg back to get off. I nearly lost my balance and almost fell to the ground. Eddie got off, and together we ran after the others. We could hear talking as we pushed our way through the trees.

"She's been here alright," Pierre said as Eddie and I reached the three men. They were bent over, studying the ground in front of them. The dogs were standing in the creek, gulping water heavily. "See how the mud oozed up from her feet near the edge of the creek. She was here early this morning. Maybe two or three o'clock."

"How do you know that?" I asked puzzled.

"Easy, boy," Pierre said, without turning. "See, mud at the top dried out from the sun. The bottom part still moist." Pierre pointed with his right hand, showing me.

"Oh," I said, understanding.

"Don't see any blood though," Pierre said, standing up and surveying the ground around him. "She didn't cross creek here though. No foot prints on other side. She either walks up or down creek. Louie, Henri!"

The two dogs' heads snapped to attention. Pierre raised both arms up and pointed one in each direction. Immediately the two dogs separated. One headed up the creek and the other down the creek. I was surprised at how well the dogs minded Pierre.

"Which one is which?" I asked Pierre. "I can't tell them apart."

"That one, Louie," Pierre answered, pointing to the dog headed up the creek. "Other one is Henri. Easy to tell, boy. Henri has bigger feet than Louie. Ha, ha. Can't you tell?"

"Oh."

I wasn't sure if Pierre was fibbing me or not. I watched in fascination as Louie sniffed one side of the creek bank and then the other as he moved up the creek. Every once in a while, he would lap up a little water.

"Find anything in there?" a call came from the search party from the trees behind us.

"Not yet," Mr. Bucklin called back. "She's been here though. We found tracks near the creek. The dogs are trying to pick up her trail again." It didn't take long. Within moments, Henri let out a howl. Our heads snapped in his direction.

"There he goes," Pierre bellowed. "Let's get to our horses. Come, Louie."

The big red dog immediately returned at the sound of Pierre's call. Pierre raised his left arm and pointed in the direction Henri had gone. Immediately, Louie headed in the direction Pierre had pointed. Pierre watched his dog for a moment, and then, satisfied he would soon pick up the trail, he turned and started pushing his way through the brush back to his horse.

We all followed quickly and carefully behind, making sure no branches snapped back in our faces. The search party had waited for our return. None of them had gone after the dogs, which Pierre had expected. Quickly, we remounted, and, once again with Pierre in the lead and Mr. Bucklin right behind him, we were off chasing after the baying dogs.

Pierre headed his horse east along the tree line looking for an opening across the creek. Shortly, he found one and turned his horse right into it. We all followed single file through the narrow opening. When Pierre reached the top of the opposite creek bank, I saw him kick his horse in the flanks and gallop off after his dogs. He was headed straight toward the Smith place.

Maybe Jody was there, I thought to myself as Eddie and I cleared the creek bank and galloped after him. Maybe she had sought shelter at his place while we were out looking for her.

Shortly, we will know, I thought. I started to get excited.

Chapter

20

"She went in there," Pierre said, staring down at his dogs. Louie and Henri were standing, howling outside Wendell Smith's chicken shed.

"I think your dogs are crazy," Mr. Bucklin said, looking at the dogs. "I think your dogs picked up the scent of the chickens, and that's what they smell."

"If they come here," Pierre said angrily, "then your girl come here."

"Could be possible, now that you mention it," Wendell Smith said, pulling his horse up next to Mr. Bucklin's.

"What do you mean?" Mr. Bucklin asked.

"Well, I didn't think much of it at the time, but early this morning, before daylight, I heard all the chickens cackling and causing a commotion. I figured it was a fox or a coyote at the time. I got up and checked, but by the time I got out here everything had pretty much quieted down. I didn't find anything or see anything."

"She was here, see?" Pierre nodded confidently. "Let my dogs in."

"Hell, no, I won't," Mr. Smith said sharply. "They'll get my chickens."

"They won't touch one chicken," Pierre returned sharply. "If they touch one chicken, I pay for it. I know my dogs. They no chicken killers. Let them in."

Reluctantly, Mr. Smith dismounted and walked to the door of the chicken shed. The dogs anxiously waited for Mr. Smith to pull the door open. One slipped through the door as soon as it was open enough for him. The other quickly followed. The chickens inside started cackling loudly. I could hear the flutter of wings inside as the chickens flew around. Mr. Smith, now joined by Pierre, stood in front of the doorway staring inside. I couldn't see inside because of the two men blocking the doorway. The dogs weren't making any noise.

"Look," Pierre said, pointing into the shed. All of us strained from atop our mounts to see what he was pointing at. I couldn't see anything. Quickly Pierre stepped into the shed out of sight. Within moments, he reappeared in the doorway, carrying something in his hand. It was a little piece of white cloth. "Recognize this?"

Pierre held the cloth up to Mr. Bucklin to inspect.

"It's …it's part of Jody's nightgown," Mr. Bucklin said with a look of disbelief.

"Is there any blood on it?" Father asked, leaning over in his saddle trying to see better.

"No, no, there's no blood on it," Mr. Bucklin answered softly.

"Mr. Smith, is there another way out of the shed?" Pierre said.

"No, this is the only door other than the little one for the chickens. Jody couldn't get through them."

"Then she come back out this way. Louie, Henri, come."

The two dogs quickly reappeared at the command of Pierre. They both lay down near Pierre's feet and patiently waited for his next command.

"What does this all mean?" Mr. Bucklin asked, raising his head and staring off into space. "Why would she come here? What's she doing?"

"Maybe she was hungry," Mr. Smith said, trying to answer Mr. Bucklin. "Maybe she got some eggs or took one of the chickens."

"Who knows," Pierre said flatly. "Back up, everyone. Give my dogs room to find her track. We know she been here, so let them work. Back, back, everyone."

Pierre held his arms upward and pushed out at us to force us back. Eddie pulled back on the reins of our horse causing him to retreat. The rest of the search party did the same. Pierre wasn't satisfied until we were at least twenty-five yards from the shed.

"Did you find something?" called a voice to the right of us. It was Mrs. Smith. She came running up to her husband. Quickly Mr. Smith explained how the dogs had led them on a trail to their place and how they had found a piece of Jody's gown in the chicken shed. Mr. Smith asked his wife if she had seen anything and she gave a negative reply. With that, Mr. Smith asked his wife to go back to the house with instructions to keep her eyes open for any sign of Jody. Mrs. Smith obediently went back to the house.

"Find the track," Pierre called out to his dogs, pointing down at the ground. Immediately, the dogs began to sniff the ground. They crossed back and forth, trying to pick up the track. Neither was successful. They ranged out farther and farther from the front of the shed trying to find Jody's trail. Each dog went his own way, searching but to no avail. All of us watched the two dogs, spellbound.

"Louie, Henri," Pierre called out after a minute. "Come."

"What's the matter?" Mr. Bucklin called out to Pierre.

"Nothing," Pierre called back, still standing near the shed door. The dogs quickly returned to Pierre. Pierre knelt down to his dogs and pulled the white blouse from his belt. He rubbed the blouse on the noses of his two dogs. Once done, he stood and pointed out in the opposite direction with his arms. Immediately a dog went in each direction. Louie, or Henri, disappeared around one side of the shed. The other dog worked the other side of the shed as we all watched. Pierre quickly ran back to us and mounted his horse.

"What's the problem?" Mr. Bucklin asked.

"Nothing," Pierre said, flashing a big toothy smile. "We have her track in a minute now."

"What do you mean?" Mr. Bucklin asked.

"Her track on back side of shed. She go over the roof. That why Louie and Henri no find track around front of shed. Took Pierre a minute to figure it out though."

Pierre was confident he was right. He sat back in his saddle, calmly waiting for his prediction to come true. It did. Within moments after he spoke, a howl came up from the dog that was now behind the shed.

"See, Henri find her track, just like Pierre say. Let's go. We are getting closer to her all the time. I can feel it."

Pierre led us around the chicken shed after his dogs. We swung west after passing the shed. The howling dogs led us past two of Mr. Smith's bigger barns. One I recognized as the one we had had the barn dance in almost two years earlier. The sight of it quickly reminded me of that night when Jamie and I sneaked out to the barn and caught

Jody and John Northfield kissing in the moonlight. It almost seemed like yesterday.

Once past the buildings, Louie and Henri changed their direction slightly. They were headed in a southwesterly direction, almost paralleling the dirt road that lay several hundred yards to the left of us. I could see the dogs climb the hill up ahead of us and disappear over the side. The land around us was hilly and rather rough, even though it was almost barren of trees. There really wasn't a lot of cover for protection or hiding. I thought that maybe when we reached the top of the hill we would catch a glimpse of Jody off in the distance. It was possible.

"Looks like she's headed toward George Powell's ranch," Eddie said, when we reached the top of the hill. "His place lies beyond the next ridge, down in the valley. It's the last place between here and the river."

"How far is it?" I asked. My arms were clamped around Eddie's waist.

"I am guessing about a mile or so when we reach the next ridge," Eddie answered, pointing his right arm out ahead of him. "Should be pretty much all downhill, if I remember. Powell's ranch isn't all that far from the river, and the lay of the land slopes all pretty much down to the river."

As we neared the ridge, I got excited. I couldn't wait to see what was on the other side. I wondered what I would see. I hadn't been down this way to the river before, at least that I could remember. The view from the top of the ridge almost took my breath away. I never realized the ridge was so high up. I could see for miles. Way down below lay the Powell ranch. It was farther than the mile Eddie had said. I could see the ranch buildings dotted in and around a large group of trees way down in the valley. The surrounding countryside was a brilliant patchwork quilt of golds, oranges, and yellows mixed every so often with greens. Mr. Powell's ranch lay at the bottom of what looked like one half of a huge bowl. Dotted on the hillside straight behind his ranch to the north was a large herd of cattle. I wondered how many he had. Beyond his ranch at least another mile or so lay the Missouri River. Green trees lined most of the river bank as the river wound its way through the colorful countryside like a big green snake.

"What a sight," I said in awe. I never realized there was any ground so high up like this.

"Something else, isn't it? You've probably never realized it because whenever we come this way we always come down here by the road, and it is lower. See, look over there. It comes through the lowest part of the hills," Eddie replied.

"Yeah, I never noticed before."

The ride down the hill was not too bad. We could hear the howling of the dogs ahead of us. Every so often we would be able to catch a glimpse of them. They were heading straight to Mr. Powell's ranch.

"Think we're at the end of the line, Eddie?" I asked.

"Who knows. The Powell ranch is the last one between here and the river. Maybe she stopped, maybe she didn't. We'll know something pretty soon, I imagine."

As we neared the ranch, the grass we were riding in shortened. We could plainly see the backs of the dogs ahead of us. The dogs headed straight to the closest barn. It was a big barn. I could see a one-story house that sat fifty yards or so to the east of the big barn. The dogs, by this time, had entered the farmyard and were racing past the closest big barn. Their howling was louder as it echoed back to us off of the farm buildings. Beyond the first big barn was a second barn of equal size to the first. It was to this barn Louie and Henri were headed. As we reached the first barn, we saw Louie and Henri disappear into the second barn ahead of us.

"Think she took cover in the barn?" I asked Eddie as we rode on to the second barn.

"Kinda looks like it, don't it?" he replied.

Pierre was the first to reach the large double doors of the barn that the dogs had entered. He dismounted before his horse had even come to a full stop and raced inside. Eddie and I could hear the dogs howling loudly inside as we brought our horse to a stop along with the others. Mr. Bucklin and Father had already entered the barn after Pierre. Eddie and I dismounted as quickly as possible and ran the few yards to the barn door. We were motioned by Pierre and Father to stop and wait in the doorway of the barn. The rest of the search party waited in the doorway with us.

"Sh," hissed Pierre loudly at his barking dogs. The dogs quit their barking immediately. Both dogs' tails wagged back and forth excitedly.

Their heads were cocked back as they both looked up into the loft above them. "So, she got up there, huh, boys?"

"Jody, Jody, if you are up there, please come down," Mr. Bucklin called out. "It's alright, Jody. Please come on down now. Let's go home."

All eyes were on the loft. We all listened quietly for the sound of a footstep or a voice. I expected to see some straw or hay fall through the cracks in the loft floor, revealing some movement up above. There was none.

"What's going on?" a voice shot out from behind us. We all turned to see Mr. Powell pushing his way by us to get into his barn. He was a short man, with short, light blondish-brown hair. He wore gold wire-rimmed glasses that sat in the middle of the bridge on his nose. His complexion was smooth and light, and he was clean shaven.

"Don't you know?" Mr. Bucklin said, turning to Mr. Powell. "My girl, Jody, has run away. We are trying to find her."

"What makes you think she's here?" Mr. Powell said, with a puzzled look on his face.

"My dogs say so," Pierre said, pointing down to his two dogs. "They best tracking dogs in South Dakota. They say she climb up in your loft."

Mr. Powell's eyes looked up to the loft. He eyes quickly fell back on Pierre.

"Well, did you go up there and see?" Mr. Powell asked.

"We were hoping she would just come down on her own," Mr. Bucklin returned. "Have you heard or seen anything today or yesterday that seemed strange?"

"Nope, everything has been nice a quiet as usual around here. I haven't seen any sign of your girl or even any strangers for some time now."

"Jody, you can come down now. Come on," Mr. Bucklin called out impatiently to the loft.

We all waited and watched in silence. I think we all expected Jody to appear at the top of the ladder that extended down to where Pierre, Mr. Bucklin, Mr. Powell, and Father were standing. There was no sound of any kind from the loft.

"Do you mind?" Pierre said, pointing to the ladder while looking at Mr. Powell.

"No, I don't mind," Mr. Powell said, moving to the ladder.

"Thank you," Pierre said, cutting in front of Mr. Powell. Pierre grabbed a ladder rung with his left hand and slowly started climbing up to the loft. His great bulk completely hid the ladder as he climbed. Everyone waited anxiously for him to reach the top. Pierre reached the last ladder rung and stepped onto the floor of the loft. The boards creaked loudly under his heavy body. I could see the upper part of his body from where I stood. We all watched as Pierre stepped forward out of our view. The boards creaked beneath his feet as we heard him move slowly around the loft.

"Jody, Jody, it's alright, you come out," we heard Pierre call softly from above. My eyes followed the floor above me as I listened for Pierre's footsteps. After a few moments, the creaking of the boards returned to the ladder. The upper body of Pierre reappeared at the ladder.

"She's not here," Pierre called down, shrugging his shoulders.

"Are you sure?" Mr. Bucklin called back in disbelief.

"Sure, I sure. She's not here. But I think she has been here."

"I just can't believe—" Mr. Bucklin began to say.

"Mr. Bucklin," Pierre cut in, "you lift Louie up to me. We make sure."

Mr. Bucklin tried to pick Louie up. Even as big as Mr. Bucklin was, he had trouble handling the large dog. Seeing this, Father grabbed the back end of the dog and lifted. Together, Mr. Bucklin and Father raised the big dog over their heads, arms fully extended, to Pierre. Pierre knelt down and grabbed the ladder to steady himself with his right hand. He leaned over the edge of the loft floor and grabbed Louie by the back of his neck with his left hand. I couldn't believe how far the loose floppy skin pulled away from Louie's neck as Pierre swung the dog up into the loft. Pierre grunted loudly from his effort. Pierre stood up and brushed the dirt from his pants. Louie shook his head, flopping his ears loudly against the side of his head as if to resettle the balled-up skin on the back of his neck.

"Louie, find the track," Pierre ordered, pointing at the floor. Louie pointed his nose to the floor and immediately came up with the scent. "See, I told you, didn't I? Come on, Louie. Louie, come back here!"

Pierre quickly turned and disappeared from our sight. The boards creaked loudly as we heard Pierre move quickly down the loft to the west end of the barn.

"Louie, Louie, stop," Pierre yelled in his booming voice. Wide-eyed we wondered what was the matter. Outside the barn, we suddenly heard a wild howl. It was a dog yelping in pain. It was the sound a dog would only make when in pain or injured. Our eyes all focused on the west wall of the barn, the direction the whining came from. In the excitement no one even noticed Pierre returning to the ladder. "Louie, he jump out the loft. Right out of the loft, twelve, fifteen feet down he jump. Crazy dog."

Pierre was yelling almost hysterically as he practically jumped off the loft to reach the ground. Some of the men behind us were already racing to the west end of the barn to find the dog.

"Come on, Ralph," Eddie said, pulling on my shirt. "Let's go see."

I turned and ran after Eddie, heading outside the barn after the other men. As we rounded the edge we saw the others standing in a semicircle around the dog. Louie lay on the ground, breathing heavily. He was not whining. Henri was calmly standing beside his partner. We ran up by the other men. Louie lifted his head up and looked over his right shoulder as if he expected it to be Pierre.

"Oh, look at that," Eddie said, pointing to Louie's right shoulder.

"I can't look, it makes me sick" I said turning away. The dog's right leg was broken. A white bone stuck out. I had never seen anything like it. I didn't want to ever see anything like it again. I felt sick to my stomach. I had to get away so I ran back to the barn, out of sight of the poor dog. As I rounded the corner I ran into Pierre. I bounced so hard off his stomach that I lost my balance and fell backward to the ground. Pierre grunted loudly.

"Watch where you going, boy," he said, stepping past me. He disappeared around the edge of the barn followed by Mr. Bucklin. I turned and watched them run by. I felt a strong hand on my right upper arm. I turned back to see my father pulling me back up.

"Ralph, watch where you are going, dammit," Father scolded me.

"I'm sorry, but the sight of the dog just made me sick. His right leg is broken, and the bone is sticking out this far," I said, spreading my first fingers of both hands about three inches apart. "It's awful."

"Oh, I see," Father said sympathetically. "I didn't know it was like that."

"Will he be all right?" I said, fighting back the moisture in my eyes.

"Oh, I think so. You can set the legs of a dog. It's not the same as with a horse, Ralph. He may not be much of a tracker anymore, but I would imagine that Mr. Beauchard will take the time to heal him up. I'm sure he thinks too much of the dog. You can tell it."

"Think so?" I asked, comforted by his words.

"Sure."

"What's going on?" Eddie said, suddenly appearing.

"Oh, he bumped into Pierre and got knocked down, that's all," Father answered.

"How's the dog?" I asked anxiously.

"They are trying to pull the bone back through the skin. I couldn't watch; it was making me sick. Pierre says he's gonna put splints on it and wrap the leg if he can get it reset right. He says he has done it before, so he thinks he can do it again."

"Good," I said, feeling better from Eddie's words.

"See, I told you, son. It's not the same as with a horse. Pierre seems to be a good man. He'll take care of him."

Father started brushing the dust from me. His tough fingers stung my legs several times as he slapped at the dirt on my pants. It reminded me of a spanking or two I had received from time to time. When I was brushed off, Father left me and went over to join the other men watching Pierre. I stuck my head around the corner and watched from a distance. Through the legs of the men, I could see Pierre kneeling on the ground working on the dog. Men huddled around the dog with Pierre.

After a few minutes, the men stepped back. Pierre had picked the big bloodhound up and cradled him in his arms. The dog never cried out once, and Pierre, followed by the rest of the men, headed for Mr. Powell's back porch. I followed along too, but at a little distance, afraid of seeing something that would make me ill. Pierre gently laid the dog on the porch. I watched him gently pat him on the head. Pierre softly spoke to the dog. He checked the knots on the red and white neckerchiefs that he had used to tie the splints on.

Satisfied that the splints were on as good as possible, Pierre turned toward Mr. Powell. We all listened as he asked Mr. Powell to care for his dog. Mr. Powell was going to be staying around his place anyway, so there was no problem. Pierre asked Mr. Powell to get some water for Louie and to feed him whatever he could toward suppertime. Pierre said he would be back with his wagon sometime tonight to pick up his dog, whether they found Jody or not. He asked Mr. Powell if he could sleep in the barn should they not find Jody so that the men could take up the next morning. Mr. Powell said there was no problem. He would take care of the dog, and Pierre could do as he pleased for sleeping arrangements.

"Come on, men. It's getting near suppertime, and we still have a ways to go," Pierre announced, waving his left hand aloft as he pushed through the men.

"I'm gonna head home, John," Wendell Smith piped up, looking at Mr. Bucklin. "I have chores to do, and it is getting on to suppertime. If I had some hired hands, or someone that could do the chores, you know I'd stay."

Mr. Bucklin stood and looked at Mr. Smith for a long moment. I tried to study his eyes to read what they were saying. His face had a blank expression.

"It's alright," Mr. Bucklin said, breaking the silence. "I understand. It has been a long day, and I know some of you have things to do. If any of you men must leave, feel free to go. I understand. You were good enough to search yesterday and today, and I appreciate that. So you go ahead. I have no hard feelings."

"Thanks, John," Mr. Smith said. "We knew you would understand." He walked past Mr. Bucklin back to his horse near the barn. As he did so, the majority of the search party followed. Each man stopped briefly by Mr. Bucklin and gave him encouraging words. Mr. Bucklin nodded understandingly to each man. When the last man passed, Mr. Bucklin turned and went to his horse. There were only four of us left to follow—Pierre, Father, Eddie, and me. Everyone else was leaving.

"I'm starved," I whispered into Eddie's ear after mounting.

"Then ride back with one of the others. Someone will give you a ride."

"No, I want to go on Eddie. It's just that I am hungry. My stomach is growling."

"Don't feel too bad, Ralph. I haven't eaten any more than you have, and I'm hungry too."

"I'm sure we are all hungry," Father said, hearing our conversation, "but we have to see this out while it is daylight, you know?"

"We know," Eddie said, shaking his head in agreement.

"Henri, come here," Pierre called out, pointing to a spot on the ground in front of him. The dog obeyed immediately. Pierre knelt down on one knee and once again pulled the white blouse from his belt. He pushed it into Henri's face. "Find her, boy, you gotta find her now. No more scent after today. Take us to her, Henri."

The big red dog sniffed intently at the blouse. Henri turned away from Pierre and began sniffing at the ground. Quickly he moved around the barnyard until he reached the area where Louie had jumped. Within seconds, Henri had picked up the scent once again and let out a long, loud howl. He broke off in a run to the northwest, passing between the barn and a small storage shed.

"He's got her, men" Pierre said, remounting his horse. "We gonna find her now."

Together the five of us galloped off in pursuit of Pierre's dog. By the time we passed the shed and headed out into open country, Henri was at the top of a small hill. He disappeared over the hill howling all the while. Our horses' hooves pounding on the dry brown grass sounded like thunder to me.

When we reached the top of the hill, I could see the trees lining the Missouri River to the west of us. The countryside in front of us was quite hilly and prevented us from seeing any more of the Missouri. I knew that as we climbed each hill we would be able to catch a glimpse of the river. Each hill was like a finger extending out to the river. I could see Henri way up in front of us when we cleared the second hill. Some of Mr. Powell's cattle dotted the hillside to our right in the distance. They looked like tree stumps against the light brown grass. Henri had already reached the bottom of the valley and was halfway to the top of the third hill. He was actually pulling away from us as he ran.

"Look at that dog run!" exclaimed Eddie as we watched little clouds of dust rise from under Henri's feet.

"He really got her scent," Pierre yelled out excitedly. "He is closing in on her."

"I hope so. I sure hope so," Mr. Bucklin added as we all rode together after the howling dog. Henri disappeared over the third hill just as we neared the bottom of the valley. With the pounding of the horses' hooves, we could no longer hear Henri howling. It was almost like a race between the five of us on our four horses to see which one would reach the top of the hill first. Everyone was going flat out to get there. Father won, followed by Mr. Bucklin.

"Hold up," Pierre yelled loudly to Father and Mr. Bucklin.

We reached the top of the hill at the same time as Pierre. Father and Mr. Bucklin had pulled their horses to a stop.

"What's the matter?" Mr. Bucklin asked, somewhat annoyed.

"Listen," Pierre said, cupping his left hand to his left ear. We all listened intently. The only thing we could hear was the horses coughing or breathing heavily after the fast, long run.

"I don't hear anything," Mr. Bucklin said. "Come on, let's go."

"Go where?" Pierre said. "You gonna chase dog you can't hear or see?"

Mr. Bucklin cocked his head back and held it still for a long moment. Only his eyes moved as he listened.

"You are right, I don't hear him. What happened to him? What does it mean?"

"It mean he think he find something. He stop howling when he think he find something. That only problem with Henri. He stops howling."

"How are we gonna find him?" Father asked. "Look at the sage trees, brush, and grass in this valley that leads down to the river. He's gonna be impossible to see."

"I know, it be hard, but we know he in here somewhere, or we would hear him going up next ridge. Right?"

"Sounds about right to me," Father said.

"Well, let's get the hell looking, okay, fellas?" Mr. Bucklin said angrily. "Or would you rather sit here until dark to watch the moon come up. It's my daughter out there you know; this ain't no picnic we're on."

"Easy, Mr. Bucklin," Pierre said, raising his right hand in an Indian greeting sign. "Let's spread out along the hill from here, down toward the river. We will sweep down across valley up to other side. If we don't find anything, we move on line down toward river and come back through again.

"How do you know your dog is not hurt?" Father said hesitantly.

"Don't know for sure, but we hope that not the case. Let's go now."

Pierre pulled on the left rein of his bridle and slowly walked his horse along the hill that gently sloped down to the river. After moving ten yards or so, he called back to Eddie and me to stay right where we were. We were to be at one end of the line, and Pierre would be at the other. Dad and Mr. Bucklin were to drop off between us. We were to spread out about thirty to fifty yards apart, depending on how thick the cover was in front of us. It only took a few minutes to set up our line.

"It would be nice to have the other men now," Eddie said. "We would darn near be able to cover the valley in one pass."

"Yea, I know."

"I wonder what happened to his dog. Think he's hurt?" I asked, hoping not.

"Who knows. We will find out."

Pierre raised his right hand and extended it out in front of him. It was the signal for us to start across the valley. Eddie nudged our horse forward in a walk. I watched the valley that lay before us, intently looking for a sign of the dog. The setting sun cast crazy shadows of the trees and bushes before us. It would be hard to see the dog, I thought. There was only going to be an hour or so more of sunlight. My stomach growled loudly. I was tired and hungry, but I couldn't complain because I knew the others were feeling the same way.

"There he is," came a wild yell from Pierre. "I see him."

He kicked his horse in the flank and took off in a gallop down the valley. The rest of us quickly responded and were chasing after Pierre through the brown high-grass field.

"I see him. Eddie. I see him too," I yelled excitedly into my brother's ear.

"Where?"

"Right through that little patch of trees. See?"

I raised my left arm and pointed over Eddie's left shoulder to a dark spot on the opposite hillside through the trees. Standing right in front of that dark spot was Henri. He was wagging his tail back and forth. His red back stood out brightly from the sun striking it.

"Yeah, I see him, Ralph," Eddie said, changing the direction of our horse slightly to the left to head straight to the dog. Pierre had already passed through the trees in the bottom of the valley and was heading up the other side to the dark spot on the hillside. I could see Father and

Mr. Bucklin slapping their horses in their rears with their reins, trying to close the distance to Pierre.

"Come on, Eddie. Won't this horse go any faster?"

"I'm trying, Ralph, but he can only go so fast, you know?"

"Well, let's hurry. I don't want to miss anything," I said as we entered the trees in the bottom of the valley. For a brief moment, we lost sight of the others. The trees blocked our view. When we reached the other side, we could see Pierre just swinging out of his saddle. Father and Mr. Bucklin were still forty yards or so away. Eddie and I were about a hundred yards away.

"Think they found her?" I said to Eddie.

"We'll know in a minute" Eddie replied as we neared the others. When we reached the others the three men were standing in front of a small cave. The hole cut back into the hillside. There was a narrow opening, but large enough to let a person, even someone the size of Pierre, enter.

"Think she's in there?" Mr. Bucklin asked.

"Call to her," Pierre said. "We find out."

"Jody … Jody, are you in there?"

There was no answer.

"Jody. If you are in there, please come out. It's alright, honey. Please come out."

There was still no answer. We waited silently for a sound to come from the cave.

"What do you think?" Mr. Bucklin said, after a few moments.

"I think we better check inside," Pierre said, bending forward, trying to get a better look inside the black cave. "I check it out."

Pierre reached into his right front pants pocket and pulled out several wood matches. He transferred all but one to his left hand. He knelt down on his hands and knees in front of the small entrance. He took the match in his right hand and struck it against a small rock near the entrance to the cave. Flame burst from the end of the match. Pierre waited until the match burned with a steady flame before entering. Slowly he crawled into the small mouth of the cave. His large body almost completely filling the hole. His backside was really big, I thought. Pierre inched farther and farther into the hole. We couldn't see any light inside the hole; Pierre blocked it off so much. Eddie and I excitedly waited to see what he would find. Father and Mr. Bucklin had tense expressions on their faces. Mr. Bucklin wrung his hands together as if he were washing them.

Suddenly Pierre let out a wild scream that was muffled by the cave. It raised the hair on the back of my neck and gave me chills. Pierre scrambled wildly to back out of the cave. His large bottom struck the roof of the cave, and he appeared almost to be stuck. Instantly, Father reached for Pierre's left foot. He pulled hard, and Pierre fell to the ground. Mr. Bucklin instinctively grabbed Pierre's right foot, and together he and Dad pulled Pierre from the hole. They rolled Pierre over on his back. He was as white as a sheet. Big beads of sweat covered his forehead. Pierre lay there, panting heavily trying to catch his breath.

"What's wrong, what's wrong?" Mr. Bucklin yelled, shaking Pierre. "What, what did you find in there?"

"Quit shaking me," Pierre screamed angrily, ripping Mr. Bucklin's hands from his clothes. Pierre sat up and with both hands covered his face and wiped the sweat away.

"What's in there Pierre?" Mr. Bucklin demanded.

"Rattlesnakes!" Pierre yelled, his eyes bugging out. "Rattlesnakes. It's a den full of them."

"There was nothing else?" Mr. Bucklin said, shocked.

"No, nothing," Pierre said, still panting heavily. "Some of the biggest snakes I ever saw. Must have been a hundred of them."

"Did you get bit?" Father asked excitedly.

"No, no I don't think so. I think one struck out though, but he must have missed me. I don't feel no pain. Their damn eyes stuck out like firebugs in the night. Little beady bastards they were."

"Let me see your hands, Pierre," Father said, bending over him. Pierre held both of his big hands up. Carefully, one at a time, Father checked Pierre's hands, first the right, then the left. Father pulled back Pierre's sleeves to expose his forearms. "No it doesn't look like you were bit, Pierre. Save for this broken tooth in the seam of your leather coat."

"What tooth?" Pierre said, blinking his eyes. Father held his right hand out to Pierre. Pinched between the thumb and first finger was a white piece of tooth. It looked like a small fish bone.

"See that, Pierre?" Father said, balancing the tooth on his index finger. "You must have moved fast enough that the snake just missed. One of the teeth broke off in your jacket."

"Creepy little bastards, let's burn them out and get rid of them," Pierre muttered, standing up brushing himself off.

"We'll do that later," Mr. Bucklin said. "Right now we're looking for someone, remember? We haven't got much time left today, and if you want your money, Pierre, we better find her, remember?"

"I don't give a damn about the money, no more. Almost worth it to stop right here, and go home. Your girl leads us on goose chase. Go all over place, through chicken house, up barn loft; Louie break leg, I almost get bit by rattler—Henri too, if he run into cave. Good thing he smart dog. No, it not worth it to me to go on. Who know what happen next. In fact, I quit. Let's go, Henri."

"No, wait," Mr. Bucklin pleaded, grabbing Pierre's arm. Mr. Bucklin quickly released his grip and put his arm down. Pierre looked down into Mr. Bucklin's eyes. You could almost see the fire in Pierre's eyes.

"What you want?" Pierre said in a low calm voice.

"I … I'm sorry, Pierre. I know things haven't gone well through the whole day. Please don't quit us now. We're close, I can feel it. I'll pay you no matter what happens—even double the amount if you will stay. We're all tired and hungry, and the day will soon be gone. Try to imagine how you would feel if it was your daughter. You would want me to go on, wouldn't you?"

Mr. Bucklin's voice wavered as he spoke. I couldn't tell if he was begging or trying to hold back from crying. I remembered seeing Mr. Bucklin crying at the train station. It was when we were coming back with Mr. Northfield's body.

Pierre turned away and walked a few feet over to his horse. He put his left foot in the stirrup and swung back into the saddle. He pulled Jody's white blouse from his belt and threw it to Mr. Bucklin. Pierre checked the sun in the west. It was coming down fast on the horizon.

"There is not much time left, Mr. Bucklin," Pierre said in a soft voice, looking him in the eye. "Stick the blouse in Henri's face. Maybe we can go a little longer."

"Thank you, Pierre," Mr. Bucklin said with a faint smile. "Thank you."

Mr. Bucklin quickly bent over Henri and let the dog sniff the blouse. The dog sniffed the blouse for a long moment.

"Find her," Pierre ordered loudly, waving his left arm out before him. The big dog began to sniff the ground around the same entrance. Back and forth he went. "I hope there still good scent. Should be. Henri led us this far."

Within moments, the bloodhound picked up the scent above the mouth of the cave. Off Henri ran west toward the river. Pierre reined his horse after his dog. Eddie, seeing Pierre take off, kicked our horse after him. Over my shoulder, I watched Father and Mr. Bucklin mount their horses and start after us. Henri cleared the hillside quickly. Pierre was trailing his dog by forty yards. Eddie and I weren't much behind Pierre.

We rode straight toward the setting sun. It was hard to see where we were going when we were riding up the hill. After clearing the ridge, I could see the tree line of the river ahead of us. The trees were black as they were hidden by the hills on the other side of the river from the sun.

"She's headed right to the river, isn't she, Eddie?" I said, hanging on to Eddie with my arms around his stomach.

"Looks like it," Eddie replied.

"Boy, it's hard to see. The sun is right in my eyes."

"I know, but I can hear Pierre and Henri up ahead of us. Hear 'em?"

"Yeah."

I could hear Henri howling up ahead of us as we rode straight west to the river. The sun was so low it was hard to even make out the top of the tree line along the river. Over my shoulder I could see Father and Mr. Bucklin gaining on us. It looked as though they were riding through fire as the grass was a bright reddish orange where the setting sun was striking it. They were only twenty yards behind us.

The ground sloped very gently to the river. In fact, it almost seemed to level out. The sun made it almost impossible to see. The only thing that directed us was the sound of Henri and Pierre in front of us. Henri was baying louder it seemed. It was impossible to see him, or for that matter, even Pierre. Henri suddenly let out a wild howl, not the kind of baying or howling he had been doing before. It was the kind of cry a dog lets out when he has been struck or hurt. The cry he let out faded quickly, and then we heard nothing.

"He's hurt! Eddie, he's hurt! I yelled, pounding on his shoulder with my right hand.

"I hear it, Ralph, I hear it."

"Stop quick, stop," Pierre yelled loudly. "Stop."

Eddie pulled back hard on the reins, bringing our horse to a dead stop. I could hear Father and Mr. Bucklin bring their horses to a stop right behind us.

"What's the matter?" Eddie called out to Pierre.

"Look, look right there," Pierre said. Eddie and I shaded our eyes from the sun. I could make out the silhouette of Pierre pointing down in front of him. Eddie edged our horse over to him. "It's a good thing you stop, boys. Look."

I could see it, a sheer drop off down to the river. It was straight down maybe forty or fifty feet into a dark pool of water. Father and Mr. Bucklin walked their horses up to us.

"Where's your dog?" Eddie asked, concerned.

"He went over the edge. He down there somewhere. I hear him hit the water. Good thing we not go over the edge. Maybe we break our necks. You think she go over the edge, Mr. Bucklin?"

"I don't know," Mr. Bucklin said hesitantly. "I know Jody can swim, but from this height, I don't know what would happen, and who knows how deep it is."

"Well the track end here. Henri tells us so."

"There's your dog, Pierre," Father said, pointing down in the river. We could see Henri swimming in the river below. He was headed downstream looking for a place to get out.

"Thank heavens, he not hurt," Pierre said, sighing in relief. "What you want to do, Mr. Bucklin?"

"I don't know," Mr. Bucklin said, covering his eyes with his right hand. I thought he was hiding some tears, but I wasn't sure. Mr. Bucklin sucked in a deep breath of air and let it out slowly. "I suppose we ought to call it quits for today. I'll have to come down to the river and search for her tomorrow, I guess."

"You mean "we," don't you?" Pierre said encouragingly. "I not quit you now, no matter what happen. You need me and Henri's help to see this to the end. I don't quit now, whether you pay me or not."

"I'll be with you too," Father added. "What time you want to start?"

"Sunrise," Mr. Bucklin said gratefully. "Thanks, Pierre. Thanks for understanding."

"Let's bring some food; it might be a long day," Father added.

"What about us, Dad?" Eddie asked. "Can we go?"

"You boys will have chores to do in the morning, so you will have to stay behind."

"Aw, Dad," Eddie whined. "Can't we go?"

"You missed all your chores today," Father said sternly. "Now that's all there is to it."

Eddie and I didn't argue; we knew it would be useless. I sat silently on our horse, staring down into the water below us.

"Here comes, Henri," Father said, pointing to the left of us. "He looks all right."

The big red dog walked slowly up to us. When he reached Pierre's side, Henri shook himself, spraying beads of water in all directions. Pierre turned his horse and started it in a slow walk back up the slope. The rest of us turned and followed in silence. Our silhouettes stretched far up the slope in front of us. I turned and looked back over my shoulder. The sun was more than half hidden on the western horizon. I knew it would be a sad, silent ride home. I knew that there were many thoughts running through all of our minds. Each of us was trying to figure out what it all meant.

Our trail had been a strange one for sure. It had led us through a chicken shed and a barn, to a rattlesnake den, and over some rough hilly country, and our only sure clue was the bloody handkerchief on the fence with the razor inside. Yet there was no other blood to be found the whole day. And we couldn't find another piece of her nightgown anywhere, even though she went through bushes and buildings and fences. Jody's trail ended at a high river bluff. Did she jump or did she fall? I didn't know. She had acted strangely in the past, but this was even stranger, I thought. I wondered where she was, and I was saddened because I knew I wouldn't get a chance to go with them in the morning. Eddie and I would have to stay behind.

Chapter

21

"Come on, Ralph. Let's go," Eddie yelled at me, setting his hoe down against the storage shed wall.

"Go where?" I asked, setting my hoe beside his.

"To the river, that's where."

"We can't go to the river, Eddie. You heard what Father said."

"Sure, I heard what Father said. That's why we're going."

"What do you mean?"

"Father said we couldn't go because of our chores. But he didn't say we couldn't go after our chores were done, did he?"

"No, but he didn't say we could go after they were done either."

"That's true, so that's why I'm going. You coming or not?"

I stood here, silently trying to decide if we were doing the right thing. I didn't want to get in trouble, but I did want to find out what was going on. I watched as Eddie led the horse we had ridden yesterday out of the barn. Eddie lifted his left foot up to the stirrup and pulled himself into the saddle. Eddie looked at me, waiting for my answer.

"Okay, I suppose if you think we won't get into too much trouble, neither do I."

I went over to Eddie and raised my hands up to him. I put my left foot in the stirrup, and Eddie pulled me up behind him.

"We'll go to where we lost the trail yesterday, at the river bluff."

Okay," I said, adjusting my sore bottom on the back of the horse. I still hurt from all the riding the last two days, and I wasn't sure how much more I could take. Slowly, Eddie walked our horse down our lane to the road. It would take us an hour or more to get there. The sun was beginning to rise high in the sky in the east. It was about ten thirty, I figured. Once we reached the road, Eddie kicked our horse into a trot. The bouncing made my bottom hurt even more"

"Take it easy, Eddie. My butt is killing me."

"Well, I'm sore too, you know."

"Yeah, but at least you are in the saddle. That's got to make it a little easier on you."

Eddie slowed the horse to a fast walk. We rode along, discussing the events of the two days before. Eddie had tried to figure out what was going on, just as I had. He didn't have an answer either.

An hour or more had passed. Eddie and I stopped at the Powell place to ask where our father and the others were. Mrs. Powell told us that the men had stopped to see how Pierre's dog was, and, after seeing that Louie was okay, they had headed up to the bluff where the trail had ended. We thanked Mrs. Powell and told her that we were going to go up to the bluff too.

Eddie turned our horse and headed him past Mr. Powell's buildings to the rolling hills behind his place. I knew it wouldn't take long for us to get there. I started getting excited at the thought of finding something out.

"Can't you make the horse go faster? I want to get there."

"What about your sore butt?"

"Hang my sore butt. I want to get there."

"Alright," Eddie replied, kicking our horse into a gallop. The slapping of my butt on the back of the horse hurt, but I didn't complain. It wouldn't be but a few more minutes before we would be there. I could see the rattlesnake den clearly on the opposite hillside in the sun after clearing the first ridge. I told Eddie to stay away from it, but it didn't matter. He headed our horse in that direction. Eddie was smart enough not to get too close though, because he knew that snakes would be moving in and out of it as the sun warmed the ground. I hated snakes and didn't like to see them, but I made myself look when we neared and passed the den. I didn't see any.

We crossed the last ridge to the river and started down the long, gentle slope to the bluff. The sun shone brightly on the dark green leaves of the trees lining the river. Funny how it didn't look like there would be a sheer bluff before you reached the river and the trees on the other side. It looked as though there would be a small rise and then the ground would slope gradually down to the river. As we neared the bluff, Eddie slowed our horse to a walk. Within a matter of moments, we were at the bluff's edge.

"That is really deceiving," Eddie said, staring down at the water below." I thought the edge was still up there farther. I can see how Pierre's dog went over the edge."

"See anyone?" I said, sliding off the back end of the horse. I landed on the ground with a jolt that seemed to make my sore, stiff butt muscles bounce.

"No, I don't," Eddie said, dismounting. "What do you think we should do?"

"Probably ought to check the river bank downstream on this side of the bluff, right?"

"Brilliant deduction, Ralph. It would probably be unlikely she would go upstream, but you never know. Enough strange things have happened already. But we can check for footprints and see if we find any."

We walked our horse along the edge of the bluff. The ground sloped sharply down to trees and bushes that began to line the river bank at the west end of the bluff. We would see that there was a good ten-to-twenty-yard thickness of trees and bushes that lined the bank between us and the river. The tree line ran several hundred yards south along the river bank before disappearing around a river bend.

"You go on in there, Ralph, and walk along the river bank. I'll stay out here and walk the horse along. In case you find anything, we'll have the horse right with us to go."

"Gee, thanks a lot, Eddie. Give me the dirty work. Are there rattlers in there?" I asked nervously.

"Nah, rattlers don't get near the water."

"You sure?"

"Here, take this with you then," Eddie said, picking up a large stick and tossing it to me. "Beat the ground in front of you with it if you are scared."

"I'm not scared," I yelled, throwing the stick down at his feet. I turned and pushed my way through some of the bushes. It was hard getting through them, but once I did, I found the going a little easier. There weren't nearly as many bushes along the water edge, just trees;

most were standing, but some were down, and I had to climb over or crawl under them. I looked back over my shoulder to see if I could spot Eddie. I couldn't.

"Eddie, you there?"

"Yeah, I'm here. Find something already?"

"No, just couldn't see where you were, that's all. It's kinda thick in here between me and you."

"Well, get looking. We haven't got all day, you know?"

Slowly, I made my way south along the river bank. With logs and sticks from dead trees lining the bank, it was difficult going. The dead branches would crack and snap beneath my feet. It would be hard to find tracks here, so I checked for broken twigs and sticks on the ground before me. I checked my tracks to see how I had broken sticks and then checked to see if there was anything like it in front of me. Nothing.

"Don't find anything yet," I said, rising to get the ache out of my back. Ahead of me something caught my eye. It was bright and shiny against the sunlight that managed to strike it through the trees. Whatever it was, it swayed gently back and forth in the light breezes. The object held my eyes like a magnet. I went to it as fast as I could, cracking twigs and sticks loudly as I went. When I had moved to within a few feet of the object, I knew what it was. It was Jody's locket! The gold locket she had worn on her wedding day. The locket I had seen her wear on other occasions. I stared at the locket as if hypnotized. There it was, hanging on a large dead tree trunk. There were barefoot prints leading to the river's edge ten feet away.

"What's going on in there, Ralph?" Eddie yelled. "Ralph, Ralph."

"Ralph, Ralph, what's the matter, dear?"

I blinked my eyes.

"What do you mean?" I said, looking about me. "Where, where am I?"

"You're at the fair, dear. Don't you remember?"

Oh, yeah. I ... I remember, but what happened?"

"Why, Ralph, you mean to tell me that you sat right here and asked that man a question and didn't even hear what he said?"

"No ... no, I didn't. I ... I started recalling all of those things he said about the torches and the razor and ... and everything. I was back there again, living it all over again. What did he say? What did he say?"

"Well, if you didn't hear it, I'm not going to tell you," Martha said, crossing her arms defiantly. I looked around the hot, stuffy tent. Everyone else had gone. Beads of sweat rolled down my face.

"Where is that Mr. Darden anyway?" I asked anxiously.

"He already left until evening," Martha answered.

"Well, what the hell did he say?" I said angrily, staring straight into her eyes.

"If you must know, I'll tell you. But I will tell you this. I think all of this is nonsense, you hear, nonsense."

"Okay, okay. It's nonsense, but I asked the question, so let's hear what he said."

"All he said," Martha started with a big sigh, "was that maybe you could find the answer at Shell."

"At Shell? What the hell does Shell mean?" I asked excitedly.

"Shell is Shell, Wyoming. Darden said it's a little town about sixty or seventy miles or so up in the Bighorn Mountains. He said he didn't know the road number but it was on the road to Greybull."

"What will I find?" I asked, grabbing Martha's right arm.

"He didn't say you would find anything for sure. He said to park at the general store and walk about back one hundred yards or so behind it and that maybe you would find your answer."

I looked at my wife with a puzzled face. What did that mean? What she said didn't make a whole lot of sense to me.

"Are you fibbing to me?" I asked sternly.

"No, Ralph, that's exactly what he said," Martha said with a straight face. "But it's nonsense. What could be there? I think he made it up to send you on a wild goose chase."

I listened intently to my wife's words. She was right. None of it made sense. I had never even heard of Shell, Wyoming. It wasn't anywhere near where Jody or I had lived. Why would Darden mention that place? But, yet, he was right about the other things, the initials and all that.

"You're right, dear, it doesn't make sense," I said, standing up.

"Well, it's about time you listened to me."

"Let's go, dear," I said, tugging on her right arm.

"We're going home now?"

"Hell, no, we're going to Shell," I answered, pulling her along with me to the tent exit.

"What?" Martha cried out, planting her feet solidly on the ground like a stubborn mule.

"That's right, Martha, Don't you see? All these years I never knew the answer. I wondered and wondered what happened to her. I was there, Martha. I went with the others. I wanted to know just like the others. If it were you, wouldn't you want to know?"

"No," Martha answered stubbornly. "It's hogwash."

"Well, I have to know," I said angrily. "I know his answer doesn't make any sense, but he was right about some of the other things. Maybe it is a wild goose chase, but I would kick myself the rest of my life if I didn't check it out."

"Well," Martha said, giving in a little. "Alright, Ralph, but I will tell you this. If we don't find anything, you will never ever hear the end of it. I'll never let you, understand?"

"Thanks, honey," I said happily, giving her a peck on the cheek." Let's get going."

I pulled my wife's arm as I led her as fast as possible to our Plymouth car. It was getting on toward evening, and I knew we would have to hurry if Martha and I were to get to Shell with any daylight left. I hoped and prayed more than anything that my old car would make it up the mountain to Shell.

Chapter

22

"Gosh, there isn't much here, is there?" I said, turning off the car. It was about half past six when we reached Shell. I patted the dashboard of my car and thanked it silently for getting us here. Shell wasn't much of a town. There were only eight buildings in the whole town, and six of those were old run-down houses. One was an old hotel that had the words "Old Shell Hotel and Diner" painted across the top of it. The other building was the general store that had a big sign hanging from the top of the front porch painted with the words "Bertha's General Store." There was one gas pump in front of it.

I got out of the car quickly and waited for Martha. When she reached me, I took her arm and together we walked past the old general store through the long, brown grass. My heart was racing. What would I find?

A dirt path sloped gently up the hill behind the general store. One hundred yards, I thought. I tried to count my steps, but I kept getting mixed up on my count in my excitement.

"Look there," Martha said, pointing with her left arm. "See that iron fence?"

"Yes," I answered, my chest pounding wildly from either the altitude or my excitement.

Martha and I walked straight to it. As we neared, I made it out to be a small cemetery. I let go of Martha's arm and quickened my pace to get there. I passed through the narrow old rusty gate and under a sign that read "Peaceful Place." The grass was high enough that only the tops of the gravestones appeared. I could see the cemetery hadn't been cared for in a long time.

I started checking the headstones excitedly.

Mildred E. Lebo
Born July 3, 1808
Died Jan. 9, 1900
Age 91 Yrs., 6 Mos., 5 days

Sarah Ethington
Daughter of Todd and Kimberly
Born Feb. 12, 1884
Died March 8, 1887
Age 3 Yrs., 24 days

Jerry Bryant
Born Unknown
Died July 3, 1872

And so it went. I searched the small cemetery looking at tombstones. None of them meant anything to me as far as I was concerned, but I continued to check the headstones one by one.

"Ralph, come here," Martha called excitedly to me. "Look at this one."

I snapped to attention at the sound of her voice. I looked at Martha, who was waving her right arm wildly above her head for me to come over. I ran to her as fast as I could through the high grass. I had to lift my knees high.

"What do you think of this?" Martha said, pointing to a wood grave marker in front of her. I bent over and pushed some of the grass aside so I could read it.

Unknown Woman?
Born Unknown
Died Unknown
Buried Dec. 6, 1909

"Wow," I whistled softly. "That's strange, isn't it?"
"What do you think, Ralph?"

"I … I don't know for sure, but you wait here for a minute." I stood up and ran through the high grass back toward the general store. I was hoping someone would be there—someone who I could ask about the unusual grave marker. There had to be someone there, I kept telling myself as I neared the store. I quickly rounded the side of the building and went up the three front steps that led to the front door. I grabbed the door handle and turned the knob. Locked.

"Damnation," I said out loud. I started banging on the door, hoping someone would answer. I peered through the door window, trying to see inside. It was dark inside, and I couldn't see much. Again I banged on the door, so hard that the whole door shook, vibrating every window in the front of the store.

"Hold yer horses," came a screeching yell from the back of the building. Through the window, I could see light pour through a door that opened in the back part of the building. I tapped my foot impatiently on the porch floor as I waited for the person to come to the door.

As the person neared, I could see it was an old woman. She was very small and her hair was completely white and scraggly. I wondered when she had combed it last. Her face was brown and very wrinkled. I was almost sure she was Indian.

"I'm closed, Sonny. What do you want?" the old lady called in a high screechy voice from the other side of the door.

"I need to ask you a question. I don't want to buy anything."

"What did you say, boy? Speak up," the old lady whined.

"Open the door," I hollered at her through my cupped hands. The old lady flipped the lock on the door and opened it about a foot.

"What do you want, boy?" the old lady squealed through a mouth half full of rotten teeth. Her breath almost took mine away.

"That grave back there behind your place, the one of the unknown woman with no name on the wooden marker."

"Yeah, what about it?"

"What can you tell me about it?" I asked nervously, not knowing what to expect.

"What do you want to know?" the old lady said, letting the door swing open a little bit. She crossed her arms in front of her and leaned against the door frame gently.

"Just tell me everything you can about that grave up there," I said, backing up a bit to get away from her breath. "Were you here when she was buried?"

"Sure was, boy, I buried her," the old lady said, pointing a thumb at herself. "I damn near ran this whole town, if that's what you want a call it, for fifty years or so. There was a lot more than what you see here now, Sonny, a lot more. It was either burned down or was torn down over the years. Every man for miles around would come here just to see me, old Beulah. Yes, sirree, they would. I was a "looker" in those days, boy. Yes, sirree." Big smile on her face.

"Please tell me about the woman," I said, trying to get her mind back on the question I had asked.

"Well, we think it was a woman," she said licking her lips. "Some hunters found her up here in the mountains. There weren't a whole lot left of her. She had been badly mangled or mauled or something. We couldn't tell which."

"Why?" I said excitedly.

"Because the body was decayed bad. Must of been out there for a long while, maybe years. We were most sure all sorts of varmints had eat on her too. There weren't much meat on the bones at all, in fact, it was almost all bones. The bones were scattered all about."

"Then you have no idea how the person ... how she died?"

The old lady raised a crooked little right index finger in the air as if to make a point. "Strange thing about it though," she went on.

"What's that?" I asked intently, staring into the old woman's brown eyes.

"Well, there weren't no clothing. You know, like you would wear in the wintertime. It was winter when the body was found, you know. Who knows how long them bones been laying out there. Who knows when she died. Maybe it was summer. Maybe a lot of it was tore off or blown off. Maybe, maybe, too many maybes. Anyway, that was one thing, but the thing that gets me was that we couldn't ever find out who it was. All the people who lived around here never had a kin disappear. Never had nobody disappear other than to run off and get married. We checked with people at Greybull and Sheridan and everywhere around. No one seemed to lose anybody or be looking for anybody. For years we asked every stranger that come through here if they was looking for someone. Never got one reply. Not one. So anyway, we had to bury her just like you saw out back. Anyway, boy, that's the whole story."

"Have any idea how old she might have been?" I asked her, not knowing what to make of what she told me.

"Oh," the old lady said, pausing, "She weren't old. There weren't much left of her. She was mostly bones. All her teeth were there."

"Why do you think it was a woman?" I asked intently.

"Well, because what little was left wasn't big. The hair that was found on the ground was long. Longer than a bears, and the bones were small and short, not tall like a man's would be."

"What color was the hair?" I asked excitedly.

"Oh, it was red or brown or something like that."

"Or maybe a combination of both?" I asked.

"Could be, boy, really can't remember for sure. Well that's all there is to tell ya. Gotta go now."

My mind went blank trying to find a question to ask that might tell me if it might have been Jody for sure. But before I could think of anything, the old lady had slammed the door shut and flipped the lock.

"Wait," I called out for her to stop. She paid no attention to me, and she turned and walked away. I stood in silence and watched the old lady walk to the back of the store and disappear through the back door.

"Damn," I said, slapping my right fist into my other hand. I turned and slowly walked off the porch. I was going over in my mind what the old lady had said. It might be her, but then again, it might not. Only the hair color and the small bones made it possible, plus the fact no one ever came looking for a woman that had disappeared. Yet, why here, I thought. Never could I recall Jody ever having even left South Dakota, let alone finding a desolate spot like this.

My thoughts changed to Martha. I remember I had left her back at the cemetery. I ran back up the hill to her.

"Well, what did you find out?" Martha asked as I neared. She was still standing by the wood grave marker.

"I don't know for sure," I said, staring down at the marker. When I had related the woman's story, we both stood silently staring at the marker.

"Well," Martha spoke, after a few moments, "after all of this and what happened back at the fair, what do you think now?"

"I really don't know," I said softly. "But you know, the river banks were checked on both sides and up and down. There were no tracks, no nothing was ever found. But I guess there is one person knows for sure."

"Oh, who's that?"

"Only Jody knows, for sure… I wonder what ever happened to Chris Jennings?"

About the Author

The author, Craig B. Ewald is a graduate of Parsons College, where he was president of his dormitory and on the campus governing board. He is an inventor, having a US patent. Incredibly, he has been credited with saving the lives of three people, each one on a separate occasion Craig was a banker for a number of years before joining Caterpillar Inc., where he was called "The Banker" by his coworkers. He likes to hunt, fish, and look for mushrooms. When he got out of college, he began collecting antique furniture pieces. Craig is an avid collector of Currier & Ives lithographs, Planters Peanut memorabilia, and hunting advertising collectables.

About the Book

*O*nly *Jody Knows* is based on a true story about a girl who disappeared after a series of events in her life in 1900. It is told by a young boy who lived through her disappearance and participated in events to find her. Travel with him as you start at the Wyoming State Fair in the late 1930s and flash back thirty years earlier when he lived the adventure. A gold locket, burning torches, bloodhounds, and much, much more are part of this story about Jody. Read it, and enjoy it.

Lightning Source UK Ltd.
Milton Keynes UK
UKHW012007220621
385995UK00001B/19